DARK
COUNTRY

Other Books by Monique Snyman

The Night Weaver Series
The Night Weaver (The Night Weaver, Book 1)
The Bone Carver (The Night Weaver, Book 2)

Forthcoming from Monique Snyman

The Sin Eater (The Night Weaver, Book 3)
False Prophet (Dark Country, Book 2)

Awards for The Night Weaver Series

Bram Stoker Awards Nominee
Superior Achievement in a Young Adult Novel

Independent Publisher Book Awards (IPPY)
Silver Medal Winner: Horror

Foreword Reviews
Indies Book of the Year Awards
Finalist for Young Adult Fiction

OZMA Book Awards
(Genre division of the Chanticleer International Book Awards)
Semi-finalist

Screencraft CINEMATIC BOOK Competition
Quarterfinalist, The Red List #3 in Horror

DARK COUNTRY

COUNTRY

MONIQUE SNYMAN

Dark Country

Copyright © 2022 Monique Snyman
All rights reserved.

Original Cover Art and Cover Design by Scotty Roberts
ScottAlanRoberts.com

ISBN: 978-1-64548-073-0

VESUVIAN BOOKS

Published by Vesuvian Books
www.VesuvianBooks.com

Printed in the United States of America

10 9 8 7 6 5 4 3 2 1

For Manus:
Who finds a way to guide me to the light, even in the darkest of times.

Author's Note

Reality is often more horrific than fiction, which is the case when it comes to muti-related crimes in and around South Africa. While you may recognize many of the routes and landmarks ahead, certain buildings and enterprises don't exist.

Some of the case studies presented as real, fortunately, also haven't occurred.

However, a large portion of this book is based on real events and circumstances, some of which South Africans deal with on a daily basis.

Dark Country is thus a fictional tale with one foot in reality.

A list of South African specific terms can be found at the end of the book.

CHAPTER 1

Too often people mistake monsters for gods.

In the distance, several uniformed police officers are clustered together. A few whisper in languages I can't understand. A couple of them have the audacity to look bored. It's a façade, though. False bravado. The other policemen are tinged green around the cheeks—a perfectly normal response, and much more acceptable under the circumstances. Then there are the two teenagers who'd called it in. The blonde girl is huddled up in the boy's arms—a blubbering mess. Tears and mucus streak her otherwise pretty face, knotted hair sticks to her skin where the day's heat still clings against her small form. She trembles, but nobody can blame her. The boy looks in better shape, though not by much. He's pale, and stares into the distance, maybe wishing he could relive the day and do things differently. Perhaps he wishes he'd taken his girlfriend to another secluded field for some alone time.

God knows this wouldn't have been my pick for an outdoor quickie.

The burnt orange skies illuminate the world in a warm glow as dusk comes to a close. Several stars already shine against the romantic evening backdrop, where orange turns to mauve and then drips into navy blue. And the moon has a Cheshire Cat quality to it.

I feel like Alice in Wonderland—or more accurately, like I'm walking through the proverbial Valley of Death. Long, yellow grass reaches up to my hips as I push my way through the open veldt between WF Nkomo Street and the Magalies Freeway.

An eerie sound—a warped version of Mandoza's upbeat hit, "Nkalakatha"—drifts through the area as a taxi drives past. Someone else honks in approval. Then there's just the lull of traffic, the chirping crickets, and the rushing water of the swelled Skinnerspruit to drown out the silence.

Le parfum de la mort, the unforgettable fragrance of decay and fecal matter, wafts through the air like cheap perfume.

My stomach churns, but I manage to keep my lunch down like a professional. The atmosphere is thick with despair, though—almost palpable—and even the least superstitious police officers can feel it. Something most South Africans—regardless of race, religion, intellect, and profession—don't acknowledge, out of fear.

"You again," Detective Mosepi, a robust, middle-aged man with a brusque temper, asks when I near him. He glances back to his notepad and scribbles something down. "Not wearing our Gucci heels today, huh? Good thing, too, I guess. I know how women get when they ruin those expensive shoes."

I give the scene a fleeting look, curious about what lies beyond the shrubbery and uniforms.

"How's your pa?"

"Enjoying the new job, sir," I say.

People always ask and the answer never changes. Dad's more alive now, in an accounting office, than when he'd thought he had a calling at the South African Police Service. My father is not *that* old—he's only forty-six—but the force didn't agree with him. Too political and too soul crushing, he'd called the job. Nobody had disagreed.

A shadow of a smile crosses Detective Mosepi's face. He and my father had worked together for years—most of my life, truth be told.

"What's the story here, Detective?" I ask to get the ball rolling.

"Those two"—he gestures to the teenagers a few feet away—"were up to no good in the grass when they found the victim. It happened about an hour ago. The victim is a black female in her mid-twenties."

I raise an eyebrow in question. "And?" These types of cases tend to make police curt and impolite, but I need more to go on if I'm going to do my job.

Detective Mosepi sighs in defeat. "Possible rape, definite mutilation, and murder. The usual stuff you're called out for."

"Is the forensics unit coming?"

"Maybe, but don't bet on them being any help. You know we don't have the funding for fancy CSI gadgets."

I nod because it's true. The forensics team only comes out for prolific crimes, and this murder won't make the local newspapers' headlines if reporters are informed of the true nature of the case. It's much too sensitive for the media, the government, and the people.

"Have you found any identification for the victim?" I ask.

He looks over his shoulder and barks out a command in isiZulu. An officer shouts something back before the detective returns his attention to me.

"They bagged a purse which might've belonged to the victim. I'll send you the details after processing," he says.

"Thank you."

With a huff, Detective Mosepi pockets his notebook and heads for the shrubbery. "Come on. Let's get this over with."

I'm already behind him, stepping only where his feet have landed and mentally bracing myself for the inevitable shock that's coming. Even though I've seen dozens of homicide victims in the past few years, each one remains unique. I fish my cell phone out of my purse and search for the audio recording app to capture my initial thoughts of the scene.

Detective Mosepi steps out of the way when we've reached the taped-off area while the rest of the hovering officials clear out, leaving me with the full, grotesque picture.

The victim is sprawled on her back; her misery in those last few minutes—or hours—on display for all to see. And with those empty eye sockets and her slack jaw, the woman's expression is frozen in a silent scream. Her nude form might have been exposed to the elements for a couple of days, judging by the insect activity surrounding the body, but I won't wager on my accuracy. After all, I'm not an entomologist.

I can't become too emotionally involved, though—not if I want to stay sane. So I push my emotions away, however heartless it may seem, and continue in a monotonous voice.

"Esmé Snyder, Occult Crime Expert, Case Number 137. It is approximately 1800 hours on Friday, 4 September 2015," I say to my phone, moving around the border of the crime scene. "The victim is a black female between twenty-six and thirty years, of average height and weight. Clothing includes a turquoise peplum top and matching pencil skirt—cut off and discarded roughly two meters from the body—as well as black underwear and a pair of black open-toe heels.

"Pre-mortem mutilation is obvious. Defensive lacerations on her palms may confirm theory. DNA evidence of assailant or assailants might be present underneath fingernails. Eyes, tongue, and lips are also missing."

I walk around the body again, studying the evidence as thoroughly as I can beneath the single erected spotlight.

"Further investigative information is required to determine whether the victim is, beyond any reasonable doubt, another muti-murder fatality. The preliminary evidence, however, is overwhelming."

I stop my recording and take a few pictures of the scene, as well as the victim, for my records. Once I'm done with that, I make my way back to where Detective Mosepi is waiting with the kids.

He gives me a worried look, but doesn't ask the question I know he's dying to ask—*Are you okay?*

Am I okay?

I don't know. I've seen worse, but it never gets any easier. Every victim suffers in incomprehensible, inhuman ways. It's part of the ritual—the more they suffered, the more potent the ingredient is believed to be for the witchdoctor's magic. Of course, murder isn't always the intended outcome, but the victims' wounds are usually of such a nature that death is imminent.

"This is Mina van der Schyff and Adhir Ibrahim." He introduces the teenagers who'd found the body.

They still look like their worlds have ended, but at least the girl has stopped crying.

"I've notified their parents of their whereabouts, and we'll take them in for questioning, but I don't think we'll get anything useful out of them tonight," Detective Mosepi whispers.

I nod in agreement.

"Do you want to sit in on the interview?"

"It's unnecessary. Just send me their details with the rest of the files,"

I whisper back. "But I would like to read the victim's family and friends' statements. If you can arrange it for me, I'll owe you one."

The detective glances over my shoulder, looks back, and nods. "I'll walk you back to your car."

I begin to protest, but the look he gives me says not to bother. I swallow my words and head back to the Sasol garage, where my car is parked alongside the police vehicles. We walk together in silence until we've distanced ourselves from the activity surrounding the crime scene.

He steals a look at me again. "It's getting worse, isn't it?"

"The ritual murder rate has risen, regardless of the official statements the government releases. So, yes."

"How bad?" Detective Mosepi asks.

I grit my teeth. The statistics aren't pretty, not by a long shot, and seeing as I am one of the few occult experts on the continent, I've gotten to see the majority of the violent crimes committed. It's become a pandemic of sorts, and *everyone* is at risk, but nobody talks about it. "Do you have any leads as to whether this is an organized crime ring?"

"No, but I won't be surprised if it is. Muti-murder cases are popping up more frequently in every corner of the world, so it's plausible. Who knows? Maybe the sex-trade rings have branched out into this sinister trade."

"That is not a comforting thought, Esmé."

"Oh, believe me, I know."

We make out way up the steep hill, past the blue devil's fork fence surrounding the back of the Sasol garage.

Detective Mosepi, huffing and puffing from the exercise, leans against the side of my car to catch his breath. After a minute, he recomposes himself and looks around the busy petrol station before his lips thin into a tight line.

He shakes his head and says, "Tell me why these things happen."

This statement catches me off guard. Detective Mosepi is more than twenty years older than me. Surely those types of questions are the ones I should be asking him.

"Murder?" I ask, unsure.

"Muti-murders," he clarifies. "Why are those bastards almost never prosecuted when we catch them?"

I inhale deeply and reconfigure my thoughts. Before I can answer, Detective Mosepi shakes his head again and puts up a hand to silence me. If he hadn't, I would have told him how socio-economic circumstances played a huge role in the cultivation of superstitions. I would have gone on to say the feeling of hopelessness bred fear, which often led to violence or idleness, depending on the person. I could also have explained how humans, in general, *want* to believe in something greater than themselves; something to fix everything in a blink of an eye. But I don't say any of these things because I suspect he has already contemplated and considered these points.

He fumbles in his breast pocket for a packet of Marlboros, takes a cigarette, and holds the packet out toward me.

I decline with a raised hand.

"Aren't *you* scared of these things?" Detective Mosepi grimaces as he lights his cigarette. He blows out a cloud of smoke. "Don't you believe in witch doctors' powers?"

I shrug. "I believe that if a person believes hard enough in those things, their beliefs might come back to bite them in the ass."

In order to be invincible, one needs only to be invisible.

The so-called victim, Valentine Sikelo, went out of her way to avoid a group of particularly troubled-looking youths on her daily route to the taxi rank this morning. But she never spared a second glance at her killer. He wasn't anyone special. He didn't look like a threat. In fact, she'd barely noticed him whenever they passed one another in the street.

Did she know him? No. Would she have been able to accurately pull him out of a line-up without an inkling of doubt? No. Does he look like a killer? No.

Anonymity was an integral part to the implementation and success of his murderous intentions.

The next pivotal step was not half as difficult as it might sound, but it could scare off the victim if the execution was flawed.

In Valentine's case, a young mother who still relied greatly on her maternal instincts, luring her in was simple. All he did was create an emergency situation to draw her attention away from her usual routine. This was accomplished by scouting out the local school children in search of one with a serious condition like diabetes, epilepsy, or a deadly allergy. The information was not easy to come by, much to his dismay. Thus, he had to improvise a minor accident for a lonesome boy who'd been unlucky enough to enter his immediate vicinity.

This wasn't ideal, but it had worked all the same.

Valentine Sikelo rushed away from her regular route to help a child in need, and her killer snatched her out of the crowd without anyone being the wiser.

Valentine had put up a good fight, as he'd known she would, but her efforts were futile.

He'd been stalking her for months, biding his time and smoothing out the kinks in his plans until they were both ready for the inevitable. She'd never stood a chance.

He'd knocked her unconscious with a swift blow to the head, carried her limp form to his van, and bound and gagged her. Then they'd made the ten kilometer trip to an abandoned agricultural holding near Erasmia, a slaughterhouse conveniently located on the premises.

Four hours later, she was long cold and ready to be moved.

Good muti was always so hard to find. Fortunately, Valentine yielded a sacrifice that even his vicious, bloodthirsty ancestors approved of.

It's a messy business, trying to stay in his ancestors' good graces, but whenever he makes a grand gesture, they reciprocate by blessing him with the power he desperately craves. And offering them Valentine's most valuable organs had given him a boost of energy few others had yielded.

An electric current filled with ancestral magic rushes through his body. Every molecule lights up with renewed vigor. *More. More. MORE!* His spirit is exalted to new heights. For the briefest time, he feels as though he might levitate and float away, but even he could not defy the laws of gravity. Not yet, anyway.

The exceptional payoff from his ancestors, however, isn't the highlight of his day.

People generally accept that the killer always returns to the scene of the crime. In this case, it's not completely true. He could kill anywhere, but he prefers to return to where he'd dumped the body. To him, the dumping sites were their last resting places. There, he can visit and reminisce when they've long since been buried elsewhere. The magic happens *there*.

Watching the cops as they chase their own tails is just bonus entertainment.

That's how it always is, until he sees her.

She looks competent enough to be a worthy opponent, the perfect adversary. She will be the one he can finally test his accumulated powers and wit against.

A name is all he needs.

File: Case53-ES_interview.wav
Duration: 0:15:39
Date: 01/06/2012

Esmé: This is an informal interview with Solomon Mahlangu, a muti-crime survivor. Please note that Solomon's name and voice were changed to protect his identity in the event this recording is accessed unlawfully. With us is my coworker, Howlen Walcott, a BA Criminology graduate from Oxford University, who is currently researching his doctoral dissertation.

[Paper rustles in background]

Solomon, could you please take us through your experiences of the day you were attacked?

Solomon: I stayed home from school with a toothache on the 23rd of March, 2009. My mother went to work, promising to make an appointment at the dentist for the next day. So, I was alone. Everyone in the flats was away, except the old woman who lives on the first floor. Our flat was on the fourth floor.

[Pause]

I went back to bed after my mother left for work and my brother went to school. But it was too difficult to sleep because of my tooth. I remember I went to the sitting room and put on the TV, but

I can't recall what I watched. Then, I fell asleep for a while on the chair.

[Pause]

Esmé: Did they break down the door?

Solomon: No, they came in through an open window in the bedroom.

Esmé: I thought you said your flat was on the fourth floor?

Solomon: It is. It was. There's this ledge where the pigeons used to sit and make noise around every floor. They broke into the flat beneath ours, climbed out on the ledge, and somehow scaled a story before entering through our flat's bedroom window.

Esmé: Okay, what happened next?

Solomon: There were two of them. One had a scar over his lip, like a cleft-lip, but not entirely. He also had these maniac eyes, demon eyes. Yeah? And I remember him having monster feet. He wore big, black boots, filthy with dried mud, and around his neck hung a leather necklace with a human tooth. I will never forget it, because it hung in my face when he held me down.

The other one was scrawny—my age. About sixteen, at the time. He looked worried, like this wasn't something he really wanted to do. But he was acting brave in front of the other guy for brownie points.

[Pause]

Esmé: Take your time.

Solomon: I screamed at them in Sotho, *"Fuck off! Get out of my house or I'll call the police! Leave!"*

On and on I screamed, before the big guy punched me around a bit to subdue me. I was scared when he took out his gun and said I should strip naked. I couldn't move. My whole body shook. I thought he wanted to rape me, but when I was naked he held me down on the couch and the little guy brought out a knife instead. He didn't look well, but I was too worried about myself to care about him.

Esmé: Who didn't look well?

Solomon: The little one. He didn't want to be there.

[Pause]

> *"Take his penis,"* the big guy said in Sotho.
>
> *"I can't,"* said the kid, shaking his head.
>
> *"Do you want to get paid or not? Take the fucking dick."*
>
> [Sob]
>
> It's difficult for me to relive what happened, because the pain is still fresh.

Esmé: Should we stop?

Solomon: No, I'd rather rip the Band-Aid off one time.

[Pause]

> My whole ordeal has been painful, the aftereffects, too. I thought I would die often, since they took what doesn't belong to them.

[Inaudible]

> They didn't castrate me completely, because the kid couldn't stomach the blood. And although I've had reconstructive surgery, the doctors told me I will never be able to have children.

Esmé: What else did they take from you, Solomon?

Solomon: After the little one cut me, and made a mess of it, the big one took my hand, too. They would've skinned me alive and murdered me if they hadn't been spooked by the police sirens outside. Turns out, the old woman on the first floor had heard my screams and called them. I would've been another statistic if she hadn't. Well, a statistic on another list, I suppose.

Esmé: Were they caught? Did the police catch these men?

Solomon: Yes, one was. The kid is serving a long sentence in prison now, for an unrelated crime.

Esmé: And the other one?

Solomon: He's still out there. I still have nightmares about him.

Howlen: For what reason do you think they targeted you?

Solomon: As you can see, I'm an albino, otherwise known as a "ghost" or a "zero." In Africa, we're believed to be spiritually powerful, and our body parts are used for a variety of muti spells. They use our blood, skin, hair, bones, and all the other parts to improve their own lives while disregarding ours completely. Also, if you're black and are born with red hair, you'll be targeted. It's just the way it is.

Esmé: Are you still being targeted?

Solomon: While I live in Africa, I'll always be a target because of my skin. It's not only here. It's everywhere. In Mozambique, Nigeria, Kenya—anywhere there's a traditional following, there'll be people wanting albino muti. The albino community is dropping like flies, man. Especially now, with the recession and economic problems, it's becoming too hard for people to cope, so they reach out to sangomas for help.

Esmé: What are your feelings toward traditional healers, sangomas?

Solomon: In general, I hate them. I hate how they prey on the fears and weaknesses of people. It's greedy how they take people's money and then sit back and feel guiltless about the lives they've ruined or ended. But I also know not all of them are like this. It's the bad ones who use human parts for their muti. The witchdoctors, I mean.

Esmé: So, you believe there are good and bad traditional healers?

Solomon: Yes. The real ones, the ones who were gifted the ability to heal people, the ones who don't care about the money rather than helping the people, aren't usually killers. They use traditional medicines made from plants, herbs, and other natural ingredients, to heal. These other ones, though—the witchdoctors [pause]—the ones who did this to me and the other people [pause]—they aren't *real* sangomas. They are imposters preying on desperate people.

Howlen: Have you taken preventive measures to stay safe?

Solomon: No matter what you do or where you go in the world, there's always the possibility of being killed [pause], or worse [pause], for whatever reason. Nobody's ever truly safe—not here. Not anywhere. Not me and not you.

END OF AUDIO TRANSCRIPT

F ear is a rational response.

The crimes are savage and arcane. Many believe the occult to be regressive in this day and age, which is why it's such a hush-hush topic. People don't talk about muti or sangomas or tokoloshes around the dinner table because they fear they'll let evil into their homes. But walk around any major city center in South Africa and you'll see the homemade posters glued to lampposts and electricity boxes with blunt slogans like:

WANT BIG STRONG ERECTIONS?
I CAN HELP!

There are numerous services on offer to a person who is willing to spend money.

Plagued by bad luck? No problem! There's a potion to help you out. Want to find a lost lover? Easy! Here's a concoction to drink. Are you ill? No medical doctor knows more about your illness than the local witchdoctor. Do you want to make your employer suffer a bit? Great! Let's conjure up a tokoloshe to make his or her life a living hell. It's that simple. Whether your money will be enough to procure whatever potent remedy you need is a whole other matter, but sometimes inexplicable, *real* things do happen.

If you're not scared, you're an idiot.

The occult is a pseudoscience not easily explained in layman's terms. It changes often, is misunderstood, and accurate information is impossible to find. Hard facts about muti killings are also basically non-existent unless you want to sift through religious mumbo-jumbo from so-called "Warriors of God" who still can't differentiate between Satanism and devil worshipping. There is a difference, like there's a difference between Islam and ISIS, Christianity and the KKK. Like there's a difference between witches, witchdoctors, and sangomas. The problem is that people rely too much on their indoctrinated beliefs to see where one blurry line ends and the next blurry line begins.

The agency I work for is located in Stanza Bopape Street, in a house dating back to the 1940s that's been converted into office space. There's nothing special about it, even with the renovations. High walls surround the property, CCTV and motion detectors keep most intruders from breaking in, and if criminals aren't deterred, there's always the alarm system and armed response security company to come to the rescue.

The original hardwood floors are always polished to a gleam. A large reception area hardly sees any action from walk-in clients. There's a new face at the front desk every other week because receptionists quit as soon as they find out what the work entails. Upstairs, there are four offices, all decorated in their own unique styles. Past the reception area is a reasonable-sized kitchen, as well as my grandfather's office and the conference room where the video equipment is stored. The swimming pool is situated near the lapa, with its built-in braai. The braai gets used often because sometimes the only way to handle everything is with a beer in hand and a blue bull steak on the coals. And then there's the quartered-off part of the backyard, used as a designated smoking area.

Snyder International Religious Crime Investigative Services (or SIRCIS, for short) has one secretary who's been here since the agency doors opened nine years earlier, when I was seventeen.

Precious Bloom doesn't take nonsense from anyone or anything, human or otherwise, but she never goes out into the field, either. Her hawkish eyes could see through bullshit a mile away, and those infamous predatory glares are almost always accompanied by a sharp tongue. She smiles easily enough, though, and she likes a good joke as much as the next person. But Precious is quick to remind everyone, "There's a time to work and a time to play, and now's not the time for *kak*."

Profanity just sounds better in Afrikaans, as Precious likes to point out.

Christiaan Snyder owns the agency, but he only occasionally works on cases. Typically, his job entails being abroad to talk about the occult at universities and police conventions as an academic, or he helps out with tough cases so the agency breaks even every quarter.

The services SIRCIS has on offer are paid for on an ad hoc basis, whether it's for murder investigations, occult training, or speeches about the paranormal. Neither the government nor the church fund SIRCIS, but the agency's expert services are often sought after and paid for when the need arises.

Take note: SIRCIS has *no* affiliation with the South African Police Service Occult Related Crimes Unit, established in 1992 and reinstated in 2012, in any way. Snyder International Religious Crime Investigative Services is a private organization dedicated to finding answers, rather than creating a second wave of Satanic Panic in the general populace.

Father Gabriel is a Catholic priest and mandated exorcist sent from the Vatican to South Africa, years ago. He became part of the team by accident after Grandpa's path crossed with his in Soweto nine years ago. A quick call to the Vatican for permission to employ Father Gabriel on a part-time basis procured him for the agency.

Father Gabriel is on his own mission, though, and only assists in our investigations when the workload becomes too much or too weird, but it's a symbiotic relationship. He gets the resources he needs, which the local church cannot afford, and we have an exorcist at our beck and call when we need one.

Howlen Walcott, who started off as an assistant to my grandfather to research his doctoral dissertation, decided to stay on. His office is next to mine, pimped out in clichés from noir detective agency novels, and it doesn't suit him in the least. He's not exactly detective-looking, if there is such a thing. He's too tall, too intelligent, too serious, and too fit. He might've been Scotland Yard's most handsome criminologist had he stayed in Britain, but apparently he didn't like the weather. So here he is, still learning the ropes of the business and the culture of this foreign land. People are instantly taken by his suave accent, his eloquence, and the way he carries himself—almost like Benedict Cumberbatch. He wears suits and ties no matter what the weather's like, has a five-hundred-rand haircut, and carries around a pair of designer sunglasses. Howlen's posh, yes, but behind the clean-cut façade is something else. Something dark.

I Googled him when we first met three years ago, but all I got were a couple of social media listings. His Facebook profile is somewhat impersonal—quotes of notable writers qualify as status updates, and a photograph of him and his buddies from university appears from time to time. There are a few films tagged in his "Favorites"—mostly horror and sci-fi flicks—and the odd YouTube cat video also shows its face once in a while. He has a few hundred friends, nothing to write home about, and there's nothing more. His Twitter is pretty much the same as his Facebook, with vague updates of his day-to-day life appearing every couple of weeks. Otherwise, Howlen Walcott is non-existent on the internet.

Fast forward three years, a dozen drunken nights spent together, and I still don't know a thing about the guy.

I enter an in-between stage where I'm not a liquid or a solid. My legs tingle with needles and pins running down from my thighs to my toes and my mind responds with a euphoric release of don't-give-a-fuck. Aftershocks still rush through my body as I try to catch my breath and cool off. It's not an easy feat when the air conditioner is on the fritz and a working fan isn't in the vicinity. The cool breeze entering through the bedroom window helps somewhat, but a glass of ice-cold water would be nicer. My legs are jelly, though, and I'm on the brink of blacking out. Besides, I'm being held hostage by a naked Brit who's already fallen asleep after our stellar performance between the sheets.

Howlen has been blessed with Atlas' stamina, but when he's done, he's *done*. Out cold. Hell, so am I.

I fall asleep with his arm draped over my waist and his crown nested in the nape of my neck. No nightmares infiltrate my unconscious state for a change, no panic attacks or sudden startles. It's a deep, dreamless sleep that'll properly recharge my batteries for Case #137-ES.

All is well, almost blissful, until—

"Esmé, don't open your eyes." A hint of anxiety laces Howlen's murmur, his thick British accent still laden with sleep.

I grumble an incoherent question and his hand moves over my mouth to muffle the sound.

"Don't," he breathes.

Panic jolts me away from the dreamless oasis, then bubbles into my veins. My chest feels heavy with dread and indecision. Should I open my eyes and face the intruder who made it past all the security measures without being heard or seen? Or should I play dead?

Howlen's heart pounds where his chest is pressed up against my shoulder and he breathes shallowly, quickly, against my cheek, even though we're both completely silent.

Curiosity killed the cat, Esmé. But curiosity gets the better of me anyway.

My eyelids flutter open and my pupils adjust to the darkness in seconds.

I see it.

A shapeless *thing* a shade darker than night hovers over me, its face inches from mine. The shadow *feels* sallow—I can't explain it—somehow gaunt and corpulent at the same time. Menace exudes from the swirls of black dripping from nothingness into nothingness. A deathly glare fixates on me, but there are no discernible eyes in the face. A gaping maw breathes sour-smelling air into my personal space.

Adrenaline pumps through my body with each frantic heartbeat. But no matter how badly I want to move, my limbs are frozen. Whimpers escape my throat and get stuck in Howlen's palm. Trembles of fear affect each molecule of my being. Yet, I can only stare at the unfathomable creature.

It picks up on my fear, and satisfaction crosses what passes as a face. Suddenly it shrieks one indistinct word in a high-pitched scream before the blacker-than-black shadow dissolves into the night.

My body is my own again.

I sit upright, casting Howlen's hand aside in the process, and inhale thick, warm oxygen. My hands shake, and tears prick the corners of my eyes, but I'm only rattled. Nothing I can't handle.

"Is this the first time this has happened?" Howlen asks.

I don't trust myself to lie out loud yet, so I nod. I've seen worse than a perverted shadow—in the daylight no less. At night, though, I've had my fair share of glimpsing strange things in my house.

"Are you okay?"

"Give me a sec," I say, still weak.

We sit in silence for a few minutes as I gather my thoughts and analyze the event, wondering what to make of this intrusion.

"We'll have to get Father Gabriel to bless your house or something."

I cast a disapproving glance over my shoulder. "Sure, let's tell the Catholic priest there was a malevolent spirit in my house while I was having premarital sex. Then he can report it to God, or worse—my grandfather."

Howlen doesn't mean to smile, but he does.

"Shut up, Howl."

The alarm clock's neon red numbers read 02:32 a.m., which means I haven't been asleep for more than an hour. There's no way in hell I'll get to sleep again. Not tonight. I push my fingers through my hair, brushing out the knots.

"Are you okay, May?"

I calm down when he calls me by the nickname he only dares to uses during our more intimate moments. "Fine, fine. It's nothing but a warning. You know how it goes."

These things happen often to me, though he's a skeptic through and through when it comes to the supernatural, regardless of what he's personally witnessed. These entities are conjured up to warn people like us away from digging around. They can't hurt anyone, just freak us out.

The bedside lamp switches on with an audible *click*, casting an artificial yellow glow across the bedroom. Shadows recede into the corners of the room, not disappearing entirely.

I'm reminded to buy a 100-watt light bulb tomorrow, because the 60-watt I purchased just doesn't cut away the gloom. The wattage, however, is ample enough to make me feel better. Pieces of clothing lead into the room from the hallway, randomly strewn across the floor. The duvet is halfway across the foot of the bed and hangs haphazardly on the gray tiles. My dressing table is a mess, with perfume bottles lying on their sides on the silver tray while the necklace tree stands at an awkward angle. The empty Durex box somehow ended up near my closet on the other side of the bedroom. The discarded foil packaging and used condoms are probably on Howlen's side of the bed, then.

A blush creeps up my neck and settles on my cheeks as I study the disarray, but the embarrassment is quickly replaced with claustrophobia and disbelief.

"May," Howlen says as he sits upright.

I steal a glimpse of him and notice worry lines creasing his forehead.

"What case did you get called out for this afternoon?"

"Tonight's little event is not related to my new case," I insist. It's an unconvincing lie because *everything* is related in one way or another. I stand and make my way to the wardrobe, where I find a T-shirt dress to cover myself. "I'm 78% sure of that."

"I'd like to see how you came up with your number."

I grin and pull on the washed-out Garfield shirt for modesty's sake. "I suck at math."

"I know." Howlen lies back on the bed and folds his arms behind his head, appreciating the view from afar. "Where are you off to?"

"To get a glass of water," I say. "Can I get you something from the kitchen while I'm there?"

Howlen sits upright again, checks the alarm clock, and stands. "I'll join you in a minute."

I flip on the hallway's light switch and pass the oblong table, where framed photographs are positioned around a large crystal vase. A mirror hangs against the wall, an intrinsic part of the décor.

My hand automatically reaches out to switch on the kitchen light, but a gut instinct tells me stop. The whole house feels alive and wrong.

The toilet flushes.

"Howl?" I call, my voice involuntarily shaking.

"Yes?" he answers.

I'm being an idiot, jumping at shadows, worried about what can't hurt me. Since when am I afraid of the dark? I don't answer him. Instead,

I ignore the shiver crawling up my spine and switch on the kitchen light.

Bad idea.

Every item in the utility closet—several brooms and mops, a bucket, the long-handled feather duster, and the vacuum cleaner—are assembled in the center of the kitchen. The inanimate objects stand upright with no human assistance, and the bucket is levitating a few feet above the ground. The first thing that pops into my head isn't *run,* but rather *The Sorcerer's Apprentice,* a poem by Johann Wolfgang von Goethe.

"Howl," I call again, my voice edging on hysteria this time.

I keep my eyes fixed on the assembly of cleaning products as he moves down the hallway, bare feet slapping against the light gray tiles.

"Jesus," he hisses when he reaches my side. "What the fuck, May?"

The spell breaks.

Brooms, mops, and the long-handled feather duster clatter to the floor at once. Loudly. The bucket drops, making a hollow plastic noise as it spins to a stop.

And then, when I think it can't get worse, it does.

The kitchen's lightbulb shines brighter and brighter before it explodes with a deafening *pop.*

A crash in the hallway makes me spin away from the kitchen. A photo frame lies shattered and broken on the opposite side of the narrow passage. Another one flies from the table and crashes against the wall before it drops dead beside its mate. Then another. One by one, the frames are thrown aside by something unseen, something violent.

Howlen grabs me around the waist and spins us around so that his naked back faces the table and I'm protected between him and the wall. Glass bursts. Shards rain down in a tinkling melody.

Pop.

The hallway darkens.

I'm trembling worse than when I'd come face-to-face with the shadow not five minutes earlier. The house feels like it's breathing. In, out, in, out. Acrid air fills the spaces between here and everywhere. Kitchen cupboards, drawers, and doors violently slam open and shut for thirty seconds or so before the house descends into utter silence.

"What did you get yourself into?" Howlen asks, bundling my

trembling body up against him.

I don't know what he means. Case #137-ES is unspectacular in a throng of unsolved muti murder cases, however macabre it seems.

I've seen worse. Hell, Howlen's seen worse. If anything, it's an old case coming back to haunt us.

The question is, which case?

Sangomas are legally recognized in South Africa as traditional health practitioners under the *Traditional Health Practitioners Act of 2007* (Act. 22 of 2007). They are diviners, healers, traditional midwives, and surgeons who openly practice their beliefs in accordance with the constitutions and laws of the country.

According to several reports, formal health sectors have shown an interest in the role of sangomas as well as the effectiveness of their herbal remedies. Public health specialists even enlist sangomas in the fight against HIV/AIDS, diarrhea, and pneumonia—some of the major causes of death in rural areas, especially amongst children.

Real certified sangomas aren't usually a problem.

You get the odd one dabbling with dark forces, but generally the *Traditional Healers Organization for Africa* (THO) regulates and minimizes malpractice in the traditional healing community.

The problem occurs when charlatans don't adhere to ethics and laws and then screw around with forces they can't control.

"Those bastards controlled this attack just fine," I mumble.

"Did you say something?" Howlen calls from the kitchen, where he's making us fresh mugs of coffee.

"Nope." I lower my head into my open palms.

We'd spent the remainder of the night clearing away glass, cleaning up destroyed objects, and throwing away any evidence of our time together. Then we'd sat in silence, drinking coffee. Now, with dawn on the horizon, my weariness has returned with a vengeance.

SABC 1 is broadcasting a rerun of some educational kids show in Xhosa. I think it's a Xhosa show, considering the joyful tongue-clicking and beautiful lilt of the unfamiliar words, but I don't know the language well enough to be sure. SABC 2 is running the same infomercial fillers as always. SABC 3 is at the end of its AM shopping programming. This leaves E-TV as my only option, but *Medical Detectives* isn't exactly the type of show to unwind with after seeing a mutilated corpse less than twelve hours earlier. I use it as background noise for my thoughts, though, nothing more.

It's been three hours since the attack and my nerves are shot. I systematically rake through memories of old cases to find a link to the attacker or a reason for the attack, but I come up blank on both.

We're usually so careful when we're investigating ritualistic crimes. Careful in the sense that we give the police credit for bringing in the culprits, whoever he or she or they may be. We try *not* to bring attention to the agency.

We don't slip up.

Slipping up could lead to more danger, more deaths, more shit in general. Still, it's possible someone fucked up somewhere along the way. We're human and humans are flawed, after all.

"May," Howlen says.

His voice snaps me out of my thoughts.

I look up to where he holds my cell phone.

It didn't ring, I'm positive.

"It's Mosepi," he states.

Whatever small amount of energy I had left is diminished at the mention of Detective Mosepi's name. It's never a social call when the police are involved, no matter how long I've personally known some of them.

"I'll deal with it," he says.

"No," I say before temptation can take root. Something weird happened, what's new? If I had to take a day off every time my reality bordered on becoming crazy-town, I wouldn't get any work done.

I took the phone from Howlen and read the vague text message: 227 MALHERBE STR, CAPITAL PARK – MOSEPI. The text sends new chills down my spine as I realize the importance of the address.

I stand, letting loose a string of under-breath curses, the sort of language sailors would blush over. I reread the street address to make sure my eyes aren't playing tricks.

When I've regained my composure, I look at Howlen, who waits for an explanation.

"Get dressed. We've got problems," I say.

"What's the significance of 227 Malherbe Street?" Howlen asks.

As I make my way to the bedroom, I'm already wondering if I should wear my black dress or black power suit. There would undoubtedly be reporters. Many news vans, dozens of journalists, photographers for blogs and newspapers, and God knows what else will flood the area. There's no way around the media for this one.

"Do you know the story of Gert van Rooyen?" I ask in response, opening the closet door as Howlen enters the bedroom.

He shakes his head.

"You're a criminologist living in South Africa. How do you not know about Gert van Rooyen and his mistress, Joey Haarhoff?"

"Okay, let's skip the lecture and get to the point." He picks up his shirt from the armchair in the corner of the room.

"Allegedly, Gert van Rooyen was a pedophile and serial killer who was never convicted and who, together with his mistress, Joey Haarhoff, abducted and apparently murdered at least six young girls between 1988 and 1989. The pair committed suicide when they were faced with arrest, after the escape of their last kidnapped victim. Their other victims have never been found. It's one of the country's greatest unsolved crimes, Howl," I explain, retrieving the black dress from my wardrobe. "There's been a lot of speculation over the years and only a few hard facts, unfortunately."

Howlen shakes out his shirt to rid it of creases. "Don't tell me—that's his address?"

I glance over my shoulder. "Sorry, but yeah." I try reaching back to the zipper of the dress.

Howlen walks over, pushes my hands away, and zips me up in one swift movement. His hands linger on my shoulders before he goes back to dressing himself.

"Anyway, I can guarantee it'll be a media circus out there today, so let's not talk about the case in the field." I slip on my black heels and walk toward the dressing table to do my hair and put on some makeup.

Howlen is ready by the time I'm done, and he looks rather dapper for someone wearing the previous day's clothes. Few people can do the walk of shame so confidently.

We drive to the crime scene in his car, listening to Jacaranda FM's breakfast show. The volume is low, but the news about the murder at the old Gert van Rooyen house breaks at 06:00 a.m. sharp.

"Does Pretoria have a copycat killer on its hands? Is this murder in any way related to the original missing girls? Who is the victim?"

The radio presenters continue to speculate while Howlen searches for a parking spot alongside news vans and random vehicles. So many faces have come out to see this morose cat-and-mouse game between a faceless foe and the good men and women in blue.

I switch off the radio, annoyed by the nonsense of having to circumnavigate other people's theories when the cold, hard facts haven't even been established yet.

Howlen parks his silver Yaris almost a block away from the crime scene, away from the mob's curiosity. Together, we walk in silence, the previous night a distant memory. Right now, we're the epitome of professionalism.

A few people look at us as we pass through the barricade keeping the fanatical audience at bay, but nobody says anything of value. There's a "hello" or a nod, or a polite wave from the officers who know us. There are also hushed conversations amongst the civilians—nothing concrete, just rumor and gossip, and disbelief at this travesty. Otherwise, we're left to our own thoughts.

I always like listening to the din of the crowds. They might know something the authorities don't, something we can use to further an investigation. It helps to keep one's ears open.

The property is hidden with seven-foot-high concrete walls and a metal gate in serious need of a new coat of paint. Dead shrubs have grown wild over the years and peep across the property's defenses. A magnificent bottlebrush tree blooms large red flowers, which hang precariously against the peeling white backdrop of the wall. There's a metaphor in there somewhere, I'm sure.

The atmosphere is disgusting.

Multiple layers of excitement, insecurity, fear, and death thicken in the air, the cocktail threatening to suffocate me.

"This feels wrong," I say, more to myself than Howlen.

He agrees with a mumbled, "It does."

"*Finally,*" Detective Mosepi says when we approach. He's irritated, that much is clear. "Come in."

The gate slides shut behind us as we follow Mosepi inside. There are homicide detectives everywhere, a few uniforms, and even the forensics team has shown up. The crime scene is partitioned off with a white tent which will become increasingly uncomfortable as the heat rises with the sun.

Detective Mosepi talks as they walk. "The victim is a twelve-year-old girl from Danville who went missing out of her bed last night. She looks … Well, I'm not certain what to make of this one, to be honest."

"Let's start with the obvious, then. What's the victim's name?" I ask.

"Carol-Anne Brewis," Detective Mosepi says, and hands me the photograph of a beautiful girl in her school uniform. "Blonde hair, blue eyes. Basically van Rooyen's type, if you know what I mean."

I nod as I bite the inside of my cheek. I glance at the tent, then look back at the detective.

"It's bad." He confirms my suspicions without needing to be asked, and my stomach does a summersault. "The first officers on the scene say her body was still warm when they touched her, meaning she was murdered between three and four-thirty this morning."

"Any witnesses?" Howlen asks.

"Mrs. Potgieter, who lives across the street, took her dog out around four-thirty this morning when she saw a suspicious car drive away. She hasn't been much help, but I …"

Mosepi's words travel off to the recesses of my mind as I stare at the photograph.

Carol-Anne Brewis seems small for her age, but her determined blue eyes shine intelligently in the photo. Her demure smile looks hopeful for a future she will never have. From this photograph, I can't deny that there's a definite resemblance to what Gert van Rooyen liked in his supposed victims. Carol-Anne was the right age and type. The telltale inconsistency of how she disappeared from her home—from her own bed—is far too brazen an act for a lowly pedophile-slash-murderer like him, though.

I turn around to look at the mammoth tent hiding the little girl from further humiliation. White canvas flaps lazily in the breeze. I spot a crumpled figure on the ground.

There lies Carol-Anne, dead.

I can't see much from my position, except for a bare foot turned at an awkward angle. It's more than enough to make me feel sick.

I don't want to go into the tent. I don't want to see the terrible things that poor child had to endure during her last hours on earth. But if I don't do my job, Carol-Anne's killer may never be found.

So, I go.

Satanism Link in Multiple Pretoria Murders
2015-09-05 | 09:23
8 Comments

Pretoria–Police are staying tight-lipped about an investigation into two murders in Pretoria this past week, but inside sources have revealed these cases may be Satanic in nature. Speculation as to whether the cases are related has been neither denied or confirmed by a police spokesperson.

"The investigations are at a critical stage, and giving out such information could be harmful to everyone involved," said Lieutenant Colonel Moses Dlamini.

Valentine Sikelo, 28, was found brutally murdered yesterday afternoon when two teenagers stumbled into the field where her body was discarded. Sikelo, a vibrant newlywed and young mother from Atteridgeville, was said to have disappeared early Friday morning on her way to work.

"I don't understand how this happened. We live a block away from the taxi rank," said Joseph Sikelo. "How does a full-grown woman get kidnapped on a busy street, less than a block away from her home?"

It is unclear, as of this time, whether the second murder victim, Carol-Anne Brewis, 12, is connected to Valentine Sikelo. Sources say Brewis disappeared late last night from her bed in Danville and was found early this morning in the abandoned lot of the late notorious serial pedophile Gert van Rooyen.

"We have our best detectives on both cases," said Dlamini.

– News24/7

COMMENTS:

AtheistsUnite – September 05, 2015 at 09:24

You have to believe in god to believe in satan.

Lettie.Myburg – September 05, 2015 at 09:24

I don't see the connection. The victims' ages are too far apart, and they aren't even of the same race. Don't serial killers usually have a 'type'?

> _DanTheMan_ – September 05, 2015 at 09:25
>
> @Lettie.Myburg – Agreed. It seems like the SAPS is reaching on this one.

Matt@DaWorld – September 05, 2015 at 09:25

Nothing in this corrupt government works, da SAPS included.

SylvieGotte – September 05, 2015 at 09:26

Rest in peace Valentine and Carol-Anne, you're home now, in the arms of our Lord and Savior.

> _AtheistsUnite_ – September 05, 2015 at 09:26
>
> @SylvieGotte – If there was a god, why did he let this happen in the first place?
>
> > _SylvieGotte_ – September 05, 2015 at 09:27
> >
> > @AtheistsUnite – There is a God, and His reasons are not to be questioned by humanity. We should accept that He knows best.

Silver&Gold – September 05, 2015 at 09:26

This is sensationalism at its best. Why does News24/7 always jump on the Satanism bandwagon the first chance they get? Whatever happened to good journalism?

Molester's Ghost Haunts Neighborhood
Alicia van den Berg | 05 September, 2015 10:00

THE discovery of Carol-Anne Brewis' body, 12, on the property of infamous pedophile Gert van Rooyen has again raised the possibility that the mystery of the disappearances, that occurred 23 years ago, of six schoolgirls might be solved.

However, the girls' families do not want to get their hopes up yet. There have been numerous futile leads over the years, but the investigations have not shed any light on the fates of their youngsters thus far.

Early on Saturday morning, the police were called to a property in Capital Park, Pretoria, by a concerned neighbor who had seen a suspicious van speed away from the area.

A relative of Odette Boucher (11 when she disappeared), who wishes to remain anonymous, was hesitant when asked about the discovery.

"I have so much sympathy for Carol-Anne's mother," she said, "but I doubt her murder is linked to Gert van Rooyen."

None of the families can be blamed for being skeptical. Over the years, their hopes have been raised countless times, only to be dashed once more.

In 2007, similar claims were made when the remains of some girls were found at Umdloti, KwaZulu-Natal, after massive storms unearthed bones along the coastline. These allegations, however, were proven to be false with the help of forensic testing and DNA analysis. That same year, current affairs TV program *Carte Blanche* reported claims by investigator Danie Krugel and clairvoyant Marietta Theunissen that the girls' bodies were buried merely a few kilometers from Van Rooyen's demolished home in Malherbe Street. No conclusive evidence has been found to validate these claims, either.

Van Rooyen committed suicide in January 1990 after a police chase. According to reports, he first shot his lover and accomplice, Joey Haarhoff, and then himself.

Kobie Wagenaar, whose daughter, Anne-Mari, went missing, said: "I really don't know what to think anymore."

Police spokesman Lieutenant Colonel Moses Dlamini said they cannot yet rule out the possibility that Carol-Anne Brewis' murder is connected to the Gert van Rooyen cases.

"Because of its sensitive nature, [Carol-Anne's case] will receive top priority," he said.

Dlamini warned against speculation and asked the public to wait until all forensic tests had been completed. This could take weeks.

– LiveTimes

Comments have been disabled for this article.

12-Year-Old Girl Found Dead at Van Rooyen's House
05 Sep 2015 10:07
55 Comments

The body of Carol-Anne Brewis (12) was found at the home of pedophile Gert van Rooyen in Capital Park, Pretoria police said on Saturday.

Lieutenant Colonel Moses Dlamini said that a neighbor saw a suspicious van speeding away from the crime scene early Saturday morning, and immediately contacted the police.

Homicide detectives and forensic experts visited the site, and the material evidence will be sent for forensic testing, said Dlamini.

"What we would like is to have the police's work go unhindered. We know the country is waiting in anticipation for our results, and for us to find the person responsible—we ask for patience," he said.

Van Rooyen and his accomplice and mistress, Joey Haarhoff, were linked to the disappearance of six girls between 1988 and 1990.

They allegedly kidnapped Joan Horn (13), Odette Boucher (11), Anne-Marie Wapenaar (12), Yolande Wessels (12), Fiona Harvey (12), and Tracy-Lee Scott-Crossley (14).

Van Rooyen killed Haarhof and then committed suicide in January 1990.

– Mail & Guardian

Comments:
Rooney Kavanagh – *two minutes ago*

DARK COUNTRY

Whoever's responsible for Carol-Anne's death is one sick puppy.

    Riana Smith – two minutes ago
> @Rooney Kavanagh – I was just thinking the same thing. What type of monster would not only kill a little girl, but also dump her body in the one place where so many other families' entire lives were ruined? It's horrific.

Vincent – two minutes ago
I think the killer did it on purpose, to make a name for himself.

CascadingClive – two minutes ago
Seriously screwed up.

HelloKitty128 – two minutes ago
This is one messed-up world.

Rachel Nkandla – a few seconds ago
Couldn't agree more. RIP Carol-Anne.

JazzMan – two minutes ago
RIP Carol-Anne.

Henrico Kruger – two minutes ago
Why do the media think Carol-Anne's murder is related to cold cases from 23 years ago? Gert van Rooyen and Joey Haarhoff are both dead. Nobody's proven they had any other accomplices. The conspiracy theories are just that: conspiracies. I don't get it.

Yvette Badenhorst – two minutes ago
Maybe it's because Carol-Anne's body was found on Gert van Rooyen's premises? We don't know all the facts, that's why those are cold cases. Maybe van Rooyen and Haarhoff DID have an accomplice and he/she was lying low until now?

Jake Fugard – two minutes ago
Maybe it's a copy-cat killer?

    CascadingClive – one minutes ago
> @Jake Fugard – Yeah, my first thought was that it was a copy-cat killer, trying to get some attention.

    Yvette Badenhorst – two minutes ago
> @Jake Fugard – A copy-cat killer usually has something to copy. In this case, we don't know for sure what happened to those girls. In other words, there's nothing worth copying.

33

<u>Lovejoy Matsepe</u> — *two minutes ago*

The cops should give the killer to the people for 5 minutes. We don't need more time than that.

<u>Harlequin49</u> — *two minutes ago*

I heard the police called in an occult crime unit to help with the investigations. Can anyone confirm or deny this?

> <u>Hannes Vermeulen</u> — *two minutes ago*
>
> @Harlequin49 — Well, we live on Malherbe Street, and I can confirm there were occult specialists on the premises, but they declined comments to every reporter they came across. I think the police want to keep their involvement in the case quiet.

<u>Francine White</u> — *one minute ago*

I wouldn't put it past the police to call in specialists. The SAPS is up to &@^! except when they're taking bribes. They can take bribes better than anyone else.

<u>ArmchairDetective</u> — *one minute ago*

Carol-Anne Brewis looks a lot like the type of girls Gert van Rooyen targeted back in the day. It's eerie.

[view image]

> <u>RickyRockyRoad</u> — *a few seconds ago*
>
> She DOES look a lot like Odette Boucher.

> <u>Vincent</u> — *a few seconds ago*
>
> Okay, that's uber-creepy.

Continue to Read Comments?

Pink Ladies Show Up in Support of Carol-Anne Brewis
Bianca Otto | September 5 2015 at 11:45am
25 Comments

Pretoria has been in a state of uproar after officials discovered the body of twelve-year-old Carol-Anne Brewis earlier this morning on the property once belonging to infamous pedophile Gert van Rooyen.

There was a heavy police presence at the scene as neighbors and concerned citizens flocked to the site to show their support. A row of police officers blocked off one part of Malherbe Street, creating a barrier between van Rooyen's house and the upset crowd. Police vehicles lined the other side of the street to keep the crowd at bay.

Around nine o'clock, the Pink Ladies arrived, all dressed in pink T-shirts.

The Pink Ladies, an organization of predominantly women who first started rallying against child abuse, child kidnappings, and child murders when Sheldean Human went missing in 2007, arrived on the scene to show their support for Carol-Anne Brewis and her family.

The color pink was chosen by the Pink Ladies, as Sheldean Human was last seen alive wearing a pink T-shirt and a denim skirt.

Human's decomposed body was found at a storm water drain outlet near the Tshwane Fresh Produce Market in 2007, two weeks after she disappeared from outside her home in Pretoria Gardens. Andre Jordaan was tried and convicted of Human's rape and murder and died in prison when another inmate attacked him.

Sheldean's name has become synonymous with the fight against crime in South Africa.

"Today is a very sad day," said Pink Lady, Lynette van der Graaff. "Not only does Carol-Anne remind us of the terrible deeds Gert van Rooyen committed back in the 1980s and 1990s, but little Sheldean wasn't found too far from here, either."

The Pink Ladies protested peacefully in Capital Park today, out of respect for Carol-Anne Brewis and her family.

"This little girl was kidnapped out of her bed in the middle of the night. If children aren't safe in their own homes, where are they safe?" said van der Graaff. "Enough is enough. The government needs to start listening to us and keep our babies safe."

– SA News

Log in to read and leave comments.

I't's painful to be beautiful, but it's absolute murder to be lionized.

In life, Carol-Anne Brewis had been just another impoverished child with an alcoholic for a mother and a deadbeat for a father. She'd shared the same origin story with countless other children. What makes her special?

Her future had not been as bright as everyone claimed. If she had been lucky, her parents *might* have enrolled her into one of the better schools on the other side of the Daspoort Tunnel. *Maybe* she would have kept her nose clean and gotten good enough grades to attend the University or the Technicon, but it's highly unlikely from what he'd witnessed. And if the stars were in her favor, *perhaps* Carol-Anne would have found herself a mediocre job somewhere, settled down with a mediocre man, and had a bunch of equally mediocre babies. Then the whole cycle would begin anew.

She wasn't going to cure AIDS or perfect Nikola Tesla's intercontinental wireless transmissions. She wasn't going to be a supermodel unless she drastically altered her appearance with plastic surgery after she hit puberty. Her genetics simply weren't up to par in *that* regard.

No.

If she had died when she was an old lady with a handful of regrets and a wasted life in her rearview mirror, only close friends and family would mourn her. Eventually, though, even they would have forgotten her. No matter how badly people want to believe it, Carol-Anne Brewis was *never* going to amount to much.

Thanks to him, Carol-Anne doesn't have to be a disappointment to herself or to anyone else. She will be remembered. She will be celebrated.

By all means, let her be the poster child for everything wrong in this country.

He will admit this: There might not have been greatness residing within Carol-Anne, but there had been power. He had craved that power.

For months, he had stalked the little girl. For weeks, he had searched for every vulnerable part of her parents' property. For days, he'd contemplated taking her life—and ultimately her power.

He'd almost released Carol-Anne after devouring every bit of Valentine's essence. Almost. He'd very nearly moved on to one of his other targets. That was before he realized how badly he wanted to play his morbid game with Esmé Snyder.

That's her name—Esmé Snyder.

She's the one who exudes the greatness he'd been waiting for. *She* is worthy to play his game, even though she doesn't know it.

He has big plans for her.

Wonderful plans.

CHAPTER 3

Cicadas buzz in harmony as the African sun ascends to its peak. Sweat droplets accumulate on my upper lip and snake from my hairline down the back of my neck, causing my hair and clothes to cling to my skin. The air is uncomfortably stagnant, dry, and hotter than the seven levels of hell. The warm breeze carries an echo of exhaust fumes with it. Whenever a large truck or Putco bus roars past, sputtering carbon monoxide into the atmosphere, nature's sounds are drowned out.

The strange symphony of nature versus man offends my ears as I stand in the shade of a feeble-looking tree. Fat blowflies sluggishly float through the sky before landing on my bare legs for a quick reprieve from their flight. They move only when I do, and return as soon as I'm still.

The sun-bleached road is lined with weathered buildings which date back fifty years or more. People swarm amongst the informal vendors, weaving in and out for a chat or a smoke or a quick purchase of whatever is on sale. Taxis swerve dangerously across the lanes to pick up or unload passengers.

Marabastad is the type of place Americans would describe as "downtown."

But Marabastad isn't anywhere near as dangerous or as frowned upon as Jo'burg's inner-city slum, Hillbrow. It is, however, the closest equivalent Pretoria has … Well, there's also Sunnyside to take into account, not to mention the CBD. Come to think of it, Pretoria is quickly turning unrecognizable, with new crime hotspots popping up all over. Nevertheless, Marabastad has a lot of history. Mostly forgotten history, but interesting stories surround the township.

Formal businesses are situated in the old run-down buildings, sharing customers with informal vendors on the sidewalks, often run by refugees from diverse backgrounds. Vacant lots have been turned into mini shanty towns by the destitute, where corrugated metal gleams atop unsound structures built from plywood, plastic, and cardboard. It's a poverty-stricken neighborhood where you can find knockoffs of anything. Here, drugs of every flavor are available if you know who to ask. Shops sell poorly made clothes at cheap prices, because South Africa has turned into China's product dumping site. Chop-shops hide in the backyards of proper businesses, but everyone who grew up around these parts knows what's happening after the taxman leaves. You could find a new identity, citizenship, a hitman, or anything black-market for a relatively good price.

People eyeball me whenever I walk around Marabastad by myself. I can only speculate on their thoughts when unsubtle glances, full of suspicion or surprise or curiosity, catch my attention. Proper white girls don't walk around here without a chaperone. Usually, said chaperone is classified as a bullish Boer with a rattan cane lying somewhere in his oversized pick-up truck—a *bakkie,* as they're more commonly called.

Good thing I'm not entirely proper.

Truthfully, the only reason I ever come to Marabastad is to meet with one of my informants who trades between Marabastad and Hillbrow. Her name is Feyisola—or so she claims. I don't care. As long as Feyisola gets me information on illegal human organ and body part trades, I'll call her whatever she wants. Feyisola's information is expensive, but her tips pan out. The only problem I have with the arrangement is the risk we take every time we met.

Feyisola works with shady characters; the type who kills first and don't give two shits later.

I walk across the street to a small tailor shop located in a relatively busy side-street. The shop is dark and smells musky when I pass through the front door, but the heat overwhelms all of my other senses. Rails of clothing and shelves of shoes, most likely manufactured by little hands in an Asian sweat shop, are on display. And although I greet the shop owner with a flash of teeth and a half-wave, the woman turns her back on me and busies herself with clothes on a rack, like always. There's no reason to take it personally. Clandestine meetings frequently occur in the shop's back room, and this was her way of saying she didn't want to become more involved than she already was. I can respect that.

The back room, which is even darker, hotter, and muskier than the front, is separated with a curtain of beads and a wooden accordion door. Not very secure. Maybe Feyisola would be open to meeting at the Casbah Roadhouse across from the Pretoria Show Grounds? At least then there's the option of air-conditioning. Here, there aren't any windows, and no back doors. There's only the ancient plastic patio furniture squeezed into the tiny room where Feyisola is already waiting with stale biscuits and cheap cooldrink.

She is dressed in a crimson pantsuit paired with a sheer black camisole underneath her jacket.

I'm certain if her shoes were in view, I'd covet them.

Feyisola's plump lips are colored in scarlet, and they twitch into an uncomfortable smile when I approach. Fake eyelashes brush against high cheekbones whenever she blinks. Feyisola is drop dead sexy, and painfully intelligent. It's best not to get on her bad side, though. She knows people—the type of people you don't want to run into in the middle of the night.

"Juice," she asks in an indistinct accent. A manicured hand waves across the perspiring glass jug when I take a seat beside her.

"No, thank you," I reply.

Feyisola's face smooths out and she shifts in her seat. "I would have sent a text, but you know how it goes."

She doesn't have to continue. A message delivered via courier works just as well as a text.

"Don't worry about it," I say in the most reassuring tone I can muster. "What do you have for me today?"

Feyisola leans closer and begins in a hushed voice, "When I heard about the girl and woman who recently got killed, I asked around town about any dealings you might be interested in. Turns out, none of the usual suspects are involved. I did, however, learn of a large shipment of body parts making its way into the country from Namibia."

"When?"

"In the next few days," she says. "From what I gather, the shipment is expected to be distributed from Johannesburg to various parts of Southern Africa." She slides a small manila envelope across the table. "Some names you might want to look into."

I pocket the envelope without looking at its contents. "Do you think the killer placed an order?"

"I have no way of knowing, but your killer took a chance by murdering a white child. Ain't no way the police will let that shit fly," Feyisola says, her accents shifting to something resembling a lower-class American gangster's dialect. She sits back in her chair. "I also heard that your grandfather will be back in town next week."

I raise an eyebrow and purse my lips together in disapproval. My grandfather is off-limits, as Feyisola knows.

"Don't worry. He's got a reputation as a bad ass. Nobody will fuck around with him."

"Good," I mutter, not bothering to correct her on my grandfather's true persona, which is as far from bad-ass as it gets.

"You, on the other hand, are considered to be fair game." She twirls a braided weave around one of her fingers as she regards me. "Good thing you haven't stepped on any crime lords' toes."

"The narcotics unit can deal with the drugs. I'm not interested."

"More than drugs are smuggled into the country."

"Yes, but unless there's a shipment of cursed voodoo dolls coming into South Africa, I really don't need to know about it." I stand. These meetings need to be kept sweet and short if they are to be beneficial to both parties. "How much do I owe you?"

"This one's a freebie if you can convince your priest to listen to my confession. Normal priests would have a fit if they hear my sins, but yours might survive the ordeal, considering what he does."

I can just imagine this feral woman confessing her deepest, darkest sins to Father Gabriel, and it brings a smile to my face. "I'm sure Father Gabriel won't mind listening to your confession. His times at the church vary, but he's almost always there on a Thursday. I'll tell him to keep an eye out for you."

Feyisola nods. "I appreciate it. Be safe, Esmé."

"You too, Feyisola."

Once outside the claustrophobic store, I sigh with relief. The hustle and bustle of Marabastad continues unhindered, even though the heat of the day seems to intensify with each passing minute. Between me and the main road is a group of people in the middle of what seems to be an intense debate. Their body odor invades my olfactory senses as I pass, the smell pushing me almost to the point of nausea. Various degrees of ripeness clings to their clothes and skin, ranging from a sweet-smelling musk to an oppressive moldy stench. Their faces glisten with perspiration and their clothes are damp with moisture. This heat wave is a nuisance to everyone today.

Dark faces turn darker as the UV rays wreak havoc. Fair faces, such as mine, turn several shades of red regardless of whatever SPF factor one wears. Blood boils and the merest irritation can turn to full-blown violence, all thanks to the weather. This persistent heat turns humans into animalistic versions of themselves.

It's not a day for outdoor undertakings.

I make it to the main road before my cell phone begins buzzing in my purse. "Esmé speaking." I answer the call without looking at the caller ID.

"Where are you?" Howlen's voice has an edge of urgency to it, giving me pause.

"Marabastad. What's wrong?"

"Could you describe the state in which you found Valentine Sikelo on Friday?"

"I think everything you need is in my report," I huff. The traffic light blinks red for pedestrians. My car sits across the street, parked parallel against the curb.

"I meant the state of the area, not the body itself," Howlen corrects himself. "Describe it."

"The grass was yellowish-green and overgrown. There were a lot of bugs. A cluster of rocks was situated close to the body, and the teenage lovebirds were sitting on a nearby log."

"Okay, well, you need to come down here and explain something to me."

"Explain what?" I check for traffic before jaywalking. "It's a veldt,

Howlen. It looks like every other veldt in Pretoria."

"I'll wait for you at the Sasol garage." He ends the call without further explanation.

"Do you know how busy I am?" I ask the dead phone, my voice pitching higher than usual. With a sigh, I drop my cell phone into my purse and find my keys as soon as I'm safely across the street.

Fifteen minutes later, my car is parked beside Howlen's at the Sasol garage. Around me, taxis flock to fill up their tanks and pedestrians wait for their lifts, chatting and shouting. The unabated cacophony shows no sign of stopping anytime soon.

Do any of these people even realize what happened not five hundred meters away? Do they care?

I spritz more sunscreen onto my face while looking in the rearview mirror.

Howlen's already waiting, appearing more disheveled than ever with his rolled-up shirt sleeves, loose tie, and uncombed hair. I can't figure out if his unkempt look is due to frustration or because of the temperature.

I find a baseball cap in the glove compartment and fit it onto my head before evacuating the car again, missing the AC.

"Your report made no mention of ecological anomalies in the area," Howlen accuses me before I'm even properly out of the car. He carries Valentine Sikelo's case file, where her name is spelled out in thick red letters against the brown cardboard sleeve. Howlen opens the file to my typed report, pushing his index finger against a paragraph. "Explain."

"Ex—" I cut myself off as soon as I hear the indignation in my tone. I take a deep breath and try once more in a more civilized manner, "Howlen, there were no ecological anomalies in the surrounding area. If there were any, I would have made a note of it."

"Come with me." He closes the file and heads downhill, into the field.

I follow without argument, although I'm burning for a fight.

Beads of sweat roll down Howlen's temple, while a vein furiously throbs in his forehead. His knuckles are white from clutching the file, setting my nerves on edge. I've seen him angry before, but never because of something as insignificant as an overlooked note. An ecological anomaly might've been a gross oversight on my part, I admit, but unless such an abnormality would directly influence the outcome of a case, there was no need to document it. Therefore, I decide, he must have stumbled on something that wasn't noticeable in the first place, making it inconsequential.

As we venture closer to where Valentine Sikelo's body had been found, the scenery—as I remember it being—changes considerably. Where healthy blades of yellow-tinged grass once grew tall, wilted patches of brownish-gray grass now lie instead. Where nature once played a song of chirruping crickets, a void replaces all sounds. Even the air tastes sour, the nearer we get. The irregularities are hair-raising, profoundly … wrong.

"You failed to mention the whole area seems to have had its life force sucked out of it." Howlen breaks the silence in an I-told-you-so manner, derogatory to my already-frayed patience.

"Maybe the grass died from natural causes? The heat wave has been unbearable, and—"

I stop talking when he crouches down in front of me and points to a dead crown plover beside its nest. The bird looks to have had everything sucked out of it before dying—blood, organs, anything remotely life-sustaining. There is no decomposition, but it appears to have been dead a while, which doesn't make sense whatsoever.

"Oh," I whisper.

He picks up one of the bone white eggs in the nest, carefully cracks it open, and holds it up to show me the inside.

I crouch down by his side, studying the purplish fossilized goo within until … "What the hell is that?" I stand and take a step back, as though whatever's happening is contagious.

"That used to be a crown plover chick."

"What happened to it?"

"I have no idea. Whatever it was affected everything to its core in a three-hundred meter radius," he says, standing. "I've already collected samples, but I'd like to know why this didn't make it into your report."

"Probably because this wasn't how the area looked when I was here on Friday."

"So, you're saying this whole area died in three days' time?"

"It seems like it." I turn in a full circle, trying to get a better perspective of the perimeter. The vacuum of life, not only visible in the fauna and flora, is apparent in the air and soil, too. This whole place feels evil. Such superstitious nonsense shouldn't even enter my mind, yet I can't describe it as being anything other than *evil*. "Did you find something else worthwhile?"

Howlen grunts an affirmative and sets off to where Valentine's body had been found.

Even the sky has a grayish tint to it, as if the sun can't penetrate the layer of morbidity in the veldt. As an investigator, it's imperative to be objective in every regard, especially when throwing around words like *evil*, *ritualistic murder*, or *muti*, but tiptoeing around the obvious when something wicked lurks beyond the veil of normality is just plain stupid.

Howlen stops in the clearing and points to the exact spot that Valentine Sikelo had last occupied.

I stifle a surprised gasp.

The crimson life force which had seeped out of the victim's body post-mortem hasn't been absorbed into the earth. In fact, the blood hasn't coagulated at all. Aside from the thin jellying top layer, the blood is as runny as though it was spilled a minute ago.

"Do you have a scientific explanation for this?" I ask.

"I'm not aware of scientific explanations for anything I've seen at this site," Howlen says, worry entering his voice. "This is your jurisdiction."

Yes, this is my jurisdiction, but I'm at a loss for relative plausibility. "I don't know how to start figuring out what can cause this type of destruction. How do we debunk any of it?"

He shrugs. "I'll do my part by coming up with some sort of logical explanation for the police, but the rest is up to you, May."

"Maybe it's time to bring Father Gabriel in on the case, too?" I mean it as a statement, but it comes out as a question.

Howlen turns to me and I notice my own doubts reflected in his eyes.

He says, "Well, if anyone's going to bring up the controversial issues we're pussy-footing around, it's Father Gabriel."

CHAPTER 9

Father Gabriel picks up a stick in the newly dubbed "Dead Zone" while Howlen and I stand aside, eagerly awaiting his assessment. The priest straightens after what feels like a lifetime, scratches at his salt and pepper beard, and looks to the heavens. He grunts, his harrumph sounding indifferent.

He then steps around a few randomly strewn rocks to reach the crown plover nest and investigates it in silence. Father Gabriel uses the stick to push the bird onto its side, careful not to touch the carcass. He peers underneath the crown plover, gently replaces it on the ground, and turns his attention to the nest.

The egg Howlen had cracked open for Esmé's perusal lies beside the other eggs. The priest examines it at length.

He straightens again and stares toward the sun before making his way to where Valentine's unabsorbed blood is still visible. Father Gabriel tugs at his collarino shirt, turns toward us, and reveals his disgust in a grimace.

I'm about to ask for his thoughts when Howlen gently nudges me with an elbow.

Father Gabriel walks toward the log where the traumatized teenagers sat during my initial investigation.

Howlen's hand brushes against mine, a calming gesture, and the tip of his pinky finger traces shapes in my cupped palm. The naughty smile hidden in the corner of Howlen's mouth is disconcerting.

While I appreciate his change in demeanor, I can't allow my focus to stray toward guilty indulgences.

Howlen crosses his arms and takes a pre-emptive step away before

Father Gabriel can witness our minor flirtation.

When the priest turns around to face us, however, it's clear there are bigger things to worry about.

He seems to have aged in the moments it took him to investigate the site. His shoulders sag and the corners of his lips are downturned. This is not normal.

"We are amidst the remnants of an ancient evil trying to pass into our world," Father Gabriel says. He waves a hand behind him before he swiftly crosses himself. "Whoever is responsible for channeling this dark power is either a complete idiot or an incredible sorcerer."

"Are we in any danger by being here?" I ask.

Father Gabriel surveys their surroundings and pulls his shoulders up to his ears. "I bet you've been in danger since you got involved with this case. Fortunately, whatever was here got what it came for and left," he said. "The residual wickedness will persist for days, if not weeks, but I'm going to bless the area and pray for nature's speedy recovery anyway."

My cell phone buzzes at the same time Howlen's phone rings, loud enough to wake Mount Olympus' sleeping gods.

Father Gabriel dismisses me and Howlen with a singular nod and turns away to do whatever he needs to do.

"Howlen speaking." He takes a few steps in the direction of the Sasol garage.

"Hello," I say, following a few steps behind Howlen.

"Esmé, Mosepi here." His voice is scratchy. It could be a bad connection, or perhaps he's spent the whole morning chain-smoking his Marlboro cigarettes. Either way, he sounds different. "Something strange is going on at the van Rooyen house."

"Clarify what you mean with *strange?*"

"Have you ever spent a night alone in a coroner's office?" Detective Mosepi asks, but continues before I can utter an answer. "It feels like every horrible memory, each bad experience, and all of your worst nightmares, combined into one terrifying, corporeal emotion, was draped over the site. The air even tastes sour! You need to come as soon as you can."

"I—"

"I swear it's not normal." He cuts me off, scratchy voice turning scratchier with panic. "Even the ecologists are stumped."

"You called in ecologists?" I shake my head, unsure whether I should be surprised, insulted, or chuffed. No, I feel all three emotions at once. I'm surprised this wasn't an isolated incident, insulted because Detective Mosepi didn't call me immediately, and chuffed because the ecologists can't do my job. "Listen, we've come across something similar in the veldt where Valentine Sikelo's body was found. I suggest you clear out the area until we can get there and grab some samples. Also, I'll bring Father Gabriel along."

"Please do. I have a neighborhood full of freaked-out residents who could use an explanation for …" He pauses. "Oh, just get here, damn it." The call ends abruptly.

Father Gabriel pops out of nowhere and gives me a look, while he rolls a blade of dead grass between his forefinger and thumb.

"May," Howlen calls over his shoulder, pocketing the cell phone before turning to face me. "Your grandfather's been incarcerated at OR Tambo International Airport."

"He wasn't supposed to arrive until next week. Wait. What?"

Howlen wipes a film of sweat from his forehead with the back of his hand. "Customs locked him up in an office because he refused to declare his newly acquired hand of glory, whatever that is, and he doesn't have the right importing permits."

"Sweet heavens, why *now?*" I trek back to my car. Leave it to Christiaan Snyder to be untimely with his eccentricities. "Call Detective Mosepi and get the details of the van Rooyen house situation," I call back to Howlen. "And tell Precious she needs to refill our anxiety prescriptions today—before we both follow Gramps' descent into madness!"

The most pleasant time to visit Pretoria is in September and October, when the old jacaranda trees are in full bloom and the whole city turns into one large purple-colored, fragrant sea of blossoms. The beautiful trees lining the thoroughfares—with their slender trunks, delicate leaves, and clusters of rich lilac blossoms—lend an unprecedented attractiveness to Pretoria. Pedestrians are also provided with shady retreats throughout the warm, albeit usually agreeable, spring months.

The same cannot be said for Johannesburg.

I'm positive Johannesburg's residents will disagree with my absolute loathing of South Africa's renowned metropolis, but I've never noticed a single good thing about it. The streets are too narrow and the skyscrapers too high. If shop owners don't hose down the sidewalks in front of their stores every morning, pedestrians would walk through urine and feces. Winter means a blanket of smog capable of giving a person lung cancer just by staring at it for too long. The horrendous traffic is another part of Jo'burg-living I simply don't care for.

Most tourists don't see these negatives because Sandton and Rosebank are far enough from the hell commonly referred to as The City of Gold.

First impressions are important, which is possibly why the OR Tambo International Airport sits comfortably on the edge of Johannesburg, near the suburban Kempton Park region. Here, it's relatively clean and the streets are in good shape. Here, you don't get to see the crime and ugliness giving the whole country a bad name. Here, you start your Proudly South African adventure—usually heading *away* from the metropolis and toward Sun City, the Kruger National Park, or Jo'burg's sister city, Pretoria.

As I walk through the almost clinical, distinctly impersonal airport to talk some sense into my grandfather, I'm reminded of a Douglas Adams quote in one of his lesser known works: *It can hardly be a coincidence that no language on earth has ever produced the expression, "As pretty as an airport."* The OR Tambo, even with its shiny surfaces and top-of-the-range technology, doesn't come close to being described as "pretty." I've seen worse in better-off countries, sure, but an airport is an airport is an airport. Each one looks identical to me. Even the customs officers, wearing their spotless uniforms and feeling oh-so-protected in their bubble of self-importance look the same as any other country's custom officers.

Déjà vu.

I know the drill by now.

Find the supervisor. Beg for a few minutes alone with my grandfather. Convince Christiaan I would somehow retrieve whatever it is he tried to smuggle into or out of the country in the first place. Then pay the fine. Sometimes fluttering my eyelashes helped lessen the fine. Other times, a bit of cleavage will do the trick. This time, I see customs officers glare and sneer as I'm led to the holding room. One had a recently broken nose, and droplets of blood stain his collared shirt. Another one sports a scar across his upper lip, and he has been scratched viciously on his forearms.

My usual wiles won't work.

I hear my grandfather long before I see him. The sea couldn't wash him clean from the obscenities he spits at no one and everyone. The supervisor clucks his tongue as he unlocks the door, but otherwise he's quiet.

When I enter the office, I say nothing.

What can I possibly say to explain my grandfather's actions? Should I tell them how Christiaan Snyder is a brilliant man? How he's a self-made millionaire—in Sterling Pounds instead of South African Rands? Should I explain how he's a beloved eccentric, respected by academics and police across the world? Or would it be better to say he's a collector of weird and wonderful items that give the Warrens Occult Museum in Virginia a run for its money? I can divulge how he's the best in the business where the occult is concerned. I can even go so far as to announce how Christiaan Snyder is the best grandfather a girl could ever want. This violent maniac is not who he really is.

But attributing any of the above-mentioned achievements to the red-faced grim reaper won't do anyone any good.

My grandfather looks up at me with narrowed eyes, his jaw clenched. He suddenly straightens in his seat like a proud peacock.

The door slams shut and the key turns in the lock, leaving me and the old man alone in the office.

His fisted hand moves to hover above the desk, then he drops a human tooth dangling from a leather cord onto the smooth surface. I glance at the necklace, an intricate knot tying the human molar to the leather thong, and divert my stare to the speckles of blood on my grandfather's knuckles.

Our gazes meet.

He seems unfazed by whatever retribution might come his way.

"In my defense," he says gruffly, "there's always been a method to my madness."

Never has he spoken truer words.

POLICE REPORT

Case Number: 010147858
Date: 22 June 2008
Reporting Officer: Deputy Clarence White
Prepared By: Tshabiso Hadebe

Incident Type:
Aggravated Assault / Attempted Murder

Address of Occurrence:
77 Semenya Street, Atteridgeville, Pretoria, 0006

Witness(es):
Lebo Jacobs: Neighbor. Male, 43

Evidence:
Fingerprints (taken from counter)
Footprint (size 10 Nike Air, found in mud outside point of entry)
DNA (collected from underneath the victim's fingernails)

Weapon/Objects Used:
Panga / Kitchen Knives / Iron

Summary:
On June 22, 2008, at approximately 20:38, two unidentified males broke into the residence of Lucky Zingithwa in Atteridgeville, Pretoria (through a bedroom window with no burglar proofing) and went on to assault, torture, and mutilate the victim with sundry

weapons.

The victim, Lucky Zingithwa, was overpowered by the first intruder in the kitchen. He attempted to fight back with a kitchen knife, but the second intruder came up from behind and knocked him unconscious. According to the victim's statement, when he awoke, he was bound to a kitchen chair, gagged and looking at two masked assailants, both wearing leather jackets, jeans, and ski masks.

"One carried a panga and the other one took the steak knife I had defended myself with," said Lucky Zingithwa.

Upon his awakening, the assailants tortured the victim through repeated beatings before cutting across his body with the kitchen knives. One of the assailants found a clothing iron, plugged it into the electricity socket, and used it to burn the left side of the victim's face. Thereafter, the assailants went on to remove the victim's teeth and eyes and hacked off one of his feet.

There is no sign of the victim's body parts in or around the residence or surrounding neighborhood, which makes this—possibly—a muti-related attack. Christiaan Snyder, occult-crime specialist, was called in to consult on the case (Snyder International Religious Crime Investigative Services – Case File: #23-CS).

After the assault/attempted murder, the two suspects fled through the front door. No witnesses have come forward to indicate whether the suspects had a getaway car.

A neighbor, Lebo Jacobs, heard commotion, but thought the victim was having a domestic squabble with one of his girlfriends at the time. He asserted to officers that he didn't see anything that could be used to lead them to a suspect. He did, however, call an ambulance and the police when he heard the victim's muffled cries for help around 23:00.

Deputy Clarence White was the first to respond to the emergency call and arrived at the scene around 23:10. He identified a partial footprint in the mud outside of the point of entry. A bloody fingerprint on the kitchen counter, possibly a suspect's, was also found and was sent to the forensics lab for analysis. Closer inspection of the shoeprint revealed one of the suspects was wearing size 10 Nike Airs. DNA evidence has also been collected from underneath the victim's fingernails and has been sent for analysis to the forensic lab.

Victim Lucky Zingithwa mentioned, in his statement, that one of the assailants wore a leather necklace with a human tooth hanging from it.

Notes:
Refer to Addendum D for the forensic lab's DNA and fingerprint results.

My grandfather's office is large and arbitrary.

What was once the main bedroom has been extended in width and length to contain everything he deems useful. This includes a large glass case from floor to ceiling stretching the entirety of the back wall. It houses a collection of fantastic items with equally unbelievable stories attached to them.

There is an authentic Maori Warrior Mask—one of many in the world—stationed proudly in the top left corner of the case. Maori warriors used to carve masks and statues prior to going into battle. The spirit of any Maori man who had lost his life in battle would then take over the specially carved piece. Father Gabriel baptized Christiaan's Maori Mask as Houdini when he'd first arrived, and the name stuck. It's a nice story; imagining a warrior's soul lives on in an inanimate object, except it's believed that these masks and statues bring harm to pregnant or menstruating women. So far, SIRCIS can't claim any females in the agency have been affected by Houdini, but it's a weirder-than-usual Maori Mask without the added stigma. Every once in a while, Houdini disappears for weeks at a time. Where the mask goes, nobody knows, but whenever Houdini returns, the mask often wears a smug smile. Gradually, the smugness fades and the usual frown is back in place.

To be honest, I think Houdini is a peeping pervert, but I won't dare say so in the mask's presence.

Next to Houdini sits an honest-to-God shrunken head, dating back to the late 1800s. We call him Jack for some inexplicable reason. Jack came from Peru, but ended up in Christiaan's collection a few decades ago when another collector decided the shrunken head was a cursed object. Apparently Jack mumbles from time to time, and it freaks people out. Jack's story is not half as interesting as some of the other items in my grandfather's collection, but shrunken heads are kind of cool to look at.

The rest of the top shelf is dedicated to other cursed knickknacks. There are ancient Israeli oil lamps in various sizes and shapes—none of which house a genie, fortunately. Statuettes from Mesopotamia, along with bad luck coins and plates, a Chinese vase, and a cracked Japanese teapot also litter the shelf.

On the second glass shelf are a few haunted dolls. Gretchen, a pretty porcelain one with wide blue eyes, perfectly curled blonde locks, and a cheerful floral dress, stares directly into the kitchen situated across from Christiaan's office. Though the doll hasn't done anything malicious around SIRCIS' headquarters, she has a tendency to hurt children. According to Christiaan, back in the 1960s, Gretchen attacked one of her previous owners with a Minora blade, scarring the poor child for life, mentally and physically. After the incident, other owners reported their hair being pulled, being pinched, and the doll moving around at night. Nothing of the sort has happened since her occupancy in the glass case, though.

Beside Gretchen sits the vintage cymbal-banging monkey, which comes to life all by itself. The bastard has a sick sense of humor. It loves making a racket when someone's working after hours, which tends to scare the living crap out of anyone unfortunate enough to try and get some overtime pay.

Otherwise, the monkey is benevolent.

Then, there's a voodoo doll from the 1800s, wooden blocks that enjoy spelling out colorful words no child should know until puberty, and a creepy clown with an affinity for the destruction of property.

On the third shelf stands The Crying Boy painting—a print, in this case—displayed in a special frame inhibiting its pyrokinetic abilities. The Crying Boy's story is common in England, but people in South Africa aren't familiar with it.

The boy was said to have been orphaned and abandoned on the street as a young child, circa 1950, and was found alone and crying after his parents' recent deaths in a house fire, one he supposedly started with his mind. Many claimed he had real life pyrokinetic abilities, and was thus named Diablo—devil—or The Fire Starter. An artist by the name of Bruno Amadio found the boy and painted his portrait, and rumor had it he also allowed the boy to live with him in his studio apartment. Shortly after the completion of his work, the studio burned to the ground.

The boy was then passed from family to family, and each family lost their house to a spontaneous fire.

Later, the same boy died in a car accident. No one claimed his body. People forgot about him, the painting, and the tale, until thirty-five years later. In 1985, in areas throughout England, some fifty house fires occurred, burning the houses to the ground. In each case, only one item within the house was left untouched and unclaimed by the raging fire: The Crying Boy picture. By then, the painting had been mass produced and thousands of copies were in circulation. Although the whereabouts of the original painting—there were twenty-eight so-called originals—was unknown, the curse seemed to extend to the copies as well.

Christiaan also owns a demonically possessed Ouija board, which sits beside The Crying Boy. In front of it is a magician's grimoire from the late 1700s, covered in human skin. A pearl necklace and sapphire hair comb, supposedly haunted, also make their home on the third shelf.

The newest addition to Christiaan's collection is a real hand of glory, the same one that'd gotten him into trouble at the airport. I hated the fact that I couldn't wait to hear the story behind it at our next office gathering under the lapa, especially since I'm still livid with my grandfather, but I knew it would be worth it at the end of the day.

Every few years, Christiaan changes out the displayed collection with other procured artifacts. Where he keeps the rest of his stuff, I have no idea.

I only hope he gets rid of the stupid monkey soon.

The remainder of my grandfather's office is lavishly decorated. Expensive lamps accentuate lavish furniture. Rare books from around the world in several languages line the shelves behind his desk. A post-modern art piece by some famous sculptor stands in the corner. Those are simply the most conspicuous things of the lot. Within the nooks and crannies are other miscellanies, forgotten until they are needed. Amulets and talismans are hidden in a flowerless vase. A discarded bowtie dangles precariously from a candelabrum, its purpose and owner unknown. A Carrol Boyes letter opener, positioned next to a Fabergé egg I've coveted my entire life, is on his desk. Where he found the Fabergé egg is anyone's guess, but he insists it's the real deal—part of the Romanov's lost treasures—and he promised me that if he ever wants to get rid of it, I have first dibs.

My feet sink into the plush carpet as I pace the length of my grandfather's office. "We're setting ourselves up for the South African version of an OJ Simpson trial. Do you have no consideration for the law?"

Christiaan and Howlen are working on the illegally obtained DNA evidence my grandfather had collected from the customs officers at the airport.

"And *you*!" I say, jutting my chin toward Howlen.

Howlen watches me from underneath his thick eyelashes.

"I expect more from *you* when it comes to adhering to chain-of-custody laws," I say.

"Get off your high horse, Esmé," Christiaan says.

Howlen's gloved hand swabs the customs officer's dried blood off my grandfather's knuckles.

As soon as I'd gotten him out of trouble at the airport—not including the assault charges they'd file against him at first light—Christiaan had instructed me to find a Ziploc bag so we could cover his hand, and the evidence with it.

My grandfather says, "It was probable cause, and I am a consulting specialist on the case. Besides, the guy was interviewed as a possible suspect numerous times."

"Probable cause does not extend beyond the police! You are *not* the police!"

"And you, my sweet grandbaby girl, have forgotten we live in South Africa."

"What does that have to do with anything, Pops?"

He groans and gives Howlen one of his help-me-out-with-this looks.

"Esmé," Howlen explains, "criminals find loopholes all the time, which is why the police hire consultants like us to do the things they cannot do, while under the influence of a badge. Technically speaking, with a good prosecutor on our side, Christiaan can be seen as part of the chain of custody. If we have an ignorant judge, nobody will even question the event. On another note, Christiaan also obtained video evidence of the suspect wearing the necklace, and I'm a licensed forensic criminologist. Everything counts in our favor."

"Well, I don't like it."

"Relax, May. Detective Mosepi will probably only use this evidence to get a search warrant for the suspect's house."

"*May?*" Christiaan asks nobody in particular, an eyebrow rising. "You two have grown rather chummy since I last saw you. I bet she calls you Howl, right?" He laughs at his own unfunny joke. It takes all of my strength not to go over there and throttle him. "Your mother will love that."

"You know his mother?"

"Of course I do." His shoulder twitches into a shrug. "Lady Sophia Jane Walcott is one of my dearest friends."

"*Lady* Sophia Jane Walcott?" I parrot, and chance a glance at the expressionless Howlen, who's focusing way too hard on my grandfather's knuckles. "How noble she sounds."

"I sense awkwardness," Christiaan muses, looking between us. "Did I say something wrong?"

"Nope." I cross my arms. "Howlen, will you be so kind as to take my grandfather home tonight? I have to get ready for an appointment."

All I get is a curt nod.

"What type of appointment, *May?*" Christiaan chuckles under his breath.

"The type of appointment that involves getting up close and personal with a dominatrix at a residential swingers club."

A long, heavy pause.

"I hope you're joking." My grandfather's expression is almost as priceless as Howlen's shock, which is quickly replaced with a scowl.

I answer them with a sheepish grin, and begin my exit.

"Esmé, tell me you're joking!"

"I'll see you tomorrow," I call over my shoulder, suppressing a laugh.

I wasn't joking.

Leila Fourie and I go way back.

Leila had been the popular girl in high school with a flock of rugby players tending to her every whim and need, whereas I had been the awkward girl smoking cheap Voyager cigarettes under the bleachers with other likeminded outcasts. Leila had the body of a svelte twenty-something-year-old when she was barely sixteen, while I was a bit more childish-looking. We've always been worlds apart, but an unlikely friendship had grown in the summer of 2004, after I'd held back Leila's hair while she vomited up a bottle of vodka. As remuneration for not abandoning her like her so-called friends, Leila taught me the finer points of womanhood. Before her intervention, I was clueless when it came to cosmetics and clothes due to growing up in a predominantly male environment. Now, though, I'm possibly the best-dressed occult crime expert in the world.

Before I came along, Leila had perpetually second-guessed herself and relied on others to rate her worth. Leila, however, had grown out of it. Today, she's a respected publicist for a major mobile company by day and a fetishist by night. She's more independent and self-confident than ever before.

We meet in secret because Leila gets confidential information from high-profile individuals and secure databases. She can easily be assassinated if our friendship ever becomes public knowledge. This is why we only get together on a bimonthly basis at the swingers' club, where members' secrets are kept secret.

The location for the swingers club, tonight, is in an ambassadorial mansion in Moreleta Park. It's a beautiful house with an enclosed courtyard, pool, four bedrooms with en-suites. and a fifth with its own lounge. And the whole place overlooks a private bird park, dam, and endless rolling lawns.

When I drive up, a security guard checks my credentials and membership card at the gate before he waves me through with a tip of a nonexistent hat.

Then the hard part begins.

I climb out of my car, wearing a formal red dress with a low front and an even lower back. I carry my prop-box, which is filled with all kinds of goodies Leila would swoon over, and walk up to the front door of the mansion. One knock, a second of waiting, and the doors open wide. Inside, people are already laughing and acquainting or reacquainting themselves with one another.

The soirée is in full swing.

The security guard at the door checks my membership card before he allows me entry. Familiar faces smile as I pass. Greetings are exchanged and quick tête-à-têtes are traded while I discreetly sweep my surroundings for Leila. I finally move on to the next room, and the next, falling into the usual routine of conversation until I find Leila in the kitchen. Dollied up in a Grecian-style white dress, sipping tentatively on a flute of champagne, Leila is as beautiful as ever.

She doesn't feign an iota of interest with the older gentleman who's trying to wiggle his way into her knickers, but he doesn't seem like he's gotten the message from her body language.

Only when she spots me in the door does her face brighten.

"Excuse me." Leila pushes past the tuxedo-clad man and closes the distance between us. We air-kiss and the box is handed over.

"What a boring old fart," she whispers as we exit the kitchen to explore the house. "As if someone like me would ever agree to consensual sex with someone like him. He's on the verge of bankruptcy. By God, I do have *some* standards."

I laugh. "Good thing I made the cut."

"I told you that if you ever want to change teams, I'd go steady with you." Leila winks.

I almost blush at her appraising glance, but we end up laughing it off.

"Let's mingle for a few minutes and go find a room. I'm hardly in the mood for this stuffy atmosphere," Leila says.

"Sounds like a plan."

We circulate the mansion filled with businessmen, diplomats, and billionaire foreigners with their husbands or wives on their arms. Some of these people I've seen around every gathering. Others are newcomers, possibly seeing this as an experiment and nothing more. They talk about investment ventures, global warming, ISIS, and current affairs. Some even talk about their children's recent prestigious achievements at whatever hoity-toity private school they attend.

It's all very civil—as always.

The first couple makes their adventurous escape outdoors. Another couple whisk themselves away to a suite upstairs, giggling like teenagers. Leila and I are the next people to disappear from the party, heading into the farthest room downstairs.

As soon as the door slams shut, we're laughing. Not because we're getting naked, but because we've survived the ordeal of faking it in front of an audience for the umpteenth time.

"What an insufferable bunch of hypocrites," Leila says. She searches for audio or visual equipment someone may have hidden in the room, while I lock the door and move a heavy chaise in front of it as an extra prevention measure. "Half of them advocated for the dismissal of the proposed DSTV porn channel. Did you know that?" She closes the curtains in one fluid movement, kicks off her shoes, and falls onto the king-size bed.

"I did not," I answer, falling next to her.

Leila twists around to pick up the box I'd brought along, opens the lid, and squeals in delight. She dumps the contents onto the bed, scattering candies and chocolates across the embroidered duvet, alongside miniature bottles of booze. It almost feels like old times.

I pick up a packet of sour worms and Leila chooses a roll of fireballs before we both lie down again.

"I heard about those cases you're working on." She licks on a red fireball and looks at me through half-lidded sapphire eyes. "From what I've gathered, it sounds like a dangerous killer is on the loose."

"You don't know the half of it." I bite into a sour worm and pull the candy taut until it breaks in half.

"Anything I can help with?" she asks. "The media's all over this. I could try and throw my weight around to give you some time?"

"It's okay for now, Lei, but thank you."

She turns onto her stomach, props herself onto her elbows, and regards me from afar. "Want to talk about it?"

"No," I say sharply.

"Want to talk about the sexy Brit you've been seeing on and off?" Leila wiggles her eyebrows. She licks the fireball and sticks out her red tongue. No good can come from the naughty glimmer in her eyes. "Does he butter your scone like a real English gent?"

My face grows hot, earning a laugh in response.

"Can I make you a cuppa tea, then?" Leila teases, faking a cringe-worthy British accent.

From a tittering giggle, I fall into fits of laughter.

She's relentless. "'Ave yer seen wha' those bluddy Tory arseholes are up to now?"

"He doesn't sound like an extra in a football hooligan flick!" I howl.

"Ah, yes. Of course," Leila says, wiping her expression clear of emotion. "Let me just channel my inner Downton Abbey—"

"Please, don't."

She grins, licks her fireball again, and jerks her hand away from her mouth. "I almost forgot." She pushes her free hand into her cleavage and pulls out a silver USB flash drive. "Don't lose it. Don't tell anyone you have it. Destroy it if you can't find a use for the information on it." Leila hands over the warm flash drive.

"Duly noted. Thank you." I hide the drive between my own breasts until it is out of sight and safe. "What's on it?"

Leila beams. "Blackmail on the judges who are pro-muti, if you get what I mean?"

"I have no idea what you mean." I sit upright.

"Oh, you know," she says, "just a few documents proving how certain judges faked their university degrees or some of their grades in order to get said degree. Photographs of an especially lenient judge on ritual murders who purchased muti from a witchdoctor he'd not convicted. Paper trails of payoffs between judges and felons who walked.

That type of stuff."

"Holy shit, where did you get this information?"

"There's a new genius IT guy at work. Not much to look at, mind, but he got me the info." Leila shrugs again, pops the fireball into her mouth, and cradles it in her cheek. "After I called him a dirty little nasty boy who was in dire need of a spanking, he was more than willing to do my bidding." She puckers her mouth as she moves the sweet to the other cheek. "Anyway, I already verified the information, so you have your golden ticket if you want to use it, babe."

"Holy crap, Lei," I whisper. I'd never blackmail a judge—it would be idiotic—but the prosecution could definitely use this information if push came to shove. If my grandfather's illegal retrieval of DNA can be classified as being a loophole, this USB flash drive is a freaking wormhole that planets could fall through.

"You're welcome," she says smugly, turning onto her back. "Now, we have about ninety minutes to catch up on each other's lives. Tell me all about what you've been up to with Howlen these days."

"It's not like that between us."

"Of course it's not. You're smart enough to know when a guy's just there to scratch an itch, and I am smart enough to know you don't see Howlen as a permanent fixture in your life. It doesn't mean there hasn't been a lack of scratching happening."

I sigh. "Fine, I'll tell you about the so-called scratching."

It's the least I can do, considering Leila doesn't accept money for risking her life for others.

CHAPTER 12

The darkness is overwhelming; the rancid smell even more so.

The clicks and scratches of scurrying rats set his pulse racing. Abraham Amin scrambles for a foothold on the dirt-caked floor, scuffing his polished black shoes in the process. Sweat taps down his neck, trails his spine, and accumulates at his waistband. His drenched, filthy shirt sticks to his body uncomfortably. His breath comes out in ragged pants while he works his bound wrists against the leather cuffs. Chains rattle as he tugs his arms and swings his body back and forth to loosen the restraints.

The last thing he remembers is being at the ambassadorial mansion in Moreleta Park, chatting up some millionaire widow from Dubai. Most of the night is a blur, though, which doesn't make any sense. He never consumed alcohol excessively. *Never.* Therefore, he concludes, he must've been drugged—probably by the overeager widow. But why?

"Damn it." Abraham chastises himself for his own stupidity. It's the first time he'd accepted the club's invitation. It's the first time he'd considered cheating on his estranged, lunatic spouse. Now, he couldn't help but wonder if she's behind all of this.

"Colleen!" he shouts, hoping to get her attention. She's done some pretty fucked-up shit in the past, but this was going too far. "Colleen!"

Blood runs down his arms and gathers in his armpits, staining his shirt. If he can only find a way to pull himself up and get the leather cuffs unhooked, then escape is possible. Then he can change his bloody last will and testament and exclude the demented she-devil from his inheritance. Abraham knows he's grown soft over the years—soft enough to be overpowered, soft enough to be strung up like an animal waiting to be slaughtered. Pathetic.

He works his wrists clockwise and anticlockwise, panting and grunting all the while. Abraham feels the leather cuff cut into the mound of his left palm, slick blood lubricating his restraint. He tugs harder, more violently, grinding his teeth as he endures the pain. The leather bites into the soft flesh of his hand until he hears an unexpected crack. He suppresses a scream when he realizes the crack was him dislocating his own thumb. It's surprise, not pain. He can't feel anything, really, except anger. He'd always known Colleen was a strange woman. When they were younger, her free spirit had charmed him, but as they'd grown older, the novelty had worn off and her crazy antics had become borderline violent. After twelve years of marriage, he knows her soul is as black as this endless darkness.

He needs to find a way out. Then he'll plan his revenge.

After a long struggle, he slips one hand out of the cuff and blindly loosens the other. It takes longer than he hopes, but soon his arms are hanging limply at his sides, and he's on solid ground again. The hard part comes next—finding a way out. If only he could see. If only he had a weapon to defend himself.

"You freed yourself faster than I anticipated."

The whispered voice is calm. Too calm. It's not Colleen's voice.

Abraham's heart pounds as fear courses through his veins. Every instinct tells him to run, but where?

"Then again, politicians are professional evaders. Get themselves out of tricky situations, fast?"

An uneasy quiet fell.

When nothing happens, Abraham wonders if the voice isn't a figment of his imagination. Mind games are one of Colleen's specialties. She says it "keeps love unpredictable." Maybe the stress has caught up with him.

He stretches his arms and takes a step forward again, his legs still uncertain with fear.

"Did you know," the voice says, giving Abraham pause, "I voted for you in the municipal elections."

"Then what am I doing here?" Abraham asks. "Where is Colleen?"

"To answer your first question, it was my attempt at irony, I think," the voice says. "You were always going to end up here, Abraham. *Always.*"

A long pause, before, "As for the second question, I have no idea where your wife is. She's not the person responsible for your capture and containment."

At this, the pretense of surviving vanishes. Colleen is a manageable foe, but an unknown assailant is a whole other matter.

Not caring about making noise, he runs with outstretched arms, hoping to reach something solid. He stumbles in the dark and collides hard with the smooth floor, knocking his wind out.

A humorless laugh echoes through the void. Without warning, something slides across his right heel, severing his Achilles tendon.

Abraham screams, but continues dragging himself forward with his fingertips and nails.

"I don't want to kill you yet, but if you're going to try and escape, I will render you unconscious. Do you want to prolong your own suffering, Abraham?" The blade slides across the same heel a second time, and Abraham screams again. "Shut your mouth, before I rip out your vocal cords!"

The threat shuts Abraham up. Mucus and tears stream down his face as he digs his nails into the dirt, breaking them into jagged shadows of what they used to be. Warm blood gushes across the heel of his foot, just more of the darkness already pooled around him. It's too much darkness to bear.

"When you're done throwing your tantrum, I have dinner waiting." The stranger hooks one arm underneath Abraham's and lifts him onto his feet.

"Why?" Tears stream down his face as his captor drags him to the other end of the room.

"I told you, I don't want to kill you yet."

"So you're playing a twisted game with me?"

A dry laugh. "I understand why you might be confused, given your status, but believe me when I say you're simply a means to an end. There's nothing political about this. I have no personal qualms against you or your family. No, it's merely fate, Abraham."

"Fate?"

He drops Abraham Amin into a plastic chair. "Fate," he echoes.

CHAPTER 13

All I want is a long bubble bath, to dress in my comfiest PJs, and fall asleep in my queen-size bed. But I know I won't. I'm too hyped up on facts, theories, and curiosities. Feyisola and Leila's information is burning metaphorical holes in my mind, demanding immediate attention. The unsolved homicides of Valentine Sikelo and Carol-Anne Brewis are equally important, and will certainly keep me awake.

These are my reasons for heading back to the office at ten o'clock instead of going home.

The Sikelo and Brewis cases are puzzles, the murderer an enigma.

It's infuriating.

The developing clusterfuck in Pretoria is eating me alive from the inside out. Though I'm sure my grandfather would call this situation a cakewalk in comparison to the 2008 Kei Ripper Murders in Butterworth.

When I reach the office, the lights are on. Howlen and Precious' vehicles are in their usual places as I park in my typical spot. When I walk into the building, still wearing the provocative red dress—a personal requirement for my cover—I hear my colleagues brainstorming in the conference room. I peek inside.

The conference room is in disarray. Whiteboards line the walls, with photographs and scribbles in blue marker covering them. Pictures of the crime scenes, ante-mortem portraits of the victims, and mugshots of the suspects hang on the walls along with assorted pieces of evidence. There are stacks of boxes filled with old case files and evidence on the large oak table. Discarded fast food containers lie on one end. At the other side, used mugs of coffee stand in a pitiful circle on a decorative table which used to house my father's miniature bottle ships.

"Something doesn't make sense here. The timeline is off on the Sikelo case," Christiaan says, facing one of the whiteboards in the conference room. "According to the reports, Valentine Sikelo's body was in advanced stages of decomposition consistent with an exposed corpse at three days in the African sun, but her husband's witness statement suggests she was alive the same morning. What am I missing here?"

"Albert Einstein once said: 'Imagination is more important than knowledge,'" I say, walking into the conference room. "For knowledge is limited to all we now know and understand. Imagination embraces the entire world, and all there ever will be to know and understand."

"Your point being?" Howlen turns in his seat and looks at me as though I'm a rare collectible.

I'm not sure if I liked being objectified without doing some objectification myself. Had we been alone, I might've toyed with him a bit. Alas, playtime would have to wait.

"My point is, other than sounding pretentious, we've grown accustomed to searching for answers in conventional ways. We've become complacent with searching for a particular type of killer."

I walk up to my grandfather and the whiteboards before pointing to the crime scene photos of Valentine and Carol-Anne.

"If you look at the placement of the bodies, and check their locations, you'll see these aren't run-of-the-mill muti-murders," I explain. "Valentine Sikelo was found in the veldt between WF Nkomo Street and the Magalies Freeway, which isn't a particularly good hiding place considering there are still some people who use the footbridge to get from Kwaggasrand to Danville. And dumping Carol-Anne Brewis' body at the Gert van Rooyen house is another peculiar choice. Why?"

"The killer wanted us to find the victims." Howlen stands, shakes his head, and searches through the various files on the table.

"But it doesn't make sense," Christiaan says, tapping the marker against his bottom lip. "Muti-killers and/or their lackeys typically try to hide their victims. They fail more often than not, but self-preservation dictates they at least try to get away with the crime."

"Unless we're dealing with a killer with a personality disorder of some kind," Howlen says, paging through a file. "I didn't think much of it before, but neither of the victims were raped."

"Not all muti-victims are raped, Howlen," Christiaan says.

"I know, which is why I didn't think it was important, but considering Esmé's hypothesis of how the killer wants us to find the bodies changes things."

"Why?" Precious asks.

"Well, the primary motivation for rape is usually power or it's committed out of rage. Since the victims weren't raped, it means: a.) the killer was in control of his anger the entire time, and b.) our killer already feels powerful enough not to show dominance over the victim."

"He's a psychopath," I add.

"Or has some other unspecified personality disorder," Howlen corrects me. "Narcissism, sociopathy, schizophrenia—they all apply right now."

"Wonderful," Christiaan mumbles. "You've narrowed down our suspect list to everyone in Parliament."

"We are also dealing with a killer of above-average intelligence." Howlen walks around the table with zoomed-in pictures of the victims' wounds. He sticks them up against the whiteboard and flicks his fingers against the side of the contraption. "Clean cuts on both accounts, made by a scalpel."

"How do you know it was made by a scalpel and not a very sharp knife?" I peer closer at the photograph to inspect the edges of the wounds.

"Okay, it could be a scalpel *or* a very sharp knife. I can't be sure without the lab results, but I can tell you that neither Valentine nor Carol-Anne Brewis died from the mutilation they endured." He points to their necks where coagulated blood covered thin ligature marks.

"How odd." Christiaan leans in and studies the photographic evidence. "Does fishing gut create ligature marks like that?"

"It's not impossible," Howlen responds.

"Pops, do you remember when you and Dad took me deep sea fishing when I was around fourteen or fifteen?"

The old man nods without taking his eyes off the whiteboards.

"Remember how the captain of the boat taught me how to gut a fish?"

"Of course, you smelled like fish for a week."

I turn to Howlen. "I don't know if you know anything about fishing, but the captain told me on the trip that every fisherman worth his salt has a sharp knife in his tackle box. We might be looking for someone who knows his way around fishing."

"In Pretoria, though?" Howlen grimaces.

"Yes, in Pretoria," I say. "We do have dams around here, you know. There's Hartbeespoort Dam, Bronkhorstspruit Dam, Roodeplaat Dam—"

"I never thought you'd enjoy fishing," Howlen interrupts.

"You never asked."

"The last thing we need is a creative muti-killer," Christiaan says.

"And on that note," Precious says, standing. "I think it's time for us to go home before we embark on catching this sick individual."

"But—" Christiaan is cut off by one of Precious' infamous murderous glares.

He sighs. "Fine, but I'm not happy about it."

"We'll work on your pursuit of happiness in the morning, Chris." Precious heads to the door and switches off the light of the conference room without further discussion. "Out."

Howlen groans in unison with my grandfather's breathy cusses. The three of them drag themselves into the hallway, and Precious locks the conference room's door.

By now, they know not to argue with their loyal secretary, because she *always* wins.

From Christiaan's office, the incessant clangs of the annoying cymbal monkey starts, reiterating the need to leave.

Everyone parts ways when the office building is locked up. Precious drives Christiaan homewards, while Howlen and I fumble around our cars in the parking lot.

I'm deep in thought and silent as the dead.

When it's clear that Precious won't turn back to check on them or the office, Howlen walks over.

"Where have you been tonight?" he asks as I slip out of the driver's seat and lean back against the back door.

He admires my dress, shamelessly tracing my body with his gaze.

I ignore him, feeling my own wants and needs multiply under his stare. He wants to touch me, I know, but he hesitates, for some reason. I take his hand in mine and tenderly brush my fingertips against his palm before I place it on my hip. I step closer, set my hand on his cheek, and draw his face closer.

"May." His voice is full of pain. "Where have you been?" Howlen's hand moves down my hip and toward my upper leg, scrunching up the crimson fabric in his fist.

I grin as I brush my nose against his, our lips almost touching. "I was working a possible lead, like I told you when I left."

He backs me up against my car, the dress becoming shorter with every breath we take. Hot wind licks my bare legs. The sound of late-night traffic on the other side of the wall drones in the background. It's exhilarating, whatever this is.

"You said you had an appointment with a dominatrix at a residential swingers club." Howlen's free hand glides down my neck. He cups one breast through my dress a bit harder than he'd usually dare, before moving his hand down my side.

I close my eyes and try to control my labored breathing.

"Were you joking?"

"No," I whisper, opening my eyes.

A mischievous smile tugs at the corners of my lips. My hands move down to his belt, loosening it with the precision of a pickpocket.

Howlen barely registers my quick movements. Instead, the same hand that'd been groping me through my dress snakes its way into my hair.

He pulls my locks backward until I'm forced to look into his eyes. It doesn't hurt, though secretly I think I might like a bit of pain with my pleasure.

He kisses me hard enough to bruise my lips, wedging my mouth apart with his tongue. However long this lasts, I can't be sure, but when he pulls away, I'm breathless with lust.

Howlen lets go of me and steps away. "Goodnight."

"Wha–?" I snap out of my wanton delirium and watch him walk to his car with purpose. "Are you fucking kidding me?" The screech of disbelief isn't deliberate, yet not entirely undignified. "Howlen?"

"Go home, Esmé," he says, closing his car door. "Go home, before we do or say things we'll both regret tomorrow."

I stare, dumbfounded, as he drives away.

CHAPTER 14

MISSING PERSON
ABRAHAM AMIN

Description:

Age: 39 Years	**SAPS Case Number:** OB07/09/15
Gender: Male	**Last Seen:** Monday, 07/09/2015
Build: Average	**Last Contact:** Monday, 07/09/2015
Eyes: Brown	**Last Seen Wearing:**
Hair: Black	Pinstripe suit, white shirt, purple
Weight: 98 kg	and blue paisley tie, black dress
Height: 1.81 m	shoes, platinum Rolex, and white
Ethnicity: Indian	gold cufflinks with diamonds.

Abraham Amin was last seen at an ambassadorial mansion in Moreleta Park, Pretoria, on the 7th of September 2015, at approximately 19:00. Witnesses state that an unknown person evaded security personnel on the premises and knocked several attendees unconscious with a club before abducting Abraham from the embassy.

Abraham Amin suffers from diabetes and is in need of immediate medical attention. His vehicle, a black Mercedes Benz CLA-Class Edition 1, was found abandoned on the N1 Southbound, before Lynnwood. His cell phone was found in the glove compartment, along with his wallet.

If you know of Abraham's whereabouts, or know of someone who may be able to assist us in finding him, please contact your nearest police station immediately.

Or please call: 0800-1177-1416 or email *findabraham@gmail.com* with any details concerning his location.

REWARD OFFERED

Nowadays, the Internet is widely available in South Africa, giving people the opportunity to explore other religions to their heart's content. Whether this is due to curiosity or from a valid quest for spiritual enlightenment, I can't tell. What I know for certain is that although it's a constitutional right to enquire and/or practice whatever faith you wish, it's your responsibility to adhere to the laws set forth in the *Constitution of the Republic of South Africa* (1996). Unfortunately, the notable increase in so-called vampirism, spiritual intimidation, voodoo, and a variety of other harmful religious practices—especially in schools—has many uneducated persons making wild accusations about things they don't understand. And they *don't* understand because they are too scared to climb out of the comfortable holes they've dug for themselves.

I should know. I've worked with these brainiacs more often than I'd liked.

They mostly show their faces in and around schools when the media reports on some or other "religious" crime committed by teenagers. With a catchy headline like: "TEENAGERS KILL IN THE NAME OF SATAN" or "SATANIST TEENAGERS KILL GIRL (16) AS SACRIFICE," how can one not take notice? This usually drew together "concerned" government officials, which includes the South African Police Service (SAPS), the National Prosecuting Authority (NPA), and the departments of basic education, social development and health, as well as teachers, pupils, parents, and faith-based speakers. Sadly, most of these people are as ignorant as they are idiotic, and the only things they know are what the Satanic Panic instigators of old forced down everyone's throats. This includes, but is in no means limited to, trying to discern the so-called "warning signs of possible occult-related discourse," because *obviously* the Biblical devil isn't smart enough to blend in with the times.

It's backward thinking in every sense of the phrase.

In the *Harmful Religious Practice* pamphlet, released by the Department of Justice and the Department of Constitutional Development in 2014, the ignorance and propaganda was slathered on so thick, it is amazing folks don't still burn women at the stake for menstruating. This pamphlet neatly outlines every possible symptom of "being influenced by a harmful or dangerous belief or practice." It covers everything from teenage hormonal changes—including unusual aggression, being quiet, or becoming secretive—to warning against gothic culture, and condemning hematolagnia—anyone who shows a fascination with blood, especially human blood. That's simply the beginning of the nonsense these backstreet "occultists" teach kids.

At best, people are labeled as being weird. At worst, people get killed in the name of God.

For years, academics have prompted intelligent approaches to occult-related problems, but the possibility of a modern witch-hunt makes it impossible for them to be heard over the incessant bloodlust born of ignorance.

That's why I tend to avoid those who are unwilling to learn even the basics of occult-related matters, much to my grandfather's dismay. The truth is, I don't have the patience. Christiaan could try to deprogram the country until he's blue in the face, but while the government backs "God's Warriors" or whatever the media calls them now, he wouldn't get through to anybody.

Dealing with the media is another peeve. They want sensationalism, not facts. They want the "SATANIC YOUTH BLAMES HEAVY METAL MUSIC FOR MURDER" headline, not the mediocre "ATTENTION-SEEKING TEENAGER KILLS" truth. They are a large part of the problem, which is why I give those vultures a wide berth every time I encounter them. Howlen can handle the reporters if he felt so inclined—he has a face for television.

Oh, and don't forget about social media. Thanks to Google, everyone's an expert on everything, especially when it comes to delegating how I should do *my* job. Well, fuck you very much for the comments and mansplaining. Just know that nobody's an expert until you've had to overturn a bucket, only to find a child's severed head arranged in their intestines.

There is evil in this world, yes, but evil can't be pigeonholed.

Take Jencko Graça, for instance.

Jencko Graça is a gynecologist who works at a free clinic in Pretoria West. Three days a week, Jencko works at the free clinic and the rest of the time he works at an abortion clinic in Pretoria CBD. Performing abortions doesn't make him evil. When rape statistics continue to climb and victims range from a few months old to well into their golden years, clinics where safe abortions are conducted and essential. After all, a twelve-year-old girl, raped by her uncle, is in no position to care for a baby, and children can't survive on air and water alone. As for religious standpoints, well, even if most people in South Africa don't condone abortion, I have never seen anyone picketing at the local Mary Stopes Clinic.

Jencko Graça isn't evil for doing his job.

The janitor at his clinic, however, is an evil son of a bitch.

Amorphous clouds of smoke accompany Rochester Ramphele where he stands on the fire escape's landing, staring into the alley behind the abortion clinic. He's in his uniform, sucking greedily on a cigarette, scratching his head. Nothing about the man screams criminal, and yet there's always something *off* about people in the human muti business.

I can't explain it exactly, but I always got a heavy feeling in the pit of my stomach, as though a boot has lodged itself in my gut.

Detective Mosepi and I sit quietly in an empty apartment looking out on the alleyway, watching the guy's every move. We're far enough away to observe him without Rochester being able to observe us. When his break ends, Rochester opens the back door and slips inside again, unaware of being watched.

I turn to the scowling detective, who's scribbling ferociously on his notepad. He places the binoculars on the dusty windowsill.

"I don't understand why I'm here," I say, glancing at my wristwatch. It's still early, 10:14 a.m. I should be in my office catching up on some paperwork, not sitting on a plastic chair to keep tabs on a cleaner with criminal intent. Besides, I have a bone to pick with Howlen. "Does this have anything to do with my current cases?"

"Maybe," Detective Mosepi says under his breath.

"But maybe not, right?"

"Maybe not."

I groan. "I hate stakeouts, especially if I don't know *why* we're going after small fry."

"Small fry can be used to bait big fish," Detective Mosepi says, looking up. "You're never this antsy. Even as a child, you weren't jittery. What's the matter?"

"Nothing," I mumble, and force my leg to stop jumping.

"Okay, don't tell me, but I'm inclined to assume the worst, then." Detective Mosepi goes back to doodling on his notepad. "Is it drugs?"

"What?"

"You need a fix, don't you?" He's only half serious, but it's enough to make me swear. "I told you I'd assume the worst."

"So, you think the worst I can do is drugs? You don't know me very well," I say. "And no, it's not drugs. It's personal."

"Ah." He tries to hide the amusement in his voice, but fails. "I wondered how long you and Howlen Walcott, *PhD* would be able to have this in-office romance without it affecting your work."

"It's not—"

"I'm not a BEE employee, Esmé. I earned my position the old fashioned way, by being a fantastic detective." He glances at the landing where Rochester stood earlier. "I've known about the two of you for—what's it been now, two years?"

"I hate it when you do that."

"Unlike your father, I can't turn this"—he pushes his pencil against his temple—"off." Detective Mosepi closes his notepad and sets it down on his lap. "Rochester Ramphele sells medical waste from this facility on the black market at high prices. He's an intelligent businessman, a go-between for those who don't want to get their hands dirty, but he made one fatal mistake."

"Which is?"

"Nobody can fool the taxman." Detective Mosepi steals a glance at me. "The South African Revenue Service has a nose for when the numbers don't add up, as they didn't in Rochester Ramphele's bank account. Call it dumb luck, but I know the woman who did the audit, and she said something wasn't right. So, I've been looking into the guy."

"Correct me if I'm wrong, but doesn't a homicide detective typically investigate murders? The title is kind of self-explanatory."

"I had a hunch." He shrugs his broad shoulders. "Turns out, my hunch paid off. Rochester is one of the brains behind a human body part smuggling ring. He, and a few cleaners at other medical facilities, steals small quantities of medical waste to sell on the black market. His reach is as far as it is wide, considering that the janitor at the city morgue is also involved in the scheme."

"And you got all this from your informant at SARS?"

"No, I got it from tailing the guy for the past two months," Detective Mosepi says. "The reason you're here is because I suspect Rochester Ramphele may know who our killer is. I'd like to have you here in case we find something sinister."

"Is it the only reason?"

"Yes," he answers simply, leaving no room for me to think otherwise.

I stand to stretch my legs. The apartment, a bachelor flat with barely enough room for a single bed, is as unappealing as it is small. The smell of mildew and dust does nothing to mute the tang of old piss that'd seeped into the fibers of the threadbare carpet. A rusty old sink in the corner of the matchbox flat acts as both the kitchen sink and bathroom basin for renters. The only door, besides the front door, probably leads to the toilet. No amount of money will convince me to open that door. God only knows what's swimming around in the porcelain bowl. An array of stains decorate the yellowing walls—the remnants of a long-ago oil fire which had licked its way to the ceiling. There's a splash of what could've been Fanta Grape, and another brownish splatter of what might have been blood.

"Was somebody killed here?" I ask.

The plastic chair groans under Detective Mosepi's weight. "I suspect a great many people have been killed in this place over the years."

I take my seat again. "I meant recently."

He responds with a stiff shrug, and scribbles some more in his notebook.

I look back to the landing as Rochester wheels a red plastic bin out the back door. "We have movement, Detective."

Rochester studies the alley before he rolls the bin to the stairs. Each step down is accompanied by a hollow *thump* as he carefully pushes the bin toward the allocated fenced-off dumping zone.

I count thirty-four thumps.

"Suspicious, for a janitor," the detective murmurs with the binoculars pressed up against his face.

Rochester Ramphele is out of my line of vision. "What is?" I ask.

"He's sifting through the rubbish bags in the bin," he answers. "And …"

"And?"

"There seems to be a cooler box hidden behind the dumpster. Probably to transport the medical waste," Detective Mosepi explains. "It's an unpleasant sight."

I can only imagine.

We don't speak much after that. He's always been a man of few words and I've always been incapable of engaging in small talk. The quiet doesn't seem to bother either of us, though.

The hours drag by. Now and then, the crackling of Detective Mosepi's radio breaks the silence with static-filled voices. Updates from other officers surrounding the building fill the room for brief moments. This operation is much larger than I'd initially thought, but it doesn't make sense for Mosepi to go all out to reprimand a nobody criminal. Then again, I'm not about to question his intentions.

Throughout the day, my phone vibrates with messages: My grandfather inviting me to dinner the next night, Precious with an update on the cases I'm working on, Dad asking how I am. Howlen, however, doesn't contact me.

I read an e-book I'd downloaded ages ago. When I tire of reading, I play a zombie game on my phone. Every once in a while, I get up and walk around the apartment to get the blood flowing again. I'm not exactly bored, but being cooped up in tight spaces for long periods always gives me a mild case of cabin fever.

When the working day comes to an end and the sunlight wanes, city noises are amplified as vehicles jammed with people rush to get home. From our position in the building behind the clinic, we can't see what Rochester Ramphele is up to inside. We rely on the periodic updates from the rest of the team. Where the others are located is beyond my knowledge, but their vantage points allow them to paint a pretty picture for us.

"The doctor has left the building, over."

"Last patients have exited through the front door, over."

"Ramphele is cleaning the surgery now, over."

We wait.

At five o'clock, long after the clinic has closed its doors for the day, the perpetrator finally leaves. He exits through the back door, dressed in ordinary clothing that would help him blend into the crowds. A black slogan T-shirt paired with plain jeans and white sneakers leaves Rochester indistinguishable from anyone else his age on the streets. The only tell is the Kaizer Chiefs baseball cap he wears, pulled low over his forehead. Though I doubt his choice in clothing has anything to do with paranoia, one could never be certain if a perp suspects a tail.

When Rochester retrieves the cooler box behind the dumpster, Detective Mosepi orders a couple of undercover cops to follow him. The rest are to stay well behind, but within radio distance.

I toss my cell phone and Kindle into my purse, pull my hair into a tight ponytail, and follow Detective Mosepi out. After spending the day in the shithole apartment, it's almost refreshing to see the disgusting hallway outside the door.

"He's going to meet his buyer tonight," Detective Mosepi says when we reach the staircase down the hallway. "As soon as the exchange is made, we move in. Two birds, one stone, all that."

"Do you know where he meets his buyers?"

"Yes."

It's all he's willing to give me, and I don't press for more.

Once outside the complex, we walk at a brisk pace to where he's parked his unmarked car. Hidden behind the mosque that shares the parking lot, the black BMW sits by its lonesome self.

Detective Mosepi is winded when we finally strap into the seats.

"You should quit smoking," I say as the engine purrs to life. "You're killing yourself."

He shoots me a sharp look, grunts, and reverses into the street.

I study the city I both love and loathe through the tinted window.

Classical structures with long, dark, yet fascinating histories stand alongside modern glass and steel skyscrapers that sparkle brilliantly in the sun. Trees line the thoroughfares beside the slender metal streetlights. Bronze statues, their significance lost to time, stare out at the ever-changing city from their patches of lawn. The homeless will move to Church Square later, where the statue of President Paul Kruger watches over them. Ironic, considering the current government sees the statue as an icon of Apartheid, yet the homeless are drawn to this spot for solace. Then comes the older part of the city, where centuries-old churches compete with pop-up ministries for souls.

It's a sad sight, but not sadder than the out-of-place primary school situated in the busiest—and possibly the most dangerous—part of town.

Eendracht Maakt Macht. The slogan of Eendracht Primary is etched into a faded sign at their front gate. Like the rest of the city, this school has a rich history forgotten by most. It's not the biggest school in Pretoria CBD, but it's old enough to make it an historical landmark of sorts. Back in the day, Eendracht Primary schooled almost all the children in the city, and some from well beyond the city's borders. Children from varied backgrounds, ethnicities, and religions were all treated equally.

I know this for a fact. I spent a chunk of my childhood behind that metal gate.

No more than a block away stand the eyesores of Pretoria—the Schubart Park and Kruger Park flats. Once upon a time, these buildings had been state-of-the-art apartment complexes, housing thousands of families. Unfortunately, like most of the families who had once lived there, these flats weren't granted a happily-ever-after. Stripped to the bone, the remnants of these skyscrapers look like the renditions of post-apocalyptic movie sets. Skeletal structures fenced off and manned by armed guards show the true horrors poverty has to offer.

It's here, near the entrance to Schubart Park itself, where Detective Mosepi parks.

"Stay in the car," he says, opening his door.

"You don't have to tell me twice." I gaze at the derelict towers that look like they might fall down at any time. To think: twenty years ago, people were jumping to their deaths from these buildings, and now the buildings themselves look suicidal. I would be lying if I said I'm not tempted to wander around the place a bit to see what it looks like now, but I keep it to myself.

Detective Mosepi gives me a dubious look before he climbs out and closes the door behind him. He makes his way up the few stairs to where a guard patrols the entrance. They have a quick, quiet conversation before the detective is granted access to the grounds.

"Of course," I say to myself, "maybe I would have listened if you had told me twice." I release my safety belt and open the door.

I couldn't waste an opportunity to see what had become of a place so many childhood friends had called home.

Here's the thing, though. I'm not the most inconspicuous person in the world. I'm considered relatively tall at 1.77 meters, and my fiery red locks are a beacon to anyone with eyesight. These elements make it difficult for me to hide, in general. Therefore, I don't hold much hope of entering the fenced-off, condemned building, seeing as the armed guards patrolling the perimeter seem on high alert. I am, however, prepared to bribe the guard out front.

So, imagine my surprise when I passed through without a hitch. The guy didn't so much as spare me a second glance when I waltzed up the steps and smiled my most brilliant smile for him.

Schubart Park consists of several towers linked together by a relatively big courtyard. I remember this from the one time I'd been in the complex, against my father and grandfather's wishes. Back then, the pond—a water feature lacking imagination—had sparkled. Older people would spend their days seated on the concrete benches surrounding it to feed birds or watch the world pass them by. I don't recall there ever being grass, though. My memory isn't quite as good.

I pass through the foyer of the desolate apartment complex, a box-like tunnel that had once housed hundreds upon hundreds of postboxes, and enter the courtyard. The towers loom over me, blocking the last rays of sunlight, their foreboding abandon more apparent than from outside. They're skeletons—flesh and muscle picked away by the harsh African elements. The water feature somehow survived time, but algae and some unidentifiable sludge is all that remains of the pool. The benches lie in piles of rubble, broken down to the foundation. Weeds push through the cracks in the pavement, threatening to take back the land.

"I told you to stay in the car." Detective Mosepi's voice is indifferent.

"When I was in grade one, one of my friends lived here. I think her name was Marie Fisher," I say. "I remember it was a cold winter's day when I arrived home, inconsolable and wearing only my school dress. My dad, expecting the worst, asked me what was wrong, but it took so long for me to stop crying. He asked me where my jersey and jacket were. What I'd done with my shoes and socks."

A shiver caresses my skin as the memory takes hold, and I wrap my arms around myself. I can still remember how the wind had cut through my thin school dress. I recall how Dad's face had twisted with pure dread. The devil must have whispered horrendous scenarios into his ear, because I have never seen him so scared before or after that day.

"I couldn't tell him," I continue. "I was crying so hard. Finally, after I'm sure he was at his wits end, I told him about how some children came to school without shoes or jerseys. Their lips are blue from the cold, their stomachs grumble from hunger. I couldn't understand why the world was so cruel. Why did I have so much when they had *nothing*?" I rub my hands over my arms. "Dad, ever the problem solver, got my grandfather to pitch in for a charity drive. Along with a few guys from the station— you included, Detective—they filled up a trailer with food and clothes and blankets and toys. Then you came to school during a lunch hour, and we distributed the goods to the children who needed it the most."

Detective Mosepi shows no sign of recollection or sympathy.

"It was my first lesson in humility," I admit. "From that day onward, I never threw a tantrum when Dad or Grandpa said I couldn't have something. I always ate my vegetables. I thanked God for what I had every night, and *never*, not once, did I curse Him for my mother's absence again." I turn around to face Detective Mosepi, the memory stirring another bout of gratefulness. "You have no idea how happy those kids were to not feel forgotten."

"You should have stayed in the car," he says.

I shrug. "Thought I'd look around and reminisce. I'll stay well out of the way, don't worry."

Detective Mosepi hands me a flashlight and points toward a stairwell as barren as the rest of its surroundings. "It's stable, but don't go falling into an elevator shaft. You have thirty minutes and then I want you back in the car."

I nod and saunter toward the staircase, excited and anxious to explore the remnants of recent history. After a day of inactivity, I have too much energy to burn. I burst with a desire for movement, for bubbling conversations and interesting sights.

"*Oro, plata, mata,*" I whisper to myself, counting each step as I climb the stairs. "Gold, silver, death." I ascend the next three steps. My grandfather had taught me the rhyme as an alternative to my annoying childhood obsession with *eeny-meeny-miny-moe*. He told me the rhyme was derived from an old Philippine superstition where people believed a staircase ending on *mata* is a bad omen. I'd adopted the superstition for shits and giggles. "*Oro, plata, mata.* Gold, silver, death." The beam of the flashlight waves across piles of trash and debris in the corners of the landings. In places, pieces of the metal banisters are missing, but the integrity of the stairs hasn't been compromised. I'm relatively safe as long as I don't venture too far to the edge or rely on the banisters. "*Oro, plata, mata.* Gold, silver, death." I turn the landing and head up another flight.

I'm not even halfway up the tower when my mantra's been repeated at least five dozen times, ending on *silver*. I decide then not to go any higher than the eleventh floor. Instead, I walk into one of the long, narrow hallways that stretch to either side. Some apartments' front doors hang at awkward angles, providing a glimpse into hollow interiors stripped bare of plumbing pipes, electrical wires, metal window frames, and anything else salvageable for illegal sales. Other apartments don't even have their doors anymore.

If the world ends tomorrow, this will be humanity's legacy.

I step around a discarded shopping trolley lying in the middle of the hallway and head for the farthest room on the floor.

Down the hallway, the last door on the left, I pass through a sloping threshold and enter what used to be a narrow corridor. This leads past a tiny kitchen and into a living room, where the only remnant of human occupation is a scorched plastic baby-doll. I push forward into another narrow corridor, making my way past a stripped bathroom and two small bedrooms. At the farthest side, overlooking the city, sits the main bedroom. It's exposed to the elements. There is no wall or window acting as any sort of barrier, and falling over the edge is a real possibility if I'm not careful.

The dying sun throws a deep orange, almost pink, blanket across the jagged horizon. City lights sparkle like gemstones, before the world plunges into darkness. The rhythms and beats of Pretoria ebb away until silence reigns.

Behind me, a mural of a black-and-white Jesus Christ looks out on the world.

It's beautifully tragic.

Using my cell phone, I take a picture of the sunset framed by the broken walls, chipped floor, and sagging ceiling. I snap shots of the mural, too, and post them on Facebook under the photo album heading PRETORIA – BEAUTIFUL AND FORGOTTEN PLACES.

A beat later, my phone buzzes in my hand, ruining the moment.

"Hello?" My voice rebounds from the surrounding walls.

"Wherever you are," Detective Mosepi hisses over the line, "stay put and keep quiet. Rochester and his guy slipped into the building you're in."

I fumble with the flashlight and switch it off.

"My guys are getting into position, but if anything happens, scream as loud as you can—"

"I'm on the eleventh floor," I cut him off. "I'm too high for anyone to come rescue me if something happens."

He grumbles under his breath in isiZulu. "Stay where you are until

I call you again. Please."

"I'm sitting down right now," I say, looking around for a place to sit. The floor is dusty and uneven and I will probably need a tetanus shot before the night is over, but I take a seat and look out on the City of Pretoria. "And I'm ruining my outfit in the process. Are you happy, Detective?"

Detective Mosepi ends the call.

"You're welcome," I mutter to the cell phone, already scrolling through my Facebook newsfeed again. Several likes have blinked in my notification box thanks to the photographs I've posted. One of the thumbs up belongs to Howlen. "Oh, so you do use Facebook?" I whisper. "Good to know."

My phone vibrates again. Another notification, this time from a text.

> **Howlen:** Where are you?
>
> **Esmé:** Shubart Park.
>
> **Howlen:** I won't presume to know where that is. Are you safe?
>
> **Esmé:** Relatively. Why? Want to come hold my hand? :-P
>
> **Howlen:** Can't. I'm going out on a date.
>
> **Esmé:** Did Grandpa drag you to dinner again? LOL!
>
> **Howlen:** No. I'm going out with a pathologist I met at the lab.

I stare at the last message for longer than necessary, eyebrow rising, lips pursing, blood curdling. Instead of saying something I would later regret, especially seeing as we have never discussed the specifics of our relationship, I weigh my words carefully.

> **Esmé:** Sounds like fun. Enjoy your evening.
>
> **Howlen:** Thank you. Enjoy yours as well.

Esmé: I plan on it. Cheers.

"Asshole," I hiss.

I ignore his texted response and push the piece of plastic tech into my pocket—out of sight, but far from being out of mind. I lean back against the wall and grind my teeth. We've never broached the subject of whether we were seeing one another exclusively or not. Still, I thought it was bloody obvious.

Well … okay, I didn't think it would have worked out between us anyway, but screwing around is just rude.

Eskom's load-shedding schedule kicks into gear after the sun sinks behind the horizon. The twinkling lights of the city are doused as the power grid is turned off. Utter blackness surrounds me. I resist the urge to put on the flashlight and pull my knees to my chest, wrapping my hands around my legs.

Life has suddenly become incredibly depressing.

With only the moon as a light source, I see individual rocks and bricks and other large pieces of debris surrounding me.

Shouts echo from somewhere in the building. A gunshot. More shouts. Then, silence. I jump up, fumble for the flashlight, and wait for something more to happen. Footsteps drag across concrete, loud and fast, and close. Shouted demands. Several more shots reverberate through the hollow building.

My heart pumps adrenaline. Paranoia has me considering my chances of survival. There are no hiding places available if someone runs into this apartment. I can get shot, be held hostage, or killed. I'm not entirely helpless, I can protect myself, but there's only so much I can physically do against a gun.

"Fuck," I whisper. I sit, and try to make myself small. The noise continues, closing in on my location. I shut my eyes, pray that this takedown is quickly resolved, and hope that Howlen has a terrible time on his date.

My phone vibrates in my pocket again. I find it with trembling hands and check my messages.

DARK COUNTRY

Howlen: Are you angry with me?

Howlen: You were at a bloody swinger's party last night!

Howlen: May?

> **Esmé:** I'm stuck in the middle of a shootout! Shut up already, I'm hiding!

Approaching footsteps make me hold my breath. I hide the cell phone's screen against my chest, hoping the light is muted enough not to alert whoever's stumbling around in the dark. My palms sweat, my mind races, and every single one of my regrets surface.

Please don't come in here, I pray, squeezing my eyes shut and tightening my grip on my phone. *Please, please, please.*

My phone vibrates.

The footsteps halt. Debris crushes, cracks, and grinds under feet. Labored breathing comes to an abrupt stop somewhere inside the apartment. A distinct *click* as a bullet slides into the chamber of a gun.

My lungs burn from inactivity, but I don't dare make a sound.

Footsteps close in on me, slowly.

I stand even slower, well aware that I can't save myself if I'm sitting, and no way in hell will I go out without a fight.

A figure appears in the doorway, tall and familiar—I've been studying it the whole day.

Rochester's gaze is glued on the city beyond, not on where I am hiding a hairsbreadth away.

Maybe he won't see me? Maybe he'll walk away?

Luck is not on my side.

Something must have given my presence away, because Rochester suddenly whirls around and pulls the trigger.

The shot is deafening from its close proximity, and the sound rebounds from three barely standing walls before disappearing into the night. The white light from the barrel sears the sparse surroundings into my retinas, effectively blinding me for a moment. I release a sound that's something between a war cry and a scream for help.

Shock and fear jolt me into action, adrenaline forces me to survive.

Before Rochester decides to pull the trigger again, I kick him in his midriff.

He doubles over, gasping for air, but doesn't release his weapon.

I'm ready to strike a second time, but instead of finding purchase against his lean body, Rochester's fist smashes against my eye socket.

"Motherf—" My exclamation was cut off when Rochester backhands me with the gun.

The metallic tang of blood floods my mouth. Spots dance across my vision, tears fill my eyes. I don't stop fighting for my life, though. As Rochester raises his hand for a probable knock-out blow, I see my chance to gain the upper hand.

I block him, grab his arm, and use his momentum to tug him closer. Without losing a beat, I knee his groin.

He loses his hold of the gun and it slides off the exposed edge of the room.

My elbow finds his face a second later—there's a sickening crunch as his nose gives way.

Rochester howls in pain and staggers a step backward. However, he charges forward again, hell blazing in his teary eyes, and I kick out at his legs. My heel smashes against something solid—possibly his femur—and he finally goes down.

I'd seen enough horror movies to know that bad guys are excellent at faking incapacitation, so I don't let my guard down. I can't. It's a good thing, too, because apparently he's just playing dead.

As soon as I'm close, he grabs my ankle and pulls me off balance.

I cry out as I fall to the rocky floor, collecting more bruises and cuts.

Rochester scrambles to pin me down in the debris, clawing at my clothing and skin. But desperation makes him stupid and careless, and I'm still in better shape than him.

My knuckles smash against his face repeatedly, and he responds by jabbing a fist into my ribs.

It's okay. I can endure a bit of pain if it means coming out of this battle alive. So, I pound, and hit, and batter back.

Eventually, I twist us around until I'm sitting on his chest, rendering him almost incapable of defending himself.

DARK COUNTRY

I hit harder, trying to fight away my own pain.

Voices intrude, then, encircling us where we lie on the ground. Hands wrap around my waist, pulling me off and away from the fallen criminal.

"He's down. He's down," a familiar voice repeats dully as I'm pulled back to the Jesus mural.

I see Rochester lying unconscious on the ground. His face is a bloody mess. At least he's breathing—the steady rise and fall of his chest indicates as much.

"Someone call an ambulance!"

Perhaps I should have stayed in the car, I think, before exhaustion overwhelms me.

PRETORIA – BEAUTIFUL AND FORGOTTEN PLACES
Album updated 3 hours ago

Howlen Walcott, Rumona Limbaugh and 17 others like this.
View 16 more comments

Johnny Allen: That's a beautiful view!
2hrs   Like: 5
Rumona Limbaugh: Where did you take these?
2hrs   Like: 1
Llewelyn Snyder: Please tell me you're not where I think you are.
2hrs   Like: 0
Geraldine van der Schyff: Is that the view from Schubart Park? Holy crap, I can't believe that place hasn't been demolished yet.
1hr   Like: 2
Howlen Walcott: Please pick up your phone.
1hr   Like: 1
Llewelyn Snyder: ^^What he said.
1hr   Like: 1
Llewelyn Snyder: Your grandpa can't reach you either. Get in touch, please. I'm a worried dad right now.
38 mins   Like: 0
Howlen Walcott: May, for God's sake, just tell me you're okay.
35 mins   Like: 0

     Annalize von Kleist: @Howlen Walcott – Did I miss something important?

34 mins	Like: 0

Llewelyn Snyder: @Annalize von Kleist – Esmé seems to have gone MIA. We're working on finding her.

32 mins	Like: 1

Annalize von Kleist: @Llewellyn Snyder – Okay, Mr. S. Keep me updated, please.

30 mins	Like: 1

Bernard Meenthuis: Wow, that's a creepy picture. I LOVE IT! #endoftheworld

20 mins	Like: 0

Geraldine van der Schyff: Have you guys found her yet? Now I'm worried.

10 mins	Like: 7

Bernard Meenthuis: This just popped up on News24/7.

Cops, Criminals in Schubart Park Shootout – Pretoria – There are reports of a shootout at the condemned Schubart Park flats … **See More**

5 mins	Like: 2

Ollie Rousseau: Jirre @Bernard Meenthuis, don't you think Esmé's family's worried enough as it is?

3 mins	Like: 4

Cops, Criminals in Schubart Park Shootout
2015-09-08 | 21:280 Comments

Pretoria – There are reports of a shootout at the condemned Schubart Park flats on Tuesday evening.

Police officers were tailing a suspect to the area and spotted an exchange of illegal goods for money after the area's load-shedding occurred. When police went in to make the arrest, "a gunfight ensued," said Lieutenant Colonel Moses Dlamini.

"The criminals fired shots at the police as they fled into the building and police shot back as they made chase," said Dlamini.

One suspect (found hiding in the elevator shaft, according to reports) was reprimanded for possession of illegal goods.

The 28-year-old man was arrested on the scene.

"A pistol and several [rounds of] ammunition were found on the suspect's person. He also had a cooler box with medical waste in his possession, allegedly to be used in the production of muti," said Dlamini.

The second suspect was allegedly arrested after a brief struggle on the eleventh floor of the building. The 25-year-old man was taken to the emergency room for minor injuries.

Both men were charged with attempted murder, possession of an illegal firearm and ammunition, buying of human tissue without a medical license, and conspiracy to sell human tissue without a medical license.

It was reported that several injuries had occurred in the assault.

– News24/7

COMMENTS:

Log in to leave comments.

CHAPTER 17

A braham Amin's captor is as courteous as he is cruel, as intelligent as he is insane.

Evidence of his previous murders is still present in the dimly lit slaughterhouse. The sharp copper smell pollutes the air, a constant reminder of what's in store if Abraham doesn't find a way to escape. Blood coagulates in puddles around the clogged drains, and sharp metal hooks glint precariously in the yellow light. Abraham's already convinced he'll spend years in therapy if he somehow manages to flee. Rats scurry in the shadows, searching—always searching for their next meal. He shudders to think of how soon he will be on the menu.

He has no idea how long he's been held captive; could be days or weeks, but it feels like years have passed.

His captor has wrapped a chain tightly around his waist and fastened it with a lock in the corner of the slaughterhouse. A filthy pallet and a raggedy blanket lie in a heap nearby. A fat rat sluggishly drags a piece of intestine into the dark. Seeing that, Abraham barely makes it to the bucket toilet to vomit. Fear forces away whatever semblance of courage he'd gathered since he awoke in this hellish place.

"They're more afraid of you than you are of them," the man had said in a sympathetic voice, patting Abraham's back. Abraham couldn't—no, he *wouldn't* —dignify the comment with a response. He continues to retch instead.

Eventually, his captor leaves, though not before tending to Abraham's wounded heel. "No need dying before Death's ready," he'd said, finishing up.

"Fuck off," Abraham had growled back.

They have not had a conversation since.

Now, as Abraham sits alone in his decrepit dungeon with only the rats for company, he regrets his animosity. Maybe kindness and politeness would've appealed to the man behind the monster? Perhaps there's a way to escape death after all? Abraham doesn't know.

He tugs at the padlock around his waist and wishes he'd learned how to pick a lock. "That shit only happens in books and movies," he says to himself softly.

Abraham shifts the chains a bit, first this way then the other way. He frowns, looking at the heavy chain, testing the gap between the metal and his body, and begins to wiggle the chain up his torso one painstaking millimeter at a time. Abraham sucks his stomach in as much as possible, squirming within the chain, which catches on an extra layer of fat he didn't know he had.

"Bloody hell," he wheezes.

Abraham wipes sweat off his forehead with the back of his hand and looks down at the chain which is seemingly stuck in an unsightly flap between his pelvis and stomach.

"No wonder Colleen couldn't bear to look at me."

A few breaths later, he repeats the process.

Suck in stomach. Hold breath steady. Wiggle chain up.

It's tiresome work, but it keeps his thoughts from wandering to places where failure reigns.

He vows to get fit. "Just let me escape and I'll be a better, humbler person."

When the chain reaches his bellybutton, a milestone if ever there was one, the work lessens. By the time he's shimmied the chains to his chest, his restraints have enough slack for him to remove them in a jiffy.

Free, Abraham grins as the chains pool on the floor, but he knows his work is far from over. With his ankle barely healing due to his diabetes, his escape will be slow-going. He also doesn't have a clue when his captor will return.

Abraham gets to work.

Carefully, he stands, placing all his weight on his uninjured foot. With one hand pressed against the grimy wall, he hops toward the workbench.

A selection of weapons—unclean yet sharp, on the workbench—makes his stomach churn with fear and disgust. He swallows down the bile threatening to debilitate him. Knives, saws, drills, scalpels, and even a long Phillips screwdriver are among the exposed weapons, not including those in what looks like a tackle box. He pockets a scalpel and a knife and takes the Phillips screwdriver in his hand. Better safe than sorry.

He moves to the far side of the slaughterhouse where a door leads out into the unknown. It's unlocked, opening into the interior of an abandoned office.

A sliver of pre-dawn is recognizable through the filthy windows behind the reception desk. Dust covers the surface, paper litters the floor. Old metal chairs are tipped over against the other wall, the insides of the cushions chewed out by rats for their nests. A shudder ravishes his body as he recalls the fat rat dragging the intestine.

He's close to being free. So close.

"Don't get cocky now." He drags his injured leg behind him as he crosses the office to another door. As he reaches it, he rests his hand on the door handle. "Please be open."

Abraham pushes down and out.

The door swings open.

Fresh air rushes in, cooling the sweat on his body, filling his lungs, revitalizing him. He inspects the grayish plains, where weeds and grass grow wildly. Abraham listens for the sound of vehicles, but hears nothing of the sort. Undeterred, he limps forward into the wilderness. Go straight in any direction and eventually he'll find life. Or so he hopes. All he can do is hope.

With the screwdriver in one hand, he makes the journey across the veldt, barefoot. *Kakiebos*, otherwise known as African marigold, clings to the hem of his pants and scratches against his skin. *Dubbeltjies*, or devil's thorn, digs into the soft flesh of his feet. He yelps every time, stops to pull out the offensive little thorns, and carries on.

Abraham remembers his childhood at every stop and curses himself for going soft. He recalls the thick calluses on his heels protecting him whenever he and his brothers ran across the open fields. Nothing could stop them—not even the *dubbeltjies*—and they'd run like the wind. Now, though …

"Soft," he mutters.

When he reaches the top of a hill, where a lone thorn tree stands with its bare, gnarled branches, he sees a narrow road cutting through hectares of open fields.

Abraham's heart leaps.

For an infinitesimal moment, his hopes soar. He would get out, get clean, hire more competent bodyguards and change the world! He would live. For a microscopic instant, Abraham sees the life he'd always wanted to lead flash in front of him. A loving wife—not that crazy bitch Colleen—looking back at him with adoration in her eyes instead of loathing. Kids, he always wanted kids, running around the house, laughing and playing. He sees himself helping the homeless, the impoverished, orphans, abused women and children, the SPCA. He sees *everything* that could be.

The twinkling of weakness blinds him to the trap he's walked straight into, there at the thorn tree.

A knife plunges hilt-deep into his gut, and hope turns to pain. It came out of nowhere, nowhere at all. A hand covers his mouth, muffling his scream before he could even think of making a sound. The blade tears through his flesh, centimeter by agonizing centimeter, spilling blood and viscera across Abraham's filthy pants and the brown grass.

"Irony aside, you were probably the best guy for the job. That's why I voted for you," the killer says. "Apologies, my friend, but this was always meant to be."

With inhuman precision and speed, Abraham's stomach is sliced open from one hip to the other. The blade leaves his body, and the killer steps away to regard his dying hostage.

As intestines and organs spill out, Abraham evacuates his bowels. He falls to his knees, unable to fight or speak or do anything except hold his slick innards in bloodstained hands.

Shock keeps Abraham from screaming, now. Shock and defeat.

"What a nice view we have." The killer kneels beside Abraham and pats his shoulder. Abraham falls on his side, curling into the fetal position. "It beats dying in an impersonal hospital room, huh?"

"Fuck you," Abraham whispers. "I'll see you in Hell."

Abraham Amin's killer smiles sweetly, almost saintly. "Only mortals have an afterlife, Abraham. I'm in the process of becoming a god."

CHAPTER 18

Green fog billows around my feet as I walked through Menlyn Park's deserted undercover parking lot. Gravestones rise from the invisible asphalt and in the vehicles' allocated spaces, thrown into relief by the ghastly green tinge. The stark black night doesn't mute the neon color. Shadows dance on walls and gravestones, following me as I search for *something*.

I'll know what I'm looking for when I see it. Until then, I'm on a treasure hunt without a map.

The gravestones come in various shapes and sizes. Some are extravagant, others plain. Sometimes there are no gravestones, only dead flowers to mark a body's location.

This is a dream, I'm sure. After all, I would never wear a ball gown— a black designer dress with a stifling corset and a matching black veil— to search for *something* in a parking lot. I also can't read the markings on the gravestones, a sure sign that this is a dream.

My search is a subconscious rendition of my conscious mind. I'm looking for the killer in real life. In my dream, however, I'm searching for some kind of clue to find him.

Nevertheless, the missing link is hidden somewhere in my subconscious, I know it. If only I can manipulate the dream, mold it into something less eerie. But how? At least I don't have anything to fear.

Dreams can't kill you …

How illogical it sounds. Finding a break in the case via a dream search. Ha! How ridiculous and desperate. I search one level and move on to the next, and the next. I look between gravestones, behind concrete pillars, in darkened corners.

Click.

"Hello," I cry out to the empty world, but only an echo responds. I wait and listen for what feels like years, contemplating an escape if something decides to chase me. There isn't a reasonable place to run. The gravestones will provide a semblance of cover, though. "Hello? Is anyone there?"

Nothing. No sounds, apart from my ragged breathing and pounding heart.

My search resumes.

Thick fog wafts around me, changing my skin tone from healthy pink to zombie green. I bet my hair looks even worse in this lighting.

Click.

I stop in my tracks. My bones are on fire; my skin icy to the touch.

The fog rolls across the pavement, tosses against the gravestones, and ripples around my frozen form. A chill crawls up my legs and thighs, runs over my torso, and dances toward my spine. Vapor escapes through my lips as the temperature plummets.

Search and you will find. I spin around, searching—always searching. Search and you will find, but I can't find a damn thing!

Run, a disembodied voice says.

I hitch up my dress and run toward the mall's glass doors, hoping to escape in the labyrinth of shops.

The thing behind me cackles and crows in delight, talons or claws clicking against the pavement as it chases me through the deserted parking lot.

I throw it—whatever *it* is—off by crisscrossing through the graveyard.

Pavement turns to tiles as I approach the glass doors where more darkness awaits. The doors slide open automatically when I reach the sensor. I sprint forward, aware of the fast-approaching clicks behind me.

Once I'm through, I'm no longer in Menlyn Park. Instead, I'm standing on the platform of the Gautrain station in Hatfield. The sleek bullet-shaped train sits in the field of fog, waiting for non-existent passengers.

Click.

Terrified, I board the Gautrain without a ticket.

The doors slide shut as I survey the compartment. All it holds are human-shaped silhouettes. Faces don't stare back, but from the prickles on my neck, I sense someone or something watching.

The Gautrain pulls away without a sound. The fog thickens but doesn't rise.

A solitary shadow figure shifts in its seat, a clear indication for me to sit.

I take the offered seat and thank the male silhouette.

He nods back and goes on with whatever shadow people do.

I look around the compartment, still searching. For what, I don't know, but it's important I find it soon.

An uneasy quiet fills the train as the benign shadow people sit motionless in their seats and stare into space. Outside, the black canvas of nothingness stretches on forever.

I fumble with my hands in my lap, my gaze darting around the compartment for the elusive creature. Nothing. I'm safe, for now.

If only I could wake up.

No, I need to find what I'm looking for.

The train slows until it comes to a complete stop in the Pretoria station. Silhouettes stand and exit the Gautrain in single file. My neighbor sits tight. Nobody and nothing board here. Soon we're moving again, but the scenery never changes and the fog never dissipates.

"Excuse me?" I ask the shadow man beside me.

He slowly turns his attention from the window.

"Do you know what I'm looking for?"

He shakes his head, bit by bit.

"Thank you." Trying was worth a shot. What harm could it do?

A few minutes pass before the train rolls into the Centurion station. This time, my neighbor stands, nods a greeting my way, and exits along with more shadow people. Nobody boards.

The motions repeat, station after station, until I'm the single occupant of the Gautrain.

When the last stop comes up, Park, I decide to get off. What use is it sitting on a train that doesn't go anywhere?

DARK COUNTRY

The doors slide open and I walk out, only to end up right back in the Menlyn Park parking lot where the gravestones are still enveloped in green fog, black night, and utter loneliness.

Click.

It's not hidden somewhere ahead, as I'd hoped, but comes from somewhere behind me. Near me.

Click.

Its breath tickles my nape. I can't escape, even if I run.

Click.

My courage wavers. I've been made a fool. This hunt is over. It's been over before it began. I know this.

Claws wrap around my arms.

My pulse races, my hands sweat, and my body doesn't answer my requests to run or fight.

I spin around to face the creature haunting my nightmare—a being that's neither bird nor beast. It's a man, but not a man per se. Feathers cover his entirety. Hands and feet aren't *hands or feet*, but claws. Shark-like teeth fill his mouth. His captivating ochre eyes stare at me.

My legs give in from fear.

He keeps me upright with ease and says, without moving his lips, "*So beautiful.*"

He leans in until our lips almost touch and sucks the air right out of my lungs.

My diaphragm deflates. My body aches. Lungs burn from abuse. I'm trembling. Dying.

"*Stop,*" I manage weakly, looking into malicious, demonic eyes that are too close for comfort.

He doesn't release his hold, but pulls away far enough so I can take a lungful of air.

"Please."

Stop. *Please.* The creature mimics my voice and cackles again.

The green fog comes alive, swirling and twirling, growing as it surrounds us in a funnel. The hideous being leans closer to my ear, and hot breath blows against my neck. A single claw drags its way down my throat and plays at the edge of my corset.

Run. Hide. But know that Yena watches you always.

The creature suddenly releases me, and I stumble to my knees. The green fog slams into my face, blinding me by the neon tinge. It chokes me with the toxicity of mustard gas. The fog forces its way down into my throat before settling in my lungs. Wave-like crashes deafen me as the noxious vapors search for entry at any other viable orifice. Once, twice, thrice, the fog slams down.

I'm heavy and sluggish and there's no escape, no matter where I turn or how much I thrash.

I stifle a whimper as I sit bolt upright in bed.

My hands tremble as my gaze darts from corner to corner, floor to ceiling, in search of the creature that terrorized my dream.

I'm in my bed in my room, and nothing's out of its place. I inhale deeply, press my palm against my chest to calm my fluttering heartbeat, and take a few moments to gather myself.

It's just a nightmare. It's just a nightmare. It's just a nightmare. I think the mantra until I've convinced myself that I'm no longer stuck in my own mind.

Dawn trickles into my bedroom through the uncovered window. The indigo sky is already being pushed into submission and a pinkish haze takes its place. Cornflower blue is hot on the dusty pinks' heels. Soon, the sun will emerge from its slumber, cutting through the remaining darkness with magnificent oranges and sunburst yellows. A new day approaches, unaffected by the wiles and woes of mankind.

When the dream recedes into the back of my mind, I gently lift my weight off the bed and head to the kitchen barefoot.

I switch the kettle on, unarm the alarm system, and unlock the door. I step outside and look out on the yard.

Apart from a single loquat tree in the corner, spilling its fruits onto the grass, there isn't much of a view. There's birdsong, of course, but their chirping is off-key this morning. A bad omen, if my experiences are enough to go on. The breeze blowing through the valley is barely enough to cool the sweat on my neck. Even now, with sun rising on the horizon, the weather is intolerable.

Another hot day is coming. Oh joy.

I ache all over from Rochester Ramphele's assault, but the pain reminds me that I'm alive. I survived.

My cheekbone throbs where his fist connected with my face, my left kidney is tender to the touch, but other than the few scrapes and bruises I'd sustained, I'm perfectly fine. He got off way worse. Mosepi had texted me Ramphele's injuries: two broken ribs, a broken nose, and seventeen stitches to his face and head. Being sued for assault is a possibility, but I doubt he'd win the case if it even got to court. One can hope.

The kettle clicks off loudly, startling me.

My nightmare has caused more damage than I thought. No. It's not the nightmare making me jumpy. It's something else. Something I'm not seeing.

I make my way back into the kitchen, wary of anything out of the ordinary. My gaze flicks around the room, scanning across the dish rack where a couple of clean mugs and a plate have been left out, across the kitchen table where an empty fruit bowl sits beside the kerosene lamp I use whenever Eskom implements load-shedding, across the closed cupboards and drawers that houses a myriad of kitchenware. Nothing seems out of place, yet my paranoia is not unfounded. There's an undeniable oppressiveness in the air, an evil presence of some sort. I feel it prickling on the back of my neck.

There hasn't been time for me to investigate the recent strange occurrences in the house. There's never enough time. Still, as I walk to the kettle to fill my caffeine need, I realize that putting an investigation of my own house on hold might not have been the wisest decision.

A loud crash resonates from my bedroom.

I spin around to face the hallway. Nothing stirs.

With the back door still open, I consider the variables. A slight gust might have slipped into the house, winded through the hallway and into my bedroom, and knocked something over.

Perhaps. Improbable, but maybe.

I move toward the hallway, cautious and silent. I reach the door and peer around the corner.

My heart races and my breathing becomes shallow as fear curdles my empty stomach.

Looking similar to church pews the morning after a big rugby game, the corridor is empty. I consider calling Howlen for backup, but my cell phone is still on the nightstand.

I slip into the gloom with one shoulder pressed against the cool wall. The only light comes from my bedside lamp at the farthest end of the corridor. Focusing on the strip of light, I place one foot in front of the other. Slowly, ever so slowly, I make it past the spare bedroom which acts as a home office-slash-library. Farther on, I pass the bathroom where knock-off Italian tiles and taps gleam. Another bedroom across the hallway—the guest bedroom, which is hardly ever used—stands silently with its door closed.

That door is always closed for reasons beyond my comprehension.

My bedroom is a few steps away, but I pause. Listening, waiting, I keep watch of the yellow light spilling from the open door. A gut feeling forces me to stay still.

A shadow flickers across the floor, moving with such speed it could've easily been a trick of the eye. My heart stops beating for a second. I suppress a scream as my throat constricts and a shock of adrenaline runs through my body.

Do I run away like a normal, rational human being? No, I don't. I tell myself to calm down. I rationalize the fleeting shadow as a creation of my overactive imagination, thanks to trauma. I would like to think myself inventive enough to come up with something better than shadows, but maybe exhaustion has screwed with that part of my brain.

Courage, but mostly curiosity, spurs me onward.

I scan the ceiling. Then my gaze drops to eye-level, and I gasp.

The room has been destroyed. Bedsheets, curtains, and even some of my designer clothing, lay in shreds across the floor. My pillows have been gutted and are bleeding feathers through the claw marks left behind. My dressing table lies on its side, broken into pieces. Even the wardrobe doors are hanging precariously from their hinges.

Nothing but pure, unadulterated hatred could've incited the devastation I beheld.

DARK COUNTRY

Rushing forward, ignoring the splinters stabbing into my bare feet, I grab and tear and search through the debris for my cell phone. Whatever's penetrated my house is still here, watching—biding its time. I can feel its watchful, patient gaze, and I fear it. Oh, how I fear it.

By the time I see a glint of hard plastic tucked between the mattress and nightstand, I'm trembling so much I can't operate the damn thing. My fingers keep slipping across the touch-screen, dialing incoherent numbers.

"Fuck," I growl, annoyed with how technology has devolved to make it almost impossible for a distraught person to make a call in an emergency.

Eventually, I dial Howlen's number.

"Esmé," he answers, wide awake.

I revert to speaking in Afrikaans, even though my family predominantly speaks English now.

"I don't understand you, May," Howlen says.

"Come over," I blurt out, desperate. "Please."

CHAPTER 19

The correct name of the dumping site is the Ollie Deneyschen Tunnel, although locals simply refer to it as the Daspoort Tunnel.

According to high school history teachers in the area, who sometimes touch on the subject of local history, councilor AP Deneyschen commissioned the tunnel in the late 1960s, after realizing that the Iscor mineworkers who resided in Hercules traveled a long way to work. The tunnel was thus built, connecting Claremont and Danville, to shorten their journey. It took forty months to complete, cost R1.7 million to build, and was officially opened to the public by the then-Mayor of Pretoria, Mr. G J Malherbe, on the 10th of August 1972. With a length of 537 meters and a width of 11.6 meters, the Daspoort Tunnel handles almost six thousand vehicles per day.

Even though he knows them by heart, these details are inconsequential.

The most relevant fact concerns the Daspoort Tunnel's ventilation shaft.

Positioned in the middle of the tunnel, the shaft measures approximately 4.57 meters in diameter and runs about fifty-five meters between the tunnel and the top of the mountain.

Without the shaft, someone could succumb in this carbon monoxide funnel. With it, though, the killer can get to work on making a name for himself … globally.

The half-rusted wheelbarrow wobbles from side to side across the rocky terrain, and Abraham Amin's stiff corpse shifts position in the bed.

Abraham's entrails don't spill, but balancing the bastard on one wheel the whole time is tiring. The steep incline of the mountain doesn't help, either. Nevertheless, he keeps moving, keeps racing against the rising sun, ignoring his burning shins and calves and thighs.

The thick, long bungee cord, acquired online, is coiled tightly and placed atop Abraham's leaking corpse. Shit and gore has already seeped between the fibers of the cord, defiling the expensive purchase.

C'est la vie, he thinks.

Skeletal trees move by as the wheelbarrow rolls up the mountain. Past boulders and rocks, over gravelly dirt, around mini bluffs, and up he goes. His body protests when the wheelbarrow is parked near the ventilation shaft, even if the whole drive, maneuvering, and climb lasted less than fifteen, maybe twenty minutes.

He looks around, searching for witnesses. Squatters, the homeless, and criminals frequent the area. With nobody in sight, he pulls his backpack off his shoulders and goes to work hammering hooks into various predetermined places around the shaft.

The sun rises. Traffic buzzes from either side of the mountain. Time is running out. When everything is in place, he finds the harness in his backpack and walks back to the wheelbarrow. Then he wrestles to get it onto Abraham's body, rigor mortis making everything more difficult. Next, he pushes the wheelbarrow closer and hooks the bungee cords on to the harness.

Slick with sweat, he straps Abraham into position. He couldn't care less if he left DNA evidence behind. Leaving behind evidence isn't a major concern when his ultimate goal is to be found. Of course, he wants to be found on his terms.

Esmé will need all the help she could get. Not that his DNA will get her anywhere.

He pins a hastily scrawled note to Abraham's shirt, which will hopefully inspire her to stop fucking around and play along.

"Come on, Abe," he groans, grabbing hold of Abraham's arm and lifting him over his shoulder.

Carefully, he drops Abraham's corpse near the edge of the shaft before straightening up the area. Untangled cords are checked over one final time. Tangled cords are quickly sorted out because the aesthetics of the scene will be ruined if Abraham didn't fall exactly right. The backpack is packed up and pulled on before he hides the wheelbarrow in some underbrush a short walk away.

When he returns, his gaze lingers on Abraham for a while. Glazed-over eyes stare back, judging him even from the afterlife.

"Oh, Abraham, don't look at me like that," he says, looking at his wristwatch. 07:06 a.m. "Perfect."

With a scuffed boot, he nudges Abraham closer to the edge, centimeter by centimeter, until a last mighty shove would do the trick. "*Auf wiedersehen, Herr* Amin."

The only sign of his success is the muted chaos that ensues.

Abraham Amin's killer walks back the way he came, unbothered by an instinctive urge to flee the scene. Brakes screech. Fast-moving metal collides with fast-moving metal. Glass shatters. Vehicles honk. Then silence, a momentous quiet between tragedy and realization. It stretches on beautifully. Then the screams start.

And it's the most glorious sound he has ever heard.

CHAPTER 20

I sit amidst the wreckage of my room, plucking through the contents of my underwear drawer. "Every single piece of lace clothing I own is gone." I giggle hysterically as I throw cotton lingerie—the unattractive ones women wear when the laundry's piled neck-high—over my shoulder. "Every goddamn G-string, gone." I look to where Howlen stands, staring at the destruction. "It's hilarious," I say.

"What happened in here? What happened to *you*?" Howlen takes a step forward, but hesitates. "Jesus, what happened to your face, May?"

"Oh, you know, an unseen preternatural entity decided to turn my bedroom into its lair. The perverted fucker also has a thing for lace underwear." I glower at the ceiling, as if whatever did this lives up there. It quite possibly does, but I can't be certain until I actually grew a pair and investigated. "As for what happened to me, my face, and whatever else might not look especially *rouge noir* as usual, well, I almost got killed because of you. I told you to shut up, but did you listen? Nope."

"Are you okay?"

"Do I look even remotely okay?" I ask, lying back into the fabric and feather nest. "I ache all over. I'll probably be slammed with a lawsuit because I beat the living shit out of the guy who tried to shoot me. I'm tired and I'm also now sharing my house with God-knows-what. Not to mention, you basically dumped me last night via text message. It's really the least of my problems, I know, but your timing needs improvement." Sighing, I push myself onto my elbows. "On the upside, my shoes and *some* of my clothes survived. I would have been inconsolable if they'd been …" I gesture to the room. "You know."

"I was under the impression you'd spoken with Father Gabriel over this entity long ago."

"Of course I spoke with Father Gabriel. Our meeting was scheduled between my manicure and my bikini wax," I say, sarcasm oozing from each word.

"There's no need to be snide," Howlen says, picking up a broken drawer. He turns it over to evaluate the damage before placing it on the bed. "Shall I call off work and help you?"

"Gramps won't approve if both of us took the day off," I say.

"Perhaps if you told him about your current predicament—"

"He'd tell me 'I told you so,' and I wouldn't blame him," I interrupt Howlen. "No, he's already pissed off about what happened last night. There's no need to prove my incompetence again."

"You're being too hard on yourself," he says, taking a seat beside me on the floor.

I want to rest my head on his shoulder, but my courage levels have reached zero. In front of me lies my favorite tube of lipstick, a shade of garnet red, which I pick up.

"How was your date?" I ask.

Howlen sighs. "I grabbed a drink with the lab technician working on our trace evidence, fishing for answers. Harry isn't exactly what I'd call date material."

I frown as I turn to face him. "Immature much?"

He meets my gaze, mirroring my expression. "Says the cheater."

"Cheater?" I ask. "I may not be the most conventional woman, but I've never cheated on any of my lovers. Juggling multiple partners, even when it comes to casual sex, sounds like too much work."

Howlen's phone bleeps with a message before he can respond.

He glances at the screen and his shoulders drop. "You better get dressed. We've got another body."

The Daspoort Tunnel connects two main roads—Transoranje Road and Bremer Street, leading from Pretoria West toward Pretoria North. This tunnel is a lifeline for many. Thousands of vehicles drive through the gloomy underpass once or twice on a daily basis, and brave pedestrians—schoolchildren, for the most part—walk through soot and grime to reach their destinations. Though the tunnel isn't especially long, the accidents that occur there tend to be fatal. Most drivers, however, would rather gamble with their lives in a death trap than take a pricy detour around the mountain. Pedestrians also prefer trying their luck with speeding vehicles than getting killed—or worse—by the "mountain men."

When we arrive, it's a circus. Roads on either side of the tunnel are congested with vehicles and people. A traffic officer tries to divert cars toward alternative roads, but it's slow-going. Frustrations flare and tempers rise as the heat of the day increases.

Howlen directs his car onto the sidewalk and drives up to the traffic officer. After a quick repartee, we are waved on. Howlen's chosen a difficult route to the tunnel, but there is no way around it.

The barricade comes into view and an ongoing flurry of activity is visible as we round the last bend. The mountain is crawling with police officers in their blue uniforms. Journalists are on foot, trying to get a look at whatever's happening inside the tunnel, while pedestrians gawk at the commotion from farther away.

"Closing down the tunnel is going to cost the government a small fortune," I say as Howlen parks on the sidewalk.

"At this stage, I'm more concerned over possible carbon monoxide poisoning than the South African government's purse," Howlen says.

A few moments later, we're standing side by side on the street, holding our respective equipment bags and readying ourselves for another long day.

"This isn't good," Howlen says.

I'm about to ask when it has ever been good to be called out to investigate a murder when I hear my grandfather's voice above the din of conversations. "Help me, Lord," I say instead.

At the mouth of the Daspoort Tunnel, dressed in his usual mortician suit with his gray hair slicked back against his head, Christiaan Snyder is arguing with Detective Mosepi.

"We best go see," I suggest.

Howlen responds with a nod and we amble toward them.

"Esmé." Detective Mosepi is red-faced and clearly frustrated. "What took you so long?"

"Technically, I took the day off." I look between him and my grandfather. "What seems to be the matter here?" I ask, but continue before either can answer. "You're aware there are vultures circling?" I discreetly gesture over my shoulder to where a particularly interested journalist is listening in on the conversation.

"Ah, yes, very well done, Esmé." Christiaan nods, straightening his jacket. He tilts his head as he studies my face. "I was under the impression your gallivanting last night had rendered you incapable of coming into work. You look perfectly fine, though. Care to explain?"

"Gramps," I start, trying my best not to get annoyed with his preposterously British tone this morning. "Have you been watching period dramas again?"

"Perhaps." He lifts his chin in defiance.

Howlen chuckles softly behind me, and it takes every ounce of self-control not to tell them both off.

I turn to Detective Mosepi. "Shall we, Detective?"

"Please," he answers, turning to walk back inside the tunnel.

I follow.

"This killer baffles me, Esmé," Detective Mosepi says in a hushed tone. "He staged this outrageous scene, but to what purpose? What do a mother, a child, and a politician have in common?"

"A politician?" I ask, surprised. "Which one?"

"A nobody ANC MP, but his position won't matter to wagging tongues. If we don't get something, *anything*, for the higher-ups to release to the public, there'll be a political uproar to deal with, on top of everything else. People are scared, and rightly so."

"You're being melodramatic, Detective."

"Am I?" Detective Mosepi searches for his cigarette pack in his shirt pocket. With precise movements, he finds a cigarette, lifts it to his lips, and lights it as the packet is returned to its home. "I've been punished with a rookie detective as a new partner. There have been talks, behind closed doors, about implementing a curfew. Fuck knows what they'll do next." Smoke slithers from his lungs and joins the murky interior of the tunnel. "Please tell me you have a lead on your side."

"Unfortunately not," I answer. "But I suspect we might find something, soon."

"I hope so." Detective Mosepi raises his hand, holding the cigarette between his index and middle finger, and points toward the suspended body swinging from the center of the tunnel. "Most of his innards are splattered across the vehicles and road," he says bluntly, emotionless. The man must be as exhausted as I am. "So, watch your step."

"Jesus Christ," I whisper, studying the corpse. "How the hell is this even possible?"

"Ventilation shaft," Christiaan says behind them.

"There's a ventilation shaft?" I ask, changing direction to get a different point of view, and hear a squelch beneath my feet. My gaze drops to the asphalt, where my red stiletto stands atop an unrecognizable organ that's been ground into the road by eager tires. "Well, that's unsavory."

"You should watch your step around here, ma'am," an unfamiliar voice says in a practically undetectable Afrikaans accent.

I look up to find hazel-colored eyes staring back at me. With a quick scan, I take in everything about the newcomer. I make out the shape of his service firearm holstered under his arm, his notebook and wallet sitting safely in his shirt pocket, and the badge clipped on his belt. Chestnut hair gleams even without sunshine, contrasting against his gray suit. The picture of professionalism is ruined, however, by his comic book socks, which I wouldn't have seen if he hadn't shifted to move out of my way. He's a real *boerseun,* the sort you'd likelier find on a farm than in the city.

I'm rather intrigued. I appreciate that in a person.

"There are a lot of pieces strewn about," he explains, holding out his hand.

I flush as I accept his hand, and carefully step out of the goo. No doubt, my natural coloring is visible under all the makeup covering my bruise, but I avoid looking at the young detective anyway.

"Thank you," I say.

"You're most welcome, ma'am."

"Chivalry is alive and well," Christiaan announces, loud enough to make a few people turn to the party of investigators. "Howlen, my dear man, you should take a page from this gentleman's book. Maybe then you'd find a wife while you still have need of one."

"Pops," I hiss, "wear your professional face, please."

"Apologies," he concedes, tipping a non-existent hat.

I swear the old man probably binge-watched Jane Austen movies the whole night. What's next? Crime shows?

"Howlen, perhaps you should touch base with the forensics team," Detective Mosepi suggests, grinding out his cigarette.

Howlen stalks off to where they are stationed beneath the swaying body.

"Introductions are … in order—" Detective Mosepi's face screws up in confusion, and I turn around to see my grandfather wandering away from their group. "Should we wait?" he asks.

"Don't mind him. Gramps is brilliant, but his way of thinking takes him on wild adventures." I wave it off. "You were saying, Detective?"

He huffs and gestures between me and the young detective. "Esmé Snyder, Detective Rynhardt Louw. Rynhardt, Esmé."

"Pleasure." Detective Louw holds out his hand for me to shake, which I take without hesitation. From the feel of the calluses on his palms, I can easily deduce that he is a hard-working guy, not afraid to get his hands dirty.

"Likewise," I say.

"Rynhardt, take us through the scene," Detective Mosepi says.

"Well," Detective Louw starts, "I think the victim was killed off-site, though it's difficult to be sure, given that I can't study the body up close."

"Get on with it," Detective Mosepi grumbles. "And keep with the facts."

"Yes, sir," he says, and looks back at me. "The victim's name is Abraham Amin, age thirty-nine, roundabout ninety-eight kilograms. As you can see"—he points to the corpse—"the body is suspended by what seems to be, bungee cords. We figure the killer dropped the victim, post-mortem, down the ventilation shaft in order to make a statement with all the … um … insides scattering about the place."

"You're more than welcome to be blunt, Detective. I'm made of harder stuff than most of your colleagues."

His smile, however small, brightens his whole face. "Very well."

I turn to Detective Mosepi. "I take it there's a multitude of witnesses?"

"Fifty-one witnesses, and more than half of them are traumatized schoolchildren under the age of sixteen," he answers.

I whistle in disbelief.

"Speaking of which, I need to get back there. Would you mind if Detective Louw takes you to do your thing?"

"Not at all," she says.

He gives us both a once over and shakes his head. "Children," he mumbles, and walked away.

"Eureka!" Christiaan shouts. "Howlen, bring your suitcase. I found a crucial piece of evidence!"

Detective Louw tries to hide his amusement by gesturing for me to walk ahead of him.

"He's at his happiest with the smell of death in the air. Pay him no attention," I explain. "Have you been up the mountain?"

"I have, ma'am."

"Please, call me Esmé." I rummage around for my cell phone as we near the body. "How did it look from up there?"

"Honestly?" Detective Louw asks.

"Please."

"The killer's staging is elaborate, well planned, and meticulously executed. There is a definite message being sent, but I can't seem to grasp it. But then again, this is not the usual type of killer we typically find in South Africa."

"Why would you say that?" I ready my recording app.

"We don't have creative serial killers." He shrugs. "This whole thing—the power play, the elaborate murders and staging, the intelligence in the design—sounds more like the things American serial killers would concoct."

"Firstly, serial killers usually murder three or more people, but this guy doesn't seem to need a cooling off period. Secondly, are you saying we're looking for a foreigner?" I stop, turning to face him.

"Not at all. I think our killer is a local. I'll go so far as to say he was an underachiever in school, possibly failing out before he matriculated—not because he's stupid, but because school didn't challenge him. There's a clear sign of abuse in his past, judging solely from the brutality of these crimes. Also, he's dead-set in his traditions. Some time in his life, though, he grew a god complex. It's peculiar."

"Impressive." I set down my bag on the road and look up at the high-strung body. "This is off topic, but I need to get higher."

"Higher?"

"Yes, I need to inspect the body for any anomalies while it's still up there."

"I can see if we have a ladder," he says.

"Hold up. It might be easier if I rappel down. What do you think?"

"I think you're fearless," Detective Louw says in a tone similar to when someone speaks of the weather.

My cheeks warmed.

"Your colleague looks upset." He juts out his chin and I follow the gesture to see Howlen approaching us.

Jaw set, eyes sharp, a little crease between his brows. Yes, that is Howlen's *I'm upset* look.

"What is it?" I ask. I look past him to where I'd last seen my grandfather, but the spot is vacant. "Where's Gramps?"

"He's gone to fetch Detective Mosepi," Howlen says. He hands me a plastic bag containing a smoothed-out leaf of paper.

I take it, turn the evidence bag over a couple of times, and study the chicken-scratch handwriting without reading the words.

"Read it, May." The urgency in his voice sends gooseflesh crawling over my skin.

Esmé

You are Beautiful,
With the flower in your hair.
I'll see you next time you visit Beaufort West.

Yena

DARK COUNTRY

My heart jumps like a jackrabbit. The riddle, which is probably a cruel veiled threat, changes my taut muscles into jelly barely strong enough to keep me standing.

I tilt my head back to study Abraham Amin's twisted face, caked in blood and dirt. I try to understand how a two-bit politician figured into the bigger equation.

I try, but I fail.

File: Case22-ES_interview.wav
Duration: 0:35:22
Date: 25/09/2012

Esmé: This is an informal interview with Hester Pieterse, a rape and muti-crime survivor. Hester's name and voice were changed to protect her identity, as a precaution.

Hester, please, if you feel you need us to stop at any point, just say the word. Otherwise, the floor is yours.

Hester: [audible sigh] I used to be amongst the majority of people, women especially, who naively think *it won't happen to me*, and when it did happen to me, I desperately clung to the hope I was trapped in some fucked-up nightmare. Perhaps my mind was trying to deal with what was happening. I'm not sure. Hell, I still don't know how to describe the attack without it sounding like a terrible retelling of *The Wizard of Oz*. You see, instead of blocking my whole ordeal like a regular person would, my mind warped some of my memories so badly, it sounds downright absurd when I hear myself talking about it. It sounds as if I was drugged out of my mind.

DARK COUNTRY

I wasn't drugged, but I wasn't *there* either.

It was an out-of-body experience where everything happening to my body was dull, gray, and horrendous. And everything around the scene was bright and welcoming.

[Pause]

I was walking home from a friend's house, taking the shortcut through a field—the same shortcut I always took. When I ventured into it on the night of the attack, though, it was nearing midnight, and the field was vacant.

I remember it had rained the afternoon. I could clearly see all the way to my house, and there wasn't anyone in the field.

[Pause]

Halfway through the field, I noticed a shadow. It separated itself from nothingness and approached.

He hit me over the head with something. It happened so fast ...

[Pause]

I couldn't scream. I couldn't wrap my head around it. By the time I realized this wasn't a mugging, it was too late.

My face was pressed into the grass so hard, I could only concentrate on not suffocating.

[Audible Sob]

Esmé: Should we take a break?

Hester: [Incomprehensible]

BREAK

Hester: I distanced myself from the ordeal enough to survive, I think, but I still remember certain things.

My arms were pinned behind my back. I was afraid they'd pop out of their sockets.

[Pause]

When he was done, I didn't even notice. He turned me over, pinned me down, and slapped me across the cheek a few times. I was completely out of it. I barely registered when he asked me what part I could offer him.

When he took out his knife, I snapped back long enough to wonder if I was going to die. I said I didn't understand. Then, he went on to explain he literally wanted a piece of me.

Esmé: Oh God.

Hester: When I didn't answer, he asked me then, again, what part I could offer him. Eventually, I said to him to take my breasts, and he went to work. I passed out.

[Pause]

But when I awoke, I still had both my breasts. I don't know if he was scared off before he could take his muti, or if my passing out was enough to deter him. Either way, I still had my breasts. I'm very lucky in that regard, but I doubt the scars will ever fade.

Esmé: Can you tell me anything about your attacker? How he looked, how he spoke, anything recognizable or unique?

Hester: You'd think I'd remember a lot of things, considering how bright the night was and the fact he was unmasked, but his appearance was unremarkable. He had broad shoulders—rugby player shoulders—and he was muscular. But, apart from his necklace, he looked like a regular guy.

Esmé: Necklace?

Hester: Yeah, it was this leather thong with a human tooth pendant. Hey, are you all right? You've gone pale.

Esmé: [Clears Throat]

I remember someone else mentioning a similar necklace in their testimony, a few months ago. It could be nothing. I'll have to check my facts.

Hester: Look, Esmé, I would love to find my rapist and take a baseball bat to his skull, but his eyes were

[Pause]

dead. He was soulless, inhuman. It's the single most outstanding aspect of him: his dead eyes.

Be careful when you go searching for him, okay? You don't want to end up like me, or worse.

END OF AUDIO TRANSCRIPT

I double-click on the desktop icon titled *Valentine Sikelo: Case #137-ES*, and find the recorded .wav file listed in the folder. I tap on it and wait for the recording to come to life in the Media Player. A deadpan voice I recognize as my own begins talking before I scroll through the photos located in the same file.

Esmé: Esmé Snyder, Occult Crime Expert, Case Number 137. It is approximately 1800 hours on Friday, 4 September 2015. The victim is a black female, aged between twenty-six and thirty years. Height is around 1.70 meters, and weight about eighty-five kilograms. Clothing includes a turquoise peplum top and matching pencil skirt—cut off and discarded roughly two meters from the body—as well as black underwear and a pair of black open-toe heels.

Pre-mortem mutilations are obvious. Defensive lacerations on her palms may confirm theory. DNA evidence of murderer and/or murderers might be present underneath fingernails. Eyes, tongue, and lips are also missing.

Further investigative information is required to determine whether the victim is, beyond any reasonable doubt, another muti murder fatality, but the preliminary evidence is overwhelming.

Edit: The victim has been identified as Mrs. Valentine Sikelo from personal effects found near the body. Several possible suspects have been cleared by the police in record time.

The high-definition photographs are graphic, and they pulled at my heartstrings, but I don't look away. I study each photo in excruciating detail and playing the recording on loop, searching for one overlooked piece of information that'll help me find this so-called "Yena." Who is he? What's his intended outcome? Why murder these people, these wholly different people? My eyes water before I decide to close the folder, stop the recording, and move on to the next desktop icon.

I open the folder, named *Carol-Anne Brewis—Case #138-ES,* and repeat the process. I listen to my uncertain voice with the almost inaudible gulps interrupting my sentences.

Esmé: Esmé Snyder, Occult Crime Expert, Case Number 138. It's around 0610 hours on Saturday, 5 September 2015. The victim, one Carol-Anne Brewis, is a white female, aged twelve years. Her height is 1.61 meters, and weight between forty and forty-five kilograms.

The victim's clothing is a panda bear printed onesie. From what I can tell, the right sleeve is torn at the shoulder, but otherwise her clothes are in place. No suggestion of sexual assault is present at this stage. The coroner would be able to verify.

Side note: Get coroner's report ASAP.

The victim's right ankle seems to be broken— possible escape attempt gone wrong? Self-defense is indicated by the victims' broken nails on both hands. A piece of cloth has been stuffed into her mouth, to muffle her screams.

A long pause follows these few facts, and I remember how I'd mentally readied myself to look at the child's ruined face and her fatal wounds. I'd never quite gotten a handle on seeing innocence stolen.

Esmé: A clean cut with a precision tool—possibly a cranial saw from the serration marks on the edges of the bone—was used to remove the top of the skull. A large piece of the brain is missing. It seems most of this happened pre-mortem.

I hear myself sob and someone in the background asking if I need a break. *"I think so,"* I'd said, and the recording ended.

Admittedly, even after having some time to distance myself from the actual crime scene, looking at the photographs still made me queasy. I study them, though, zooming in for close-up shots of the bruising and wounds. I zoom out, piecing the photographs together on the monitor to get an overview of the crime scene and the body.

Nothing jumps out at me as particularly unique. The killer's signature is either not there or is invisible.

Sighing, I close the folder and recorded file and move on to the newest icon, named *Abraham Amin—Case #139-HW*. Howlen's voice issues from speakers.

Howlen: Howlen Walcott, PhD. It is Thursday 10 September 2015 at 08h46. The victim has been identified as Abraham Amin, an ANC MP. His height is 1.81 meters and weight approximately ninety-eight kilograms—as suggested by the missing person's report. The victim is suspended by bungee cords running down the ventilation shaft of the Daspoort Tunnel—an elaborate setup, planned well in advance.

The victim has an infected wound running from left to right, severing to his Achilles tendon, on his right heel. The fatal wound, however, is the deep, jagged cut across the victim's abdomen. Premeditated disembowelment is a possibility, but the momentum of the fifty meter fall would've created a similar effect when the bungee cord jerked back. What bothers me is: did the killer take something, some piece of Abraham Amin, for a ritual? I cannot be certain at this stage.

The victim also sustained multiple post-mortem bone breaks and wounds. From the fall down the ventilation shaft?

Howlen's voice grows distant, thoughtful, and I can imagine him studying the victim, along with the whole scene.

"Possibly," he says. "These cords, and the harness, are professional bungee equipment. I'll look into it.

I have doubts about the victim's political status being the reason he was targeted, but one can never be too sure. Law enforcement will be investigating this particular lead, and Detective Mosepi vows to keep us updated with their findings. I'd bet a month's wages that the coroner's report is most crucial to this case.

I close the files, sit back in my chair, and chew on my bottom lip as I look around my office. The pastel colors are supposedly too cheerful, too homey, and too girly for an occult crime expert. So I've been told, anyway. A baby blue and white chevron pattern is painted across the walls. White bookshelves are built around the large window that allows for natural light throughout the year. Mauve and turquoise green vases act as bookends whilst simultaneously matching the dusty pink shag carpet and my repurposed turquoise desk. An oil landscape depicting an abstract Pretoria skyline in more pastel colors hangs at eye level across from my desk. Then there is my personal rolling whiteboard peeking out from behind the open door. The office isn't exactly me. It's an office better suited to a muted personality. I much prefer dramatic colors, severe lines, and unconventional materials for decorating, but when you're surrounded by death most of the time, that type of décor would become depressing fast.

Nevertheless, there is a lot of *me* in this office.

The chevron pattern has semi-severe lines. The repurposed desk has an unconventional design. The colors are dramatic for someone's work office. All in all, it's still me in its own weird way.

This leads me to contemplate not only the psychology of murderers and serial killers, but rather human nature in general—if one could call Yena a human being.

In almost every situation, everyone leaves something true about themselves behind. Why should a crime scene be any different?

"The riddle," I say to myself, revisiting the memorized words from the note the killer had left behind. There were grammatical errors, silly ones where capital letters were used wrongly. It shouldn't mean anything, yet …

I open my internet browser, and then type in *Beautiful in Beaufort-Wes*, which is a dual-lingual love song with Afrikaans and English lyrics combined. It isn't a big lead, but it is something new to follow up on. If anything, this clue could mean the killer is familiar with the Afrikaans language to some degree. Who knew? Maybe the killer is familiar with the popular Afrikaans song, too.

I scan the lyrics and am overcome with another dreadful feeling, the same one I'd gotten when I first read the note.

The killer has left a message, all right—a sick, creepy message hidden between the lines of a note.

I jump up from my seat and rush to the door. "Howlen," I call down the corridor.

"Yeah?" He comes into view with an open file in his hands and reading glasses perched on his nose.

"I think I've got something," I say.

He closes the file and walks over.

"That riddle the killer sent is actually an Anglicized title of a song. Well, it technically started out as a poem, but the song's more popular."

We make our way back to my desk where the laptop's still open with the lyrics page on display.

"After looking at the note's grammar, I might have stumbled onto something."

"You couldn't have mentioned it earlier?" Howlen asks as he takes a seat on my chair.

"I didn't think his note would reference anything. I thought it was a way to freak me out. Anyway, it turns out that it's a song."

"Fair enough," he says. "So, what caught your attention about this song? You know I'm useless when it comes to Afrikaans." He leans forward to study my computer screen.

"I'll quickly translate the parts I think are important."

"Everything's important, but okay, I trust you."

"The gist is," I say, "the guy's stalking me."

"You got that from a song?" Howlen presses his spectacles higher to his face.

"Stanza one, line two: 'You and I had kissed on graves, and on trains, and on the back seats of Ford Fairlanes,' is related to a nightmare I had last night. There were graves in a parking lot, some cars, and I took a ride on the Gautrain."

"That's just coincidental. What's next?"

I point at the screen. "The chorus, um, here: 'Now you can't sleep anymore, can't laugh anymore, can't do anything for yourself,' is another part relating to me. I've had—"

"Bouts of insomnia, I know. You also struggle with depression when you don't get enough sleep," he says.

MONIQUE SNYMAN

"I didn't think anyone would notice."

"I do. What else?"

"Stanza three is more provocative."

"Oh, do translate."

I roll my eyes. "It reminds me of the last time we—"

"Three coincidences are no longer coincidences," he cuts me off, clearing his throat uncomfortably. "So it's a stalker note."

"Partly. What concerns me is the imagery of stanza three's last line: 'I felt how my heart was torn right out of my body and how it floated away like a rowboat on the river.' Here, I can't decide if the killer is threatening me or giving me a clue to what he has planned next."

"It could be nothing." He sounds unconvinced. "'Yena' might just be jealous."

"Or it could be everything." I tilt my head to look up at him.

He grunts an affirmative and walks around the desk to sit in a chair opposite mine.

"Maybe I'm being too literal?"

Howlen shakes his head. "The killer is intelligent, but he lacks the finesse of a formal education." He sighs, but perks up almost immediately, as though he's had a revelation. It gives me a microscopic amount of hope. "He's not brilliant, Esmé. There's no ingenuity in his methods. He's a narcissist playing a game with us—with you, in particular."

"No shit."

"The guy is manipulating us with crude psychology. It's brilliant, but human. He's not unbeatable, he just thinks he is."

"I like your positive outlook, but it doesn't get us any closer to an answer." I spin the laptop around to the open web page and gesture to the screen. "What do we do about this?"

Howlen sits back and fiddles with his left cufflink. "We play his game, of course. That is, unless you've got something better in mind?"

Out of ideas, I shake my head.

"Then, let's work on getting the upper hand. What else have you got?"

I open the top drawer and find Feyisola's list of names. Some of them might or might not have ordered body parts from outside the country. Feyisola doesn't give bad information, even if she sometimes omits details to save her own skin. If we're lucky, one of the names could turn out to be their guy.

"I have a list of possible suspects I need to investigate," I say. "There's a big shipment of muti coming in from Namibia, and these people might be involved in some way."

"Namibia?"

When Feyisola first told me, I had a similar reaction to the news.

"That's new," Howlen says. "Usually the shipments come through the Beitbridge border."

"It's a weird turn of events, I agree. But, muti is a hot commodity these days, so why not Namibia?"

"True. Would you like some help?"

"Thank you, but no. You have enough to deal with as it is. The best way to help is to butter up the labs and get our results back as soon as possible. I'll see to the list."

He nods, stands, and opens his mouth to say something else, but doesn't.

"We're okay, Howlen," she says.

"You sure?"

Smiling, I turn the laptop around to face me again. "I'm sure. We all have our own ways to deal with this."

He smiles back, and I know that our brief quarrel has come to an end and that our friendship is re-established.

"Go home and get some sleep, okay?" he says.

"In a minute."

Howlen pushes his hands into his trouser pockets like a dismissed schoolboy and turns to leave.

"Howlen?"

"Hmmm?" he mutters.

"If something were to happen to me, you'd look after Gramps, right?"

"Nothing will happen to you," he insists.

"Yes, but if it did …"

"I will, but nothing's going to happen to you, May."

Howlen slips out of my office without another word.

CHAPTER 23

Detective Rynhardt Louw isn't the type of person who would enter a career in law enforcement without a good reason. He's far too kind, almost too polite, and a little too … innocent. His eyes, those wise hazelnut eyes, tell a story of great hardship and loss, but his past hasn't turned his soul to stone, yet. He's quick to smirk and tease and joke, but the young detective still seems guarded whenever he does.

For a week, he's acted as Detective Mosepi's personal errand boy between the firm and the precinct, and I have used the time to study him from afar. There's not much else to do while we wait for some miraculous break in the cases, or for the killer to strike again. So why not curb my curiosity about Detective Rynhardt Louw while I bide my time?

Detective Louw's gait is always determined, always proud. Even with windswept hair and a disheveled suit, he appears unyielding to the sheer force of nature. He calculates his surroundings in a single sweep. Detective Mosepi is the only other detective I know who is as thorough when the situation doesn't necessarily call for it. Then there's Louw's smile that never truly reaches his eyes. Still, whenever he looks my way, he seems to soften up a bit.

Contradictions intrigue me.

As he waits for my grandfather to look over the newest developments in the Valentine Sikelo case, I watch him from the staircase.

He moves from his seat in the vacant reception area to where I'm sitting on the stairs with a file open on my lap.

Hidden between the pages is Feyisola's handwritten message, dropped off before Rynhardt arrived, inviting me to a meeting in a shoddy part of town with one of her shady acquaintances. She doesn't elaborate on why there is a change in location, but I would be an idiot not to go. Maybe Feyisola stumbled onto something. Perhaps our old meeting place has been compromised. Who knows?

Rynhardt leans with his back against the banister, his hands in his pockets as he looks up through the openings to catch my attention.

"Sometimes I think you're undressing me with your eyes." Detective Louw barely breathes the words, never diverting his stare. Apparently, I haven't been subtle enough. "The trick," he says, relaxing his stance, "is to be as inconspicuous about your examination as possible. Make it seem as if you happen to be in the room, as if you belong, and that you don't really care what's happening around you." He's silent for a while before he turns around and flashes me a guarded grin. "You try."

I shift the open file on my lap, wondering how I can maneuver my position to appear more natural. Eventually, I decide to pick up the file and recline slightly, before I steal another glance at him.

He breathes a chuckle. "You're too tense. Also, your position does *not* look comfortable."

I sit upright. "Okay. What would you suggest?"

"Your initial position was perfect," he says. "Hunch your shoulders a bit."

"I don't hunch," I say, but do so anyway. "Now what?"

"Fake your reading of the file. Then, glimpse at the room."

I do as I'm told and, for extra effect, I act deep in thought.

"Check your breathing," he warns.

I haven't even noticed my breathing had become slightly strained, but I correct the tell.

"There we go. That's better."

A blush creeps up my neck. "Thanks," I say, closing the file.

"It takes a lot of practice, but you'll master it soon enough." He takes a relaxing stance against the banister. "Where's your partner?"

"Howlen? He's upstairs, fiddling with his paperwork." I shrug.

"Oh."

"Do you need him for some reason?"

"No, I was just wondering," Detective Louw tilts his head to catch my eye. "So, you two are … together."

"I wouldn't go that far." I clear my throat and study the now-uninteresting file in my lap.

He gives me a knowing look. "I'm not judging you," he says. "I only want to know if I can ask you out to dinner without stepping on someone's toes."

"Why?" There's enough suspicion thrown into this one word to make any interested man change his mind.

"Why what?" Detective Louw asks.

"Why do you want to ask me out to dinner?"

"When was the last time you were asked out on a date?"

"I don't date," I mumble, and stand.

"Do you want to start dating?" he asks sincerely before I can walk away.

I'm so baffled by this question, I can barely formulate a thought.

"It's dinner. Nothing more, nothing less," he says.

"Er." I look everywhere except at Rynhardt. "Can I think about it?"

He smiles crookedly. "Take your time."

My grandfather rounds the corner, asking questions about missing witness statements and coroner reports.

Rynhardt steps away from the banister.

I nod, turn, and make my way back upstairs. Instead of going to my office, though, I head to Howlen's.

"You won't guess what happened." I close his office door.

Howlen is standing in front of his rolling whiteboard when he glances over his shoulder with a single raised eyebrow.

"Detective Louw asked me out on a date."

"I heard," Howlen says.

"Were you eavesdropping?"

"No," he says, turning back to his work. "Are you going to accept his invitation?"

"I don't know." I strut to his messy desk, and scan the open files strewn across the surface. One of the files belongs to Carol-Anne Brewis. Howlen must be looking into it, seeing as I've struggled to face the little girl's picture without having a shred of evidence that'll lead them to the killer. "Maybe."

"The two of you are badly matched, you know this."

"Really? I don't know." I turn away from his desk. "It would be nice to be wooed for a change."

"If you wanted romance, you would have told your grandfather about us a long time ago." He regards me coolly.

I take a few steps toward the door, ready to leave.

He turns around, which makes me freeze in my tracks. "If I thought you would appreciate unimaginative dates, being showered with gifts, and hearing sweet nothings day and night, I would do those things. The problem is, I know mundane hogwash bores you." Howlen exhales loudly. "Tell me, Esmé, why did you really come in here? Was it to get a rise out of me? If it's the case, you've succeeded."

"I …" I begin, but immediately realize I'm wholly unequipped to deal with the rush of emotions threatening to suffocate us both. I reach for the handle. "I was fucking with you, Howl—"

"No! Don't you dare." He grabs me by my elbow to keep me from leaving. "I can't go on like this, May. Either you tell me what you want us to be or I'm handing in my resignation, today."

"You wouldn't."

"Try me."

We stare at each other for a long minute, unflinching, before I straighten.

I pull my arm from his grip and blow a hair from of my face. "You're not wrong about how I hate mundane gestures," I say, trying to salvage whatever dignity I have left. "I do like flowers, though."

"So, if I were to ask you on a date—"

"The answer would be yes," I say. "But you never asked."

"Fine," he says. "I'll pick you up at seven."

"Fine, I'll see you then."

"Good."

"Don't be boring." I open the door to leave.

"I won't," he almost snarls behind me.

It takes every ounce of my self-discipline not to smile. "We're not well-matched either, you know?"

"Tell me about it."

The stifling weather dictates my outfit for the evening—a summer's dress paired with a crocheted wrap and wedged heels—because I have no idea where we're going or what we'll do for this "date" thing. I wondered, of course, as I nervously fumble with my hands in my lap and watch the world pass by through the passenger window.

The suburb slowly opens up to the roads leading into the city. Electric lights twinkle in windows and shine down from the streetlights, illuminating the emptying streets. In the distance, neon lights flicker to life, brightening up the gloom. The cloudless night sky is speckled with starlight accompanied by a bright sickle moon.

The night is beautiful—warm, but beautiful.

"Are you always this quiet on dates?" Howlen asks.

"Yes," I say. "Silence leaves no room for misinterpretation."

He smirks.

"You're awfully quiet, too."

"Honestly, it's because I'm nervous," Howlen says.

I twist in my seat to study his face. His strong jaw is set, but a grin played on his lips. Smudges of exhaustion are present under his eyes, but it's only noticeable whenever he's cast within the shadows. He glances toward me and the slightest blush appears.

"I haven't been on one of these in a while," he explains.

"I can't imagine why. You're always so charming." My joke earns a soft chuckle.

Soon, we turn onto Stanza Bopape Street, heading west.

Jacaranda blooms rain onto the windshield of his silver Yaris, tugged from the branches by a slight breeze. The world feels strange, both new and ancient at the same time, but it might've been my imagination.

We come to a slow stop at a red light.

"Let's not talk shop tonight." Howlen checks his rearview mirror. "Please?"

"Deal," I agree. "On one condition, though."

"I'm listening."

"When the date's over, I'm going to need your help."

"What type of help?"

"The back-up kind," I say.

He sighs his, "Okay."

The red light turns green, and the Yaris pulls away.

"Let's start with something easy," he begins, stealing a glimpse of me.

I nod, force a smile, and stop fumbling with my fingers and thumbs.

"What's your favorite color?"

I roll my eyes. "You know that already."

"No, I don't."

"Blue. Yours?"

"Blue," Howlen says. "King's blue, though."

Howlen slows the car and flips on the indicator to turn right into Pine Street. "Why do I get the impression you're not in the mood for a game of twenty questions?"

"I like to think we at least know each other well enough to have the basics memorized."

"True, but it feels somewhat awkward, going on a date and not going through the motions."

"I know, right?" I clap a hand against my thigh for emphasis. "Where are we going, by the way?"

"It's a surprise."

I sigh again. "Okay, then tell me something I don't know."

"Well, one in every four-million lobsters is born with a rare genetic defect that turns it blue."

"What?" I laugh. "No. I meant tell me something I don't know about *you*."

"I know what you meant, May." He laughs softly. "Hmmm, okay, here's something you don't know. I used to be a pretty decent violinist, but I haven't played in years."

"Why not?"

"That's a story for another time."

That's all he says.

The Yaris turns left onto Government Avenue and we proceed down the street until the twinkling lights of the Union Buildings break through the canopy of green and purple. The imposing neoclassical structure, with its Cape Dutch and Edwardian style details, sits atop Meintjieskop and overlooks most of the city. Beautiful terraced gardens—planted exclusively with indigenous plants—stretch out toward the always-busy Stanza Bopape Street. Larger than life statues, memorials or monuments, are visible even if most of them are merely specks in the darkness. Then there's the Nelson Mandela amphitheater, which can seat nine-thousand people at a time. The Union Buildings remain a marvelous sight, even to those who see them every day as they make their way to work or home.

Howlen slows the car and parks. "Voila." He switches off the engine, undoes his seatbelt, and exits the car.

"Voila?" I unbuckle the seatbelt, grinning like an idiot. By the time I have the door closed behind me, he's done rummaging around in the trunk. "Can I help with anything?" I ask.

The trunk slams shut. "No, but thank you for offering."

He appears, carrying a picnic basket in one hand, a checkered blanket folded over his forearm, and a fragrant bouquet of pink daisies, baby's breath, and white roses in his other hand. "For you," Howlen says, holding out the flowers.

I accept them, battling the flush rising to my cheeks, but I can't subdue my smile.

He presses the fob to lock his car and then holds out his arm so I can hook my hand in the crook of his elbow.

Together, we make our way toward the uneven stone staircase leading into the terraced gardens. Once we reach the uppermost terrace, Howlen spreads out the blanket on the lush grass and sets down the picnic basket.

I take a very ladylike seat, cross my legs, and watch as he opens the picnic basket, revealing a bottle of sparkling grape juice and two Styrofoam cups. He then spreads out an array of Woolworths' bite-size snacks. Afterward, he set up a few thick, white candles around us and lit the wicks one after the other.

"You went all out, huh?"

Howlen opens the grape juice and fills the Styrofoam cups. "Imagine what I can do when I have time to plan."

"Hot air balloons, champagne, caviar?" I ask, taking the offered cup from him.

He tries to hide the beginnings of a crooked grin, but fails. "Too predictable," he states.

"I'm intrigued *and* impressed." I take a sip of the sweet, sparkly drink. "So tell me something else about you."

"What do you want to know?" Howlen's eyes become molten chocolate in the candlelight.

Those eyes make my inner teenage girl sigh.

"Surprise me," I say, moving my tongue across my teeth as I smile brightly.

"Okay. I have an older half-brother from my father's previous marriage and a younger half-sister from my mother's current marriage," Howlen says. "Richard is a musician and Christine is an actress. My mother is an ex-stage actress and quite melodramatic, which is why your grandfather insists on calling her Lady Sophia Jane Walcott."

"And your father?"

"My father was a musician, too, but he's recently decided to be a lyricist," Howlen answers. "Anything else you want to know?"

"Yes."

"Okay, shoot."

"Are you sure you weren't switched at birth?"

He grins and drinks some grape juice. "You'll laugh, but it was the first thing I checked when they let me loose in a lab." Howlen crosses his legs without breaking eye contact. "I think my parents figured out I was different when, for my sixth birthday, I asked for a chemistry set instead of toy cars or a guitar like my brother wanted." He takes another sip of his drink. "Mum sent me to a preparatory school when I got beat up in public school for being too nerdy. My father, on the other hand, decided it would also be helpful if I knew how to defend myself."

"Martial arts?" I probe.

"Boxing. My father's old school, even if he lives by the whole 'sex, drugs, and rock and roll' motto."

"Ah." I nod. "Do you live by that same motto?"

"Not really, but I've been known to have moments of delinquency," Howlen answers. "Apparently, I'm quite self-destructive when the mood hits, but these days I tend to work my frustrations out in the gym."

"So where does the violin come in?"

He clears his throat, and says in a deep male voice not his own: "You're a Walcott, Howlen. You *have* to play at least one instrument. Pick one, stick with it, and you'll have any woman worth having. Not that you'd know what I mean right now, but one day, son. One day."

"Your dad's a smart guy. Real classy."

Howlen laughs. "Don't tell him that. He has a big enough ego as it is."

We talk for hours about everything and nothing, getting to know each other outside of work, outside of the death and grim realities overshadowing most of our lives. It's just us and the stars and the warm spring breeze.

The candles burn out, but neither of us seems to want the night to end.

Our shoulders touch as we lie on the blanket, gazing at the stars. "I should probably take you home at some point," he says.

I turn to face him, my cheek pressing against the soft blanket, and find him staring back. My heart skips a beat and then my pulse starts to race. Before I can persuade myself otherwise, I turn onto my side and prop myself onto my elbow. I place my free hand against Howlen's cheek.

Leaning down, I brush my lips against his, tracing his jawline with my fingertips.

His breathing hitches before he places his hand against the small of my back.

My hand comes to a rest against his chest, where his heart pounds fiercely, and I smile against his mouth. I pull away too soon and those few shared moments of closeness can only be described as both infinite and insufficient.

"Does this mean I get a second date?" His voice is husky; his eyes roam my face, lingering on my lips, before our gazes lock again.

"Maybe." I'm breathless. "We'll have to see how you behave yourself in between now and when you drop me off at home."

"Then I better get you to your meeting," he whispers.

Reluctant for the night to end, yet unwilling to spoil the memory, I whisper, "Am I out of line for wanting to go home with you instead?"

"Very," he says, his hand clutching a fistful of fabric. "And that's why I'm crazy about you."

"But?"

"But you wanted romance. And romance means you'll have to make peace with having to kiss me for a while, before we do more."

His mouth muffles my groan of dismay before it can escape. I feel him smile.

I pull away to protest his definition of romance, but he cuts my arguments off again in the same way. Soon I'm putty in his hands, and relinquish the win.

The next kiss is deeper, lasts longer, and is full of promise.

I don't trust it for a second.

Yena sits in the driver's seat of his van, parked near the Yaris that transported Esmé and her shining knight to the Union Buildings. With the window cracked open for ventilation, he watches them have their evening picnic. Their heads are bent together, smiling, laughing, talking, and dining.

He sees how the snob pushes a stray strand of Esmé's long red hair out of her face, watches him caress her loose curls. That hair, oh how it reminds him of waterfalls of blood. Then, he watches her eat offered food, seductively looking at her dearest Doctor Walcott. Had Yena any emotions for the woman, Howlen would have been dead already. Lucky for Howlen, he doesn't see Esmé as a paramour.

She isn't a conquest, but an opponent. An opponent who needs more inspiration to play his game, it seems.

His stomach rumbles and he decides to eat his own dinner while observing them from afar.

Dinner consists of comfort food—peanut butter and apricot jam sandwiches, prepared that same morning with his own two hands and packaged in a large, airtight Tupperware lunchbox. Blue Ribbon brown bread slathered in Rama margarine with Black Cat peanut butter on one side, and a generous helping of Koo apricot jam on the other. Exactly the way his Gogo used to make them.

No gourmet meals come close to childhood favorites, in his opinion.

He takes tentative bite after tentative bite, relishing the flavors combining in his mouth, and reminisces over the few good memories he's accumulated in his short thirty-five years of life.

There aren't many good ones.

DARK COUNTRY

He remembers his Gogo in detail, though: a stout, stern woman, a matriarch like no other. Crocheting her brightly colored shawls and wearing them like armor whenever she left the house. Hovering over the stove like a witch tending to her cauldron, feeding her horde of grandchildren whatever she had in her shiny pots. Always willing to love someone fiercely, to defend them viciously, until she found them undeserving. All of her own children had lacked in some department or another; prostitutes, drug dealers, criminals—the lot of them. But Gogo didn't hold the sins of her children against her grandchildren. In fact, she had high hopes for the younger generation.

She'd had the gift, too, like Yena. Gogo could see *things*, hear their whispers in the dark, and sense their presence even if they sometimes hid from her. What's more, she was a human lie detector. Lie to her and you would feel her full fury.

Unfortunately, the difference between Gogo and Yena was that she decided to ignore their fearsome ancestors' calling.

It was foolish of her, he now knows.

They only kept her around long enough to make sure he didn't die young. For eight years, the ancestors spared her for him. Eight short years …

Then it all went to shit.

Thanks to his fucked-up drug addict mother, who spawned more children than one would think possible, and his unknown father, who was either a pimp or a client she'd turned tricks for, Yena and all his siblings and cousins were sent into a non-existent foster system after Gogo's death. The three youngest of Gogo's brood, Yena included, ended up with a distant relative—a long lost uncle of some sort. A sadistic bastard whenever he came home from the *shebeen*, which happened infrequently, but not seldom enough.

By ten years old, he'd known what true hunger was, what real fear felt like, what pain meant. By thirteen, all three of them had lost every bit of innocence his Gogo had tried so hard to preserve. The remaining childlike essence had disappeared when they'd burned that fucker's rickety shack down to the ground, with him still in it.

Yena was fifteen years old when it happened.

They'd run away and lived on the streets for a few years like animals, doing what they could to survive.

Nobody had cared then; nobody cares now.

He closes his empty lunchbox, places it on the passenger seat, and proceeds to brush the crumbs off his face, shirt, and trousers. Eyes glued to the PG-13 romance scene developing on the Union Buildings' lawn, he contemplates his next move, his next victim.

He needs to get her attention properly. With his mind made up, Yena turns the key in the ignition, and the van growls to life.

If she doesn't want to play, she's useless to me. Entirely useless.

W hile I admit to initially being terrified, the entity residing in my house is probably benevolent, for the most part. Annoying as it is, what with stealing anything resembling lace and destroying most of my bedroom, I see no reason to enrage it by inviting Father Gabriel to abruptly end its ethereal presence. If that particular being wanted to hurt me, it would've done so by now.

The phantom that'd stalked me on the night of Carol-Anne Brewis' murder had also moved on. So it seemed, at least.

As I told Howlen, these things are just scare tactics employed by disgruntled criminals with a knack for magic. I'd go so far as to blame the human psyche for conjuring up such fantasies due to sleep deprivation, or psychological impairments, *if* I wasn't a non-believer in the weird.

Unfortunately for me, and others plagued by the paranormal, these things do exist.

It's acquiring logical evidence which makes it difficult to prove how insignificant and insufficient humans are in the greater scheme of life, the universe, and everything.

So, although while in public I choose to actively ignore whatever pseudo-psychological attacks comes my way, I do see these otherworldly creatures as an invaluable research opportunity. Each nuisance, every disturbance, is one tiny piece of a magnificent puzzle that could solve questions mankind has never even dreamed of asking.

Snyder International Religious Crime Investigative Services wasn't established to solve murders. It was never our intention to fight crime.

But here I am, still dressed in my flowery dress and wedged heels after my date with Howlen, crossing the sticky floor of a two-bit strip club in a questionable neighborhood.

A bottle blonde bombshell expertly moves around a pole, wearing nothing more than a bejeweled G-string and a pair of fuck-me heels. A smoke machine sets the mood while the strobe lights flash with the rhythmic music. Men sit in groups around the stage—the young howling in delight, the old intense in their ogling. Wads of cash—tens and twenties—are waved around to catch her attention as she stretches her body into some extreme yoga positions to show off her best attributes. Her perky breasts glisten in the spotlight as she slowly slides down the pole. Once on the raised podium, the stripper crawls toward a group of men who've pulled out a few hundreds.

Howlen clears his throat and turns his attention away from the stage. His shoulders are stiff, his gaze focused on everything except the stage, and a droplet of perspiration trickles down his temple.

"Are you seriously uncomfortable right now?" I ask loud enough to be heard over the music.

He shrugs.

"Well, stop it already. You look like a cop."

I look back to the stripper, her expression a blank as she allows one of the men to push some money into her panties.

An oversized chest blocks my view. I look up to see the brutish bouncer with a roid-rage glare staring down. His bald head gleams with sweat, and the pungent smell of meat coming out of his pores make my eyes burn.

Howlen sticks to my side, casually snaking a hand around my waist.

The bouncer, a giant, studies us for longer than necessary.

"You Esmé?" he grunts.

"Yes."

"And him?"

"My partner," she says. "Is his presence a problem?"

"Depends," the bouncer snorts, reminding me of an antagonized bull. "Come," he says, turning around and leading us deeper into the club.

The music changes from techno to rap, and the now-naked stripper surrenders the stage to a new girl dressed in a hip hop outfit.

DARK COUNTRY

We're led through a beaded curtain, away from the strobe lights. A corridor stretches ahead, lined with doors—some closed, some ajar, some open. The carpet might have been red at some point, and it might've even been plush, but it has become distinctively brick-colored and worn through, with time.

Howlen's grip tightens on my waist as we walk a couple of steps behind the bouncer.

The bouncer opens the farthest door in the corridor and shows us into the dimly lit soundproofed chamber. More people are present than I expected, especially for a Thursday. I take in the scene of men and a few women seated around circular tables. People huddle together in their own cliques; the gamblers play poker, the drug addicts shoot up or snort the flavor of the week, the lady-boys sits on the laps of businessmen, and the ladies of ill repute search for their next paycheck.

Topless waitresses make the rounds, their erect nipples reinforced by cold air blasting through the air-conditioning. The bouncer continues his steady pace toward a well-guarded door on the other side of the chamber even as a young woman saunters up to us. She's wearing a revealing evening gown, her ample bosom almost spilling out of the flimsy fabric. Raven curls frame her oval face, bouncing with each step she takes. I would have thought her pretty were it not for the track marks visible on her arms.

"Five hundred for the night," she says in a dry whisper to Howlen, her voice sounding like wind rustling through dry leaves. She licks her plum-purple lips and flutters her fake eyelashes, undressing him with her eyes. Before he can answer, she averts her gaze and sizes me up. I can almost feel her caressing the curve of my hip and the swell of my chest. "Seven fifty if she joins in on the fun."

"Sorry, but no," Howlen says, walking us around the woman.

"Look me up when you change your mind," she calls after us.

My breathy giggles can't be heard over the reverberating music playing through speakers in the walls, but Howlen senses my amusement and pinches my waist as a warning. I return the favor by slapping his hand away.

The bouncer impatiently crosses his arms as he waits for us to catch up. The other two guards are impassive, though I doubt they would stay that way if problems arise.

The bouncer gestures for Howlen to spread his legs and arms for a body search. He does a thorough pat-down before glancing at me.

"Don't even think about it, Tarzan," Howlen says.

Perhaps the bouncer sees something in Howlen's eyes, or maybe his body language does the talking for him, because the bouncer decides not to force me into a pat-down. He nods to one of the guards and the door is opened for us.

"Whatever happens, don't say a word," I whisper to Howlen.

We enter a windowless room occupied by a large desk and two chairs, a sofa against one wall, and file cabinets stationed against the other. Behind the desk sits a man, his short dreadlocks bleached white—a heavy contrast against his midnight skin. He's wearing an immaculate white suit. With folded hands, he watches me as we dawdle near the door.

I catch sight of Feyisola seated in the corner, behind the unknown man, filing her long nails. She doesn't acknowledge us.

"Ah, yes, the Crimson Huntress and ... You brought Lancelot? Why, yes you did! What an honor to meet you both," the man says cheerfully in a thick accent—part gangster trying to sound posh, part African, nationality unknown. He rises from his seat. "You may call me The Rabbi; everyone else does. And this is Naledi." He nods to Feyisola. Of course she'd have another alias to play with, on this expedition. "Please, sit." He gestures to the seats across from him.

"Thank you." I smile my sweetest smile, crossing the room to take a seat.

"You must be curious as to why I asked you here," The Rabbi says once we're settled.

Not really, I think, but say, "Your name is whispered whenever I catch a killer—usually as a last resort, but whispered nonetheless. I suspect you need a favor of some kind, considering your recent run-in with the law."

"Our reputations precede us," The Rabbi says, folding his hands together.

I nod nonchalantly. "Unfortunately, I don't do favors for criminals."

"I am hardly a criminal. It's business, nothing more."

"But you do want a favor?"

"No." The Rabbi smiles broadly, showing off a golden tooth which glitters in the artificial light. "I asked you over to do *you* a favor."

"Interesting." There goes my entire game plan for this meeting. "What favor could I possibly want from you?"

"I've heard you're looking for a killer, a man known only as Yena." The Rabbi sits back in his chair. When I don't respond, he continues, "What if I told you I can help?"

"What if I told you that withholding any information from the authorities can be considered obstruction of justice?"

He bursts out laughing, a rough bellow which came straight from his belly.

I wait for him to quiet down.

"If this was America, I might've been worried, but this is Africa. Obstruction of justice ..." He chuckles and shakes his head, and short dreadlocks slap against his forehead. "I like you, Crimson. Your poker face is impeccable."

Of course a criminal of The Rabbi's caliber would know the law better than an appeal court judge. Fuck! There goes Plan B.

"What do you want, Rabbi?" I ask.

"A character witness," he answers, his smile never faltering. "For my trial, of course."

"Of course. Give me the information and I'll consider it."

"May," Howlen whispers to me.

I ignore Howlen, watching The Rabbi's expression instead.

"I need more than a consideration. They're trying to catch me on ludicrous charges—tax evasion, like Al Capone. Those uncreative morons," he explains. "The charges won't stick; they never do. I'm a businessman, not a fool. Still, a character witness will improve my standing with the judge."

"I can't make a deal if I can't use the information. How do I know you aren't bullshitting me?"

"Tsk." The Rabbi clicks his tongue. "Would I waste my time calling on you if I had *nothing* of worth?"

"Desperation makes people do strange things."

"Ah-ha! Exactly!" he exclaims. "I'm not desperate. You are."

"Fine, I'll be a character witness, but you better have something good up your sleeve or the deal's off."

He grins and slides forward in his chair. "I've never met anyone who knows Yena's true name. Those who knew it are either dead or too afraid to call him anything else," he says, crossing his arms on the desk. "Before I made Pretoria my base of operations, I had a club down in Hillbrow named Sodom. I never particularly cared for the place, due to the patrons' strange tastes and desires, but it made money, so I kept it running for longer than I should have." The Rabbi folds his hands together and laces his fingers. "I had a standing arrangement with the manager. Once a month, I go in and make sure the books aren't being fucked with. On those occasions, I sometimes heard things about this one's thing for young boys or that one's taste for strangulation. You know, typical whorehouse stuff." The Rabbi pauses, his gaze traveling to Howlen.

"I don't know, actually, but please continue," Howlen says.

The Rabbi shrugs. "One day, out of the blue, I get a call from the manager. 'Come in,' he says, 'It's an emergency.' I wasn't in the mood to deal with another prostitute OD-ing, so I told him to fix it himself. But the man was adamant, and eventually I was persuaded to check in at Sodom.

"Yena is a strange man, unremarkable in almost every way. If you see him on the streets, you wouldn't look twice in his direction. Look into his eyes, though, and your first instinct will be to run. He has no soul. I confirmed this when I shook his hand."

I glance at Howlen before looking back to The Rabbi. "Explain."

He holds out his hand to me. "Take my hand," he says.

Howlen moves forward, taking The Rabbi's hand in his.

In an instant, The Rabbi's eyes turn milky white, but he locks gazes with Howlen anyway.

"Will you join us for a tea party, Howly? Mr. Wiggles and Mrs. Bear requested your attendance, personally. Will you? Will you? Will you?" The voice coming out of The Rabbi's mouth doesn't belong to him. The eerie sound, saccharine and girlish, has a distinctively British accent to it, which I doubt he could fake.

Howlen tries tugging his hand away, but The Rabbi holds fast, clamping his free hand over Howlen's.

"Did you see that one, boy? What a beauty!" Another voice, an elderly male sounding excited. *"I should bring you on more of these trips of mine."*

"Stop it." Howlen tries to free himself. "Stop!"

The Rabbi doesn't let go.

Blood drains from Howlen's face until he's an ashen copy of himself. His eyes widen and his jaw goes slack.

I rest my hand on Howlen's knee. "Howlen?"

"Shit," Feyisola, or rather Naledi, says, putting down her nail file and standing.

"What shit?" I ask.

"Why didn't you hold my hand, Howlen? Mum said you should always hold my hand, but you didn't ... Don't you love me anymore?" The Rabbi tilts his head to the side, those glazed-over eyes staring without really seeing. It sends shivers up my legs. *"It's so cold here, Howly. Cold and dark ... Why didn't you hold my hand?"*

Feyisola rushes to The Rabbi's side, places one hand on his shoulder, and tries to pry his fingers away from Howlen's. "Help me!"

I grab hold of Howlen's wrist. His skin is like ice and the hair on his arm is coarse from fear. I try pulling him away from The Rabbi.

"I'm so scared, Howlen," The Rabbi continues in the little girl voice. Then he switches to an elderly man again. *"Sit down, son, and tell us exactly where you last saw Olivia. No, no, we're not angry with you, Howlen. Just tell us where you last saw—"*

Whatever connection there was breaks as Feyisola and I pull them apart.

Howlen slumps back against his chair.

Air rushes out of The Rabbi's lungs in a *whoosh* as he crumples into himself.

"That was rather unpleasant," he says in his own voice.

I kneel by Howlen's side, trying to revive him from whatever dark place he'd been forced to visit.

"Howl?" I whisper, taking his hand in mine. The calluses on his palm feels familiar against my fingertips, but his eyes are vacant. "Howl, snap out of it," I say, gently placing my other hand against his cheek.

"Give him a few minutes," The Rabbi grumbles as he massages his temples.

"What did you do to him?"

"Naledi," he says, waving a hand.

"The Rabbi acts as a conductor for the dead. Whatever happened here is the result of a guilty conscience, of not being able to let the dead sleep in peace," Feyisola explains. "Your friend's grief is what caused this. Nothing more."

"Will he be okay, though?"

"In time," she says, sounding unsure.

"This happens more often than you might think. Guilt, I mean. When I shook Yena's hand, however, the voices of his victims were in my head—begging, pleading, yelling for some release from the endless torment—but his state of mind kept them from breaking through. Yena has no soul, Crimson. None," The Rabbi says. "Lancelot's different. His guilt keeps the dead here."

"I'm fine," Howlen says, blinking as he snaps out of his stupor.

"See? What did I tell you?" Feyisola says, sitting back in her chair.

"Are you sure?" I ask, ignoring Feyisola. Howlen suddenly pulls his hand from mine and stands. "Howl?"

"I'll wait for you outside." The monotonous sentence holds the slightest hint of anger. With a single cutthroat glare, directed at The Rabbi, he weaves around me and the chair and heads for the door.

Obviously his wellbeing is important, but I decide—for the sake of not making a scene and flaunting my personal life in front of potential enemies—to let him leave.

"Do you want the information I have on Yena, or do we need to reschedule? Either way works for me. I have a motherfucker of a headache brewing now. anyway." The Rabbi opens his drawer as I sit back in my own chair.

"Continue," I say.

He pulls a Grandpa headache powder packet from the drawer, unwraps it, and drops the white powder directly onto his tongue. He chews a few moments, rolling it around his mouth while he crumples up the wrapper and tosses it in a bin under the desk.

"There are a lot of rumors as to where Yena comes from and what his deal is. They're all false. Nobody knows for sure. Nobody besides me knows, of course." The Rabbi hands over a thick A4-sized manila envelope. Something heavy lies in the bottom. The outline of an A5 notebook, perhaps? "If this doesn't buy your trust, nothing will."

"What's in it?" I take the envelope.

"I don't know." He makes a show of pulling up his shoulders. "I've never seen that envelope before in my life."

"Illegally obtained information, huh?" I stuff the envelope into my oversized purse.

"Look, I couldn't care less about the police finding out how I came about my information. It's Yena I'm worried about. If he finds out who gave you the envelope, I'm dead," he says. "So, do everyone a favor and get the fucker off the streets before he targets one of my people." The Rabbi cradles his head and massages his temples some more. "And show up to my trial on time. Judge Haskins hates me enough as it is."

"That's your cue to leave," Feyisola says.

I stand, ready to go.

"This meeting never happened," The Rabbi says before I can take a step.

"Quick question," I say. "Not to offend or anything, but why do they call you The Rabbi?"

"The Gypsy was taken, I suppose," he says.

The bouncer opens the door for me to exit, and Feyisola nods my way as I depart. Then, I'm alone with the bouncer in the VIP part of the strip club.

"Where's the guy I came here with?" I ask the bouncer, searching the faces of people in the crowd.

"He left with Cinnamon."

"Cinnamon?"

"The prostitute who propositioned you when we first came in," he says. "They left in a hurry."

"You're joking, right?"

"Nuh-huh," he grunts. "Men like him have a wandering eye. If they do stick around after they've gotten what they wanted, or after they've gotten you into trouble, they'll never be yours alone. Wandering eye, yeah?"

I find my cell phone, intending to call Howlen, who'd left me stranded in this godforsaken place.

"My advice," the bouncer says as we exit the VIP room and make our way through the red corridor, "is to move on before you're the one who's stuck cleaning up his mess."

I dial Howlen's number and wait. It goes directly to voicemail: "This is Howlen Walcott's phone. You know what to do." The beep sounds.

"Are you fucking kidding me, Howlen? A whore? You left me stranded to go screw another woman on the night of our first fucking date?" I almost yell into the phone. "I hope you pick up an STD that'll make your dick rot off! We're *done*. It's over." I end the call. "I need alcohol," I say, and the bouncer gives me a knowing nod.

"Want me to call you a taxi?"

"No, I want to get shitfaced."

A new girl's on stage, her dark skin highlighted with golden powder and an itsy bitsy golden G-string. Kohl lines her brilliant green eyes, and her black hair is straight and long and shiny. She's an Egyptian queen, a Nairobian goddess. Nefertiti in the flesh. The bouncer, seemingly disenchanted with the women and the atmosphere, says nothing. He simply leads me to the bar and leaves after having whispered something to the bartender.

"One vodka, neat," I order, glancing at my phone. I sit in an empty spot. By the time the bearded bartender gives me the drink, I've already scrolled through my contact list in search of someone to come get me. Twice.

"Wonderful." I pick up my vodka and slam it back, allowing the spirits to burn my throat and stomach for a few moments before pressing 'dial' on my choice of chauffeur.

"Hello?"

"Hi, Rynhardt. It's Esmé Snyder," I say. "Are you working?"

"No, but I'm on call tonight. What's the matter?"

"I need a favor."

The neon red light declares that there are GIRLS! GIRLS! GIRLS! inside the rectangular brick building. In truth, there are girls on the street, too.

The almost-vacant parking lot, where trash litters the asphalt and faded white lines indicated parking spots, looks desolate and unwelcoming even with the brightly dressed girls and women strutting about. There are men there, too—mostly homosexuals, from the look of things, but they aren't as prominently dressed or flamboyant in the way they try to flag down clients. Cars drive by, some speeding up to get out of the red light district as fast as possible, others slowing down momentarily to check the merchandise walking on precariously high heels.

I'm not afraid to be out here by myself, but I'm not exactly happy, either.

I pace the short walkway in front of the strip club, where a bouncer named Gillis keeps a watchful eye on me. After what feels like a lifetime—which turns out to be no more than ten minutes—a black double cab Ford Ranger turns into the parking lot. The car drives up to me and the window inches down, revealing Detective Rynhardt Louw's face.

"Thank God," I say.

"Get in." He eyes the surroundings.

I half-heartedly wave to the bouncer as I make my way around to the passenger door. Gillis, in turn, nods my way in greeting.

When I'm in, Rynhardt looks me over. "Do I want to know?" he asks.

"I came with Howlen." I hide my trembling hands in the folds of my dress. Trembling not because I'm afraid, but because I'm livid. "My informant scared him senseless, and he upped and left with a prostitute, leaving me stranded here. I couldn't call Mosepi, because he'd tell my dad. I couldn't call my grandfather, because then I wouldn't hear the end of it. My real friends, unfortunately, can't be seen with me in public, otherwise they'll get killed. And my acquaintances wouldn't understand. I could have probably called a cab, but—"

"No," Rynhardt interrupts. "You were right to call."

"I'm sorry." I sigh, embarrassed. "This is *not* how I thought tonight would go. On the upside, at least I know if things don't work out for me as an occultist, I'd be able to become a hooker. I got some creative cat-calls and colorful language while I waited. That must mean something."

"I know you're trying to be funny, but don't," Rynhardt says, picking up his GPS. "Address?"

I give him my home address, which he quickly types into the machine.

"What type of partner—no. What type of *man* leaves a woman by herself in this part of town?" It's not just talk. I can tell by the way his hands clutch the steering wheel, knuckles whitening, veins throbbing, how angry he is. "Even Detective Mosepi, who despises me, wouldn't allow me to come here without backup."

"The bouncer was keeping an eye out, and I'm perfectly capable of taking care of myself," I say.

"Well, it's still not right."

"Relax. You're not the one who was blown off because something shinier walked past in a skimpy dress."

I should've known something like this would happen. It *always* happens. How many losers were there before Howlen? Quite a few, to be honest. The difference is, usually I figure out the guy is a douche before I slowly open my heart to them.

"Are you okay, though?" Rynhardt breaks the awkward silence threatening to settle around us.

"As okay as can be, considering the circumstances," I say, forcing a smile. "Thanks again for coming to pick me up."

"You're welcome." He smiles back. "I didn't know occultists even had informants, especially ones who hang out around The Rabbi's franchises."

I shrug. "Did you think my leads came out of thin air?"

"Maybe. For all I know, you commune with ghosts."

"Ghosts? No. I've never actually seen a ghost. But I suspect there's a demon in my house."

"I was kidding."

"I know, but I wasn't."

Rynhardt frowns as he looks at me, studying my face for dishonesty. When he finds whatever he's been searching for, he turns back to the road. "All right, then."

More silence.

"See? This always happens."

"What?"

"This." I gesture between us. "I repel good guys."

"I don't think so—"

"I'm good guy bane," I insist. "As soon as good guys figure out how real my job is, they bolt. Not that I blame them or anything, but my ego can't withstand the rejections for much longer." I brush my hair behind my ear, and cross my arms. "If I didn't have any dignity left, I'd wallow in self-pity."

"I'm not repelled by you or your job, Esmé," Rynhardt says, turning onto the always busy N1 highway. "If anything, I'm more—"

His words are cut short when the car suddenly jerks, shaking us in our seats. The vehicle veers into another lane without warning. My nails dig into my palms as I watch the nose of the Ford Ranger miss the taillights of the next car by a hairsbreadth. The radio switches on by itself and runs through AM stations. The static noise is the least of our problems, though.

"Put your seatbelt on," Rynhardt orders me as he battles with the steering wheel.

"It is on. Slow down!" I watch us miss another car by centimeters.

Instead of slowing down, though, the car speeds up. We hear honking behind and beside us, threatening shouts somehow making it through the din.

"Rynhardt!" My hands move to the armrests to brace myself against impact.

"I'm trying," he screams, pumping the brake, battling the wheel, and switching on the four-way flashers all at once.

Blurs of colors streak past as the engine moans from being pushed to its limits. The speedometer's reading increases with each passing second.

I reach to the radio with a shaky hand, trying to switch the damn thing off. It's useless. Every time I come close to the stand-by button, the car swerves, bumps, or jolts my hand away.

I glance up in time to scream out "*Truck*" when the sixteen-wheeler appears directly in front of us.

The registration number of the truck grows larger and larger as we approach. Rynhardt's eyes widen like those of a poor animal caught in headlights. His one arm reaches out in front of me, a further brace for when we collide. His other hand remains on the wheel, shockingly white from clutching it.

Seconds become endless hours.

I use those hours to watch my pathetic life play itself out before my eyes. When that's done, I get to wonder what I would miss out on if my life is cut short. No husband. No kids. No growing old enough to reminisce about how different the world used to be way back when. There'll be nothing for me except a lifetime of regrets.

Even though I think of all of that, there's still time left for me to picture the wreck itself. Enough time to let me imagine the cacophony of sounds hitting us like a tidal wave, hearing the engine being ripped apart like tinfoil while metal fuses with metal on impact. I can envision the way the doors get torn apart, the windows shattering into a billion little pieces. I can already smell burning rubber and feel how we're thrown around, even though we're both strapped into our seats. What happens next? A resounding quiet? Pain?

Before any of those thoughts can become reality, the Ford Ranger jerks into another lane, away from certain death, as if the car has a mind of its own.

"Jesus," I gasp. My heart is propelling so much blood through my head, I became dizzy. Sweat trickles down my forehead, burning my eyes, blurring my vision. My throat constricts after a sob manages to escape.

Rynhardt slows the Ford Ranger and coaxes it to the side of the highway.

I have the safety belt off and the door open before the car comes to a complete halt, then I'm out. Gasping, filling my lungs with warm oxygen and exhaust fumes, I wander around aimlessly on shaky legs. My hand is pressed against my diaphragm while I'm trying to get my heart rate under control.

That aside, the world seems brighter and the air tastes sweeter.

Rynhardt walks around the front of the car, heading to where I'm still regaining my wits. His strides are long, fast, and resolute, bringing him closer before I can comprehend his intentions. He takes my face in his hands and crushes his mouth against mine. Hungry, desperate, grateful—those elements turn my skin ultra sensitive. Sparks ignite as his tongue massages mine, drowning me with vibrant sensations. Malleable lips envelope mine, the kiss growing deeper and ravenous. I fall into his embrace without considering the consequences and grab hold of his white button-down shirt with both hands to stabilize myself.

Whether it's Howlen's rejection, the alcohol in my system, or the near-death experience that are responsible for my lack of inhibitions, I don't know. What I do know is that I've never felt more alive, and there's no way I'm about to squander the opportunity to live.

Rynhardt moves his hands to my hips and takes a tentative step forward.

I've danced to this song before, but it somehow feels new, so I take a step back. My fingertips trail down his stubbly cheek and over the side of his chin. I direct one hand past his Adam's apple, over his neck, and across his collarbone.

A hoarse sound escapes his lips. He tugs me closer, closer still, until only our clothes separate us.

I shrug off my crochet wrap right there in the field beside the highway, taking another step backward.

Rynhardt guides us toward the Ranger, his one hand venturing to loosen the buttons of my dress.

Our urgency grows, along with our electricity and passion.

We somehow manage to get into the cramped back seat of the car without injuring ourselves.

I unbuckle his belt and undo the button of his pants as his hands roam over my body, exploring my form through the thin material of the sundress. Every time our skin meets, his touch sends fireworks through me. My cotton thong is hastily removed, discarded over his shoulder, and flies out the open door.

Rynhardt tugs my hips into position, his mouth never leaving mine. The dress shifts high over my thighs and he settles between my legs.

He slides himself inside me, and my world bursts with starlight and pleasure.

I grab hold of the armrest above my head, arch my back, and exhale loudly. *This* is living. Where a single touch can set your world on fire … *This* is what being alive is meant to feel like.

I moan against Rynhardt's mouth, relishing in how our bodies melt together.

When we've established a steady rhythm, his hands explore and caress in ways that drive me insane. His mouth moves away, kisses trailing along my jaw line and down my neck, and I take the time to draw in quick, deep breaths.

Rynhardt reaches the nape of my neck and finds a sweet spot … and … and—

"Don't stop." My whisper is a few decibels higher than normal.

I grip the armrest tighter as my body respond to his. Throaty moans, high and low, intermingle with loud gasps and short exhalations. My ecstasy is potent; infectious enough to send Rynhardt over the edge, too. A guttural sound is muffled in my neck as he rides his own orgasm while I come down from my high.

Our laborious breathing is the only communication between us.

After it passes, Rynhardt pushes onto his elbows and fumbles to button up my dress.

I watch him, smirking.

When he's done, he sits upright to make himself more presentable.

I swing my leg over his head and sit up beside him.

"I don't know what came over me," he says.

"Ditto." I straighten my dress, trying to ignore the slick stickiness between my thighs. I make a mental note to pick up a morning-after pill the next day on my way to work, but he doesn't need to know that. He seems like he has enough self-guilt and regret to deal with already, so what's the use of bothering him with that little piece of information? "I should"—I gesture to the open door—"get dressed."

"Of course, sorry," Rynhardt says, slipping out of the back seat to help me onto the grass.

Once my feet are on the ground, he walks to where my wrap lies, searching around. "I hope you weren't attached to your underwear."

"Don't worry, these days I have to buy in bulk, anyway," I say, accepting my wrap from him. Rynhardt frowns. "Remember the demon I told you about?"

"Yeah."

"It's a kleptomaniac with a thing for lace underwear," I explain.

He opens the passenger door. "I can never tell if you're lying or not."

"I have a tell when I'm lying," I say, reluctantly climbing back into the Ford Ranger.

"What's your tell?"

"My lips tighten when I speak."

"Noted." He forces a smile, closes the door, and makes his way around to the driver's side.

I buckle the seat belt again and throw a silent prayer to whatever god or goddess might be listening at this time of night.

Rynhardt climbs in, takes a moment to lock his seat belt into place, and inhales deeply. He glances out the window to the starry heavens. Then he turns the key in the ignition and the engine roars to life. The Ford Ranger slowly pulls away, driving back onto the always busy N1 highway.

The tension and awkwardness mutes us the entire way to my solemn, silent house.

He parks in front of the garage.

The headlights brighten the metal garage door I've been threatening with a new coat of paint for the past year, but haven't gotten around to doing. Fully intending to voice a platitude for the lift home, I turn in my seat to find him already looking back.

"Thank you for—" I cut myself off, feeling foolish on one hand and reckless on the other. "Screw it." I throw myself across the partition separating us, and onto the mercy of his lips.

My alarm clock reads 3:06 a.m.

I sit cross-legged in a pool of sheets on my bedroom floor, my back resting against the edge of the bed. I'm working by the dim light streaming in from the corridor. Distorted photographs of Yena, supposedly, are arranged in front of me according to the date they were taken by the unknown photographer. In my hands is an A5 notebook with hundreds of names and addresses scrawled inside. Hastily written notes accompany some of the names, while others are completely crossed out or only have question marks beside them. I see Valentine Sikelo and Carol-Anne Brewis among the rest, as well as Abraham Amin, but nothing is noted with their names. It's disturbing.

The bed shifts behind me, before warm hands settle on my bare shoulders and hot breath blows against my neck.

"Why don't you put on a light?" Rynhardt asks in a whisper, as if the night might shatter.

"Because then you wouldn't be able to get your beauty sleep," I whisper back. I turn to catch a glimpse of his ruffled hair.

His hands disappear momentarily before he throws one bare leg over my head and I wiggle forward so he can shift into the space between me and the bed. His arms wrap around my waist and his legs cocoon me in his body heat while he studies the information over my shoulder.

"What's this?" He picks up one of the distorted photographs.

"Yena," I say, paging through the strange notebook. "Every image is the same. Everything around Yena is in focus, but he's not. It's odd."

"Where'd you get them?" Rynhardt reaches for another photograph.

"I can't disclose the names of my informants." I hold up the notebook. "Does this handwriting look similar to the note we found at Abraham Amin's crime scene?"

Rynhardt's other hand also disappears from around my waist as he takes the notebook for closer inspection. I sit forward to empty the rest of the manila envelope's contents on the floor, waiting for his opinion.

"I can't be sure, but the *e* does slope the same way," he says, paging through the notebook.

I fish out a few stapled pages from the envelope, but before I can start reading through them, Rynhardt says, "There's an inconsistency here."

"Hmmm?" I turn slightly, brushing the tip of my nose across his shoulder.

Rynhardt holds the notebook so some of the light catches the page, and points to the "RR" with a simple note in the margin: *eliminate if compromised.*

"RR could be anyone," I say.

"True, but it sounds more like someone Yena might know."

"You've got a keen eye, Detective."

"You would have picked it up eventually," he says.

"That's highly unlikely, but thanks for the vote of confidence." I lean back against his chest, studying the pages in my hand but unsure of what the letters mean.

Rynhardt wraps his arms around my waist again, reading over my shoulder, while I decipher the needling feeling that he is on to something with that RR thing. Slowly the puzzle pieces itself together in my head. The strange things happening to me, the murders, the RR—they're all related.

We seem to have an epiphany at the same time, because he grabs the pages from my hand as I move to get my cell phone.

"Put on the lamp," he says.

I switch on the lamp as I get to the nightstand. I find my cell phone and scroll through the contact list until I land on Detective Mosepi's number.

"Damn it," Rynhardt says. "Where's my phone?"

I dial Mosepi's number and press the phone to my ear. Two rings later, a yawn greets me.

"Ja?" he says.

"Get guards assigned to Rochester Ramphele," I say.

"Esmé?"

"Is that Mosepi?" Rynhardt asks.

I nod.

"Tell him, I know where Yena will strike next."

"Is that Rynhardt in the background?" Mosepi says. I curse myself silently. "What's going on?"

"Catch," I say to Rynhardt, who's searching for his clothes on the floor.

He looks up, and I toss the phone over the bed. Rynhardt catches it in one hand, expertly moves it to his ear, and listens.

"Get him to put extra guards on Ramphele."

Rynhardt gives me a thumbs up as I walk out of the bedroom, ready to wash away the night's sins.

"This better be good." My grandfather exits his car, dressed in striped pajamas, slippers, and a paisley robe. Apart from the dawn-pink sky, which is tinted with an almost sickly green hue, night still reigns over the world. This far from the city lights, the darkness is absolute. He searches around the wooded area before making eye contact with me. "Where's Howlen?"

"Off screwing Cinnamon," I answer, shrugging.

My grandfather frowns. "That sounds both unpleasant and unsanitary. What happened to good old hand cream?"

"Gramps, Cinnamon is a prostitute's alias." I shift the lifejacket and helmet into my other hand.

"Oh," he drawls. "Now it makes more sense."

I roll my eyes, ready to change the subject. "I can handle the crime scene myself, but you're going to have to work with the witnesses today."

"There are witnesses at this time of the morning? It's pre-dawn, for God's sake." He makes a show of yawning, and looks around again as uniformed police officers tape off boundaries around the river's beach. Early risers who might've heard or seen the commotion stare on from their campsites. The onlookers' interest would diminish if they knew how horrendous the Hartbeespoort police officers made the actual crime scene sound. "Where's Detective Mosepi?" he asks.

"He's down in the river bend, helping the other detectives set up a makeshift bridge while we wait for forensics to come," I explain. "Pops, you need to go to the clubhouse downstream. The witnesses are waiting for you there."

"I'm going, I'm going," he mutters. "And if you see Howlen,

perchance, tell him that if I wanted to get called out in the middle of the night, I wouldn't have hired him."

He doesn't wait for a response. Unlike me, my grandfather enjoys his eight hours of sleep every night, and he's not a morning person if he doesn't get them.

As he leaves, I turn back to the Crocodile River where the commandeered canoes, lifejackets, and helmets are located. I've already picked out my equipment and a one-man canoe, but from looking at the beach, the police expected a small army today. Good thing I arrived early to avoid the rush. I put on my gear and walk up the shore, where an officer waits with the yellow canoe. Together, the two of us quickly get the boat into the water. I climb inside the raft, get my paddle into position, and push away from the shore. Yelling a quick thanks over my shoulder, I paddle in a wide arch to rectify my course downstream.

It takes a few strokes to establish a rhythm, but I'm soon heading toward the first manmade rapid where slick concrete is visible underneath the fast-moving water. As the canoe approaches the first rapid, I brace myself and pull the paddle out of the water. The river slowly pushes the canoe over the edge before gravity takes me down. Spray crashes against my face as I plunge into the filthy water, and I purse my lips in disgust. The paddle makes its way back into the water; right, left, right, left.

There's something soothing about white river rafting. It gives me time to think about where I've been and where I'm going. Even if the thoughts are predominantly set within the last few hours.

After Rynhardt called Detective Mosepi, sharing his hunch on where the killer might hit next, a whirlwind of synchronized policing had occurred.

Detective Mosepi called the Hartbeespoort Dam Police Department and they'd sent out a patrol. When they'd arrived at the downstream clubhouse, they'd found several witnesses who'd been out on an overnight white river rafting adventure, about to call the emergency services themselves. Before Hartbeespoort police called Detective Mosepi back, though, he'd already set up an interrogation with Rochester Ramphele for me at eight o'clock in the Pretoria Central police station. Extra guards were stationed for Ramphele's protection, too. An hour later, an onslaught of authorities had gathered at the camping grounds' beach, getting ready to evaluate Yena's newest horror show.

So many different facets need to be assessed, but at least I'm getting somewhere. At least I'm not stuck in the office, waiting for the crime labs to get back with the results we so desperately need.

I grip the paddle hard enough for my knuckles to turn white.

The canoe hits a few mini rough patches on the way to the second manmade rapid, tugging and pulling the raft, bumping over the raised rocks. I lift the paddle from the greenish-brown river, and the current pushes the canoe forward.

Irrigation has tamed whatever force this narrow river once held, but the rush of water still prickles my adrenal glands. My stomach lurches at what appears to be a ninety degree drop. I brace myself and squeeze my eyes shut. It feels as if my organs need to play catch up with gravity as the raft falls forward, spraying water everywhere. I open my eyes to see the oncoming bumps ahead and the sharp curve that lies beyond. My paddle is submerged again.

I lean left and paddle hard to avoid the looming carved-out hill where jagged rocks lurk under the shallow water. The Crocodile River bends and I follow the curve with ease. Another set of small rapids awaits me, but even amateur rafters can maneuver them without breaking a sweat. Beyond that, though, is a long stretch of tranquility surrounded by nothing but nature—or so it leads one to believe.

Squaring my shoulders, I paddle past the high embankments where tree roots hover over the polluted water. I try to look past the plastic bottles, beer cans, pieces of cardboard, and other remnants of human waste caught in the roots, but it's impossible. Once upon a time, before man corrupted the world, this must've been an idyllic spot. Now, though, the Crocodile River is another casualty in mankind's war against nature.

At the next bend, where the river's flow has deposited enough sediment to create a slim piece of a beach, policemen are squeezed together. The actual scene, however, is obscured from my view by the natural curvature and wild flora inhabiting this stretch.

An officer gestures for me to round the bend before the sickly sweet smell of death hits with such force, it brings tears to my eyes. The rancid odor, however, is nothing compared to the larger-than-life crime scene ahead.

At the highest point of the overlooking cliff is the skeleton of an incomplete mansion. Nearby stands a smaller neglected house and its matching shed. I can hear traffic from the nearby highway intermingling with the bounty of insects drawn to the Crocodile River.

It's private, for the most part.

Quiet.

Perfect for a midnight murder.

The trees grow at awkward angles from the steep slopes of bordering cliffs, their gnarled branches stretching far across the water. Limbs and organs dangle from the drooping branches like overripe fruit. Blowflies buzz around decomposing flesh and muscle. Carrion birds circle overhead. Forensic analysts climb the trees to retrieve body parts. I didn't think they would get here so soon—someone high up must've pulled them out of bed for this. Then there are the police on the jagged cliffs, who struggle to keep the media hounds from getting a closer look at what we're dealing with.

From my position on the river, I can see approximately twenty meters of chaos, but this gruesomely ostentatious display of power is nothing more than an art project for the killer. How many people suffered in order for Yena to make this ... this shrine? How many more will suffer before he is caught?

My canoe bumps into the makeshift bridge where planks have been hastily hammered together on top of car tires and secured with nylon ropes to either side of the river. It looks sturdy enough, but the first big storm would tear it up like paper.

Detective Mosepi steps into view, a Marlboro cigarette between his lips. "Shocking, isn't it?" It's rhetorical, of course, but accurate nonetheless.

All I can do is nod. The picture of the low-hanging body parts is seared into my retinas.

"Elaborate," I agree when I find the courage to speak again. "How far does it go?"

"Exactly twenty meters," Detective Mosepi says, exhaling smoke.

"And I think Rynhardt was right. This is our guy."

"Did you find anything tying this scene to any of our previous victims?" I hold my hand out for assistance.

Detective Mosepi takes it and pulls me out of the raft and onto the makeshift bridge with ease.

As soon as I stand upright, I turn to face the scene again, undoing my helmet.

"The first cops on the scene found Carol-Anne Brewis' charm bracelet, Valentine Sikelo's necklace, and Abraham Amin's cufflinks in a Ziploc bag on the beach," he says, tossing the half-smoked cigarette into the river. "I'm thinking we might have more than one killer. One person cannot get this done in a single night."

Detective Mosepi juts his chin to the forensics team rappelling down the cliffs to get to the trees as evidence of his deduction. He scratches his nose and exhales, clearly at a loss for words. Explanations fall short for this one. "Maybe he has followers helping him?"

"No, our guy doesn't have acolytes," I say. I hold the helmet. "He's probably counting on getting some in the future, but his megalomania feels new."

"Humph." Detective Mosepi glances around the area.

My mind swims with questions. There is something here, something I'm not seeing. The trees, decorated with body parts, are scratching the surface of more sinister wrongdoings. I can sense the something, but can't comprehend the killer's motives.

"Esmé?" Rynhardt's voice cut through my thoughts.

I ignore him and survey the water on either side of the rickety tire-plywood-hybrid bridge. One side is occupied by the various canoes, their journey downstream halted by the manmade disturbance stretching across the river's width. The other side is clear, or as clear as a polluted river can be. The water is murky, tranquil but flowing. A bubble appears on the surface, its pop muted by a familiar din that always accompanies a police investigation. At first I think it's nothing more than a fish—crocodiles don't inhabit this part of the Crocodile River, as far as I know—but when another bubble rises to the surface, I'm no longer sure.

I'm on all fours before I know it, leaning over to study the bubbles.

The next bubble rises at a snail's pace, and when it reaches the surface, I very nearly miss the ink black sludge it releases when it, too, pops. The river dilutes the black substance fast enough to make it unnoticeable to anyone who's not paying attention.

I remember the veldt where Valentine Sikelo was found, and the photographs and reports Howlen had handed over after they inspected Carol-Anne Brewis' dumping site—both decimated by an inexplicable *something*.

Something is happening here, now.

Another bubble rises and pops. A dead fish floats to the surface, its white belly swollen and decomposing quickly.

I stand, look at the twenty or so faces working hard on cracking the case, and realize that this display of carnage is nothing more than a trap.

"You need to get everyone out of here," I order Detective Mosepi.

Rynhardt gives me a puzzled look.

"For fuck's sake," Detective Mosepi mutters, but doesn't ask questions. He walks to the other end of the bridge and yells for an evacuation.

A flurry of activity occurs straight away. The forensic analysts are pulled up onto the edge of the cliff. Uniforms rush around, trying to clear out the collected evidence without disturbing anything else. Detective Mosepi shouts to the beach, telling them in three languages to vacate the area, while Detective Louw passes me to grab hold of the unwinding rope ladder. "Ladies first," he says.

I'm about to respond when I glance down to see more dead fish drifting to the surface of the water. A circling carrion bird falls from the sky, dead. I glance at the trees to see the body parts already withering away, emaciated by an unseen force sucking the very life out of everything in the region.

"Go. Go *now!*" I shout. "Come on, Mosepi." I grab his sleeve and tug hard. "We need to leave."

"I'm coming," he barks over his shoulder.

I point to the trees, showing him the way the body parts shrivel up, which he obviously missed.

"What the hell is that?"

"Death," I say. "Now, move it."

CHAPTER 28

They're like ants before a thunderstorm, scurrying for higher ground.

He might have found it comical under different circumstances, but Esmé Snyder's presence ruined his meticulously planned ritual. At least fifteen people, all involved with the SAPS in some way or another, were supposed to be sacrificed today. More had shown up than he'd thought, but that would've been a good thing.

It was supposed to be a denouement for the history books.

This ceremonial hecatomb would have gained him reverence. His ancestors would have rejoiced at his devotion. They would have welcomed him to their ranks with open arms and loving hearts.

And the people would have feared his majesty.

His power would have made him a god amongst men.

While watching the shrine's epicenter suck the life from everything caught in its clutches, he wonders how she'd recovered from his last attack so fast. Soon, the death will spread further, decimating the soil itself, but it won't get him what he wants.

"Sir, please step back," an androgynous police officer commands.

He takes a step away and watches as Esmé and the detectives are escorted through the gathered crowd. The fat one he knows—Detective Mosepi. The other one, however, is a new face. His attention is quickly drawn back to her, though.

Esmé's so close, he can smell her perfume, taste her anger, and feel her heat.

She stops abruptly, a couple of feet away, and turns to look at him.

When their eyes meet, his heart beats faster, but he can't look away.

He can't force himself to hide even if his every nerve shouts for him to run. He steels himself for the confrontation as she takes a step toward him. His lungs protest from holding his breath, while he hopes to disappear into the crowd.

After an agonizing moment, Esmé shakes her head and forces a faint apologetic smile before continuing toward the idling car.

He exhales in relief. He knows this could have easily been the end of his game. Luckily, the ancestors still favor him.

After a few more minutes of watching the failed ritual site, he makes his way back to his van.

"How had it gone so terribly wrong?" he asks himself, getting in.

His mind reels through every step he'd taken to procure the organs and limbs on the black market. They were of high quality; he'd made sure of it. Weeks of prayer had ensured him this would be the perfect site for what he had in mind. The planning had taken months. The fiasco had cost a fortune.

His ancestral magic still runs strong, which means the ritual itself hadn't been cursed from the get-go. So, why?

"Esmé shouldn't have been there." He answers his own question and kisses his teeth. Her intervention had disrupted what fate already promised him.

He directs the van onto the highway and slams his hands against the steering wheel, enraged. "She shouldn't have been there!"

He quiets his anger through sheer will and takes a few calming breaths.

There's a way to rectify this.

It would take time, but he can remedy the situation.

"It's gonna be fine," he promises his reflection. "She doesn't have the upper hand, yet. Everything will be perfectly fine."

But first he needs to get rid of a rat before the game tips in Esmé's favor.

EXCLUSIVE: AMATEUR FOOTAGE OF PRETORIA SLASHER'S RITUAL SITE (NSFW)
2015-09-29 | 07:2212 Comments

Hartbeespoort, the usually-serene resort town on the slopes of the Magaliesberg Mountains, was disrupted this morning when Pretoria and Hartbeespoort police forces joined together to investigate a heinous ritual site found at the Crocodile River.

According to inside sources, the ritual site is possibly the work of the Pretoria Slasher.

"Hundreds of body parts and organs were found hanging from the trees over the river," a News24/7 source, who wishes to remain anonymous, said to interviewers. "It was quite a shock to see, but it's painfully obvious that the Pretoria Slasher is taunting police by making this statement."

Whether these body parts and organs come from the killer's victims or were bought on the black market is unknown.

The Pretoria Slasher has presumably murdered at least three people since the start of September. Known victims include: Valentine Sikelo (27), Carol-Anne Brewis (12), and Abraham Amin (39).

Police have yet to release official information about the killer, the victims, and the sites.

Amateur footage of the ritual site was sent in by numerous Hartbeespoort residents this morning before police arrived at the scene of the crime.

Please note that the following footage is not suitable for work. Viewer discretion is advised:

PLAY VIDEO

– News24/7

COMMENTS:
PuddinPie – *September 29, 2015 at 07:25*
(O_O) That's … Wow. I'm speechless.
HelenaC – *September 29, 2015 at 07:25*
How the hell is this monster still walking around a free man? Look at the carnage!
   DanTheMan – *September 29, 2015 at 07:42*
   @HelenaC – Agreed. The police seem too busy picking their noses than wanting to catch killers.
      HelenaC – *September 29, 2015 at 07:45*
      @DanTheMan – I wouldn't go that far in putting them down. I'm sure the police are doing everything in their power to catch the Pretoria Slasher, but they'll need to do more, a lot faster. It looks like the guy's already branching out to the Northern Province.
         DanTheMan – *September 29, 2015 at 07:59*
         @HelenaC – You have more faith in our judicial system than I do.
NaeNae92 – *September 29, 2015 at 07:32*
WTF did I just watch? Is this a belated April Fools prank?
SkyrimKyle – *September 29, 2015 at 07:33*
FAKE! This footage is so fake, it's not even funny!
   ParaNorman – *September 29, 2015 at 07:37*
   @SkyrimKyle – I don't think so. Decomposing flesh is difficult to fake.
      SkyrimKyle – *September 29, 2015 at 07:42*
      @ParaNorman – I bet you're one of those conspiracy theorist dudes. Hahahaha! Do you see little green men in the sky, too? Or, wait. Does Bigfoot actually exist?
         ParaNorman – *September 29, 2015 at 07: 43*

@SkyrimKyle – Your response was unnecessary. I'm giving my opinion on the matter, as everyone else is doing. And yes, I am a conspiracy theorist, although we like to call ourselves something less derogatory. Asshole.

ThatStationaryGuy – September 29, 2015 at 07: 33

Whether it's real or not, this is f@#*ing disturbing.

Twerkarina – September 29, 2015 at 07:52

Are you kidding me @News24/7.

Valentine Sikelo was reported, by you, to be 28 years old, in a previous article! Are you too lazy to check the facts by using your OWN published articles?

Ugh. The journalism in this country is going to be the end of me.

They're so close to a break in the case. I can almost taste it.

Not being able to enter the quarantined area made it harder to find clues, obviously, but there are quite a few things my grandfather and I could study from afar. For example, the perimeter itself is remarkable. One side teems with life—green grass and insect activity is found in abundance, fish are alive and swimming, birds are chirping—whereas the other side is a complete void. Neither of us is able to come up with a reasonable explanation of how life had been siphoned out of the "Dead-Zone," but it's undeniably the most interesting evidence of esotericism we've ever encountered.

I pick up the borrowed binoculars from Detective Mosepi's equipment bag and stare at the trees. From afar, they look as if they've been decorated with cadaverous Christmas ornaments. Dead fish and birds dot the water's surface, floating yet lifeless. It's an eerie sight.

"If anybody believes this is the result of a chemical spill, there's no hope for the human race." I lower the binoculars and look to where my grandfather is hunched over in his striped pajamas, taking samples of the earth.

"It's not impossible. Isn't there a nuclear research center nearby?" my grandfather asks.

"Pelindaba? Yeah, I guess. It just feels like such a stretch."

His shoulder twitches into a shrug as he stands. "The tales they weave is none of our concern. We have a killer to catch. But I'm starting to think we might not be suitable for the task."

"Oh?" I ask. "Who else is there, if not us?"

"I don't know, but let's be honest; we're out of our depth," he says.

Thinking about it is one thing, hearing it said out loud by my grandfather, of all people, is different. I'm afraid he might be right, but we can't make assumptions if we haven't assessed all the facts. Besides, I still have to make my way over to the Pretoria Central police station to interrogate Rochester Ramphele. Who knows what titillating information I can scare out of him?

"This aberration is beyond our expertise," my grandfather says. "I feel we simply need a while to ponder the facts without interruption, in order to find a viable solution."

"We don't have time to ponder this stuff. Yena is out there, killing for sport, and people are anxious."

"Anxious ... yes." He sighs.

"Are you ready?" Detective Mosepi's voice comes from behind us. We turn around to face the burly detective as he checks his wristwatch. "If we don't leave now, we won't make it in time for Ramphele's interrogation."

"I'll be right there," I say.

He grumbles something unintelligible, pivots, and walks away.

"That one will never change," my grandfather says as he picks up his equipment bag.

I drop the binoculars in the open bag for him when he holds it out to me.

"I'll see you back at the office," he says. "Hopefully, I can consult with Howlen and Father Gabriel about what's going on here when I get there. That's if Howlen's decided to come into the office in the first place. What's the date?"

"It's the twenty-ninth of September."

"Hmmm. It's a bit early in the year for his self-destruction streak to shine through. Something must've happened to tick him off."

I don't respond as we walk back to the clubhouse.

"Keep close to Mosepi, okay?" he says. "I don't think it's safe for you to be alone."

"I'm as safe as I always am, Pops."

"If only," he mutters, stopping before we can make it to the parking lot. "Look, pack an overnight bag and come sleep in your old room for a while. I'll make you breakfast in bed every morning. Those strawberry crumpets you like so much?" His dazzling smile catches me off guard. "I'll even serve them with ice cream."

"I love you, but—"

"Fine." He cuts my placating excuse short. "But could you at least come to dinner tonight? SIRCIS needs to brainstorm the hell out of this case. We should have done it sooner, actually. Oh well." He directs his attention past me. "You better leave before Mosepi has a stroke."

"Drive safely."

I run to catch up with Detective Mosepi and slip into the passenger seat as he gets into the driver's seat.

He lights a new cigarette, the smoke clouding up the inside of his car.

"You need to quit your smoking, Detective," I say.

"And you need to *not* sleep with my partner, Miss Snyder," he retorts.

My eyes widen at his bluntness, but I don't dare face him.

"Judging from your expression in the side-mirror, my assumptions were accurate. Shame on you, Esmé."

"Don't start with that bullshit," I snap back, not bothering to hide my face anymore.

He backs his vehicle out of the parking spot and makes a U-turn on the dirt road.

"It's not like I sleep with every guy I meet, you know."

"You should be focused on the case, not on men," he grumbles.

"Well, if Rynhardt and I weren't focused on each other last night, neither of us would have figured out what Yena was planning on next." I blow a stray red curl out of my face and cross my arms. "So you can be pissy about this or you can be grateful we've made headway."

"Of course I'm grateful for that. I'm pissy because you can't stop bitching about my smoking," he says, ending with a throaty growl. "If you knew how much shit's been blown down my neck since Yena killed the kid, you'd be smoking too."

"You're only hurting yourself with your excuses," I say, closing my eyes. "Besides, you're not the only one who's had to deal with backlash."

"What are you doing?"

"I need to close my eyes for a while." Yawning, I shift around to be more comfortable in the passenger seat. "Wake me when we get there, please? I'm running on fumes."

Whatever Detective Mosepi says afterwards goes right over my head. Not only because he's bitching in his native tongue, but because my exhaustion sweeps me away into a well-deserved, dreamless nap.

A short while later, Detective Mosepi gently prods me awake.

We're in his car, parked in the underground lot of the Pretoria Central police station.

Still groggy, but feeling like my energy levels are much improved, I glance in the mirror. I fix my hair as much as possible, shake away the sleep that remains, and follow him out of the car and into the police station. Once inside, and once our credentials are verified, we're led to the place where Rochester Ramphele awaits our arrival.

The interrogation room is nothing as fancy as what you'd see on television. Here, you're in a square little room, sitting on an old metal chair in front of an older metal table. There isn't a one-way mirror for anyone to watch through—just stained walls and scratched metal furniture, with the culprit handcuffed to the table.

At our request, a video camera has been set up in the corner, but that isn't the norm in most interrogations.

Rochester Ramphele has seen better days, but his bruises are already fading and his skin is knitting over cuts.

When he sees me, he goes into a frenzy. He tugs at his tight handcuffs, trying to free himself, spitting curses that would make demons blush.

I don't have to quiet him down, though. Detective Mosepi quickly puts him in his place and Ramphele shuts up.

I make sure the video camera is in focus, aiming it at Rochester Ramphele. His eyes are vague and distant on-screen. I press the recording button and pull my chair over to sit beside him instead of across from him.

"Rochester," I start.

Too fast for me to react, Ramphele's hands shoot out and take mine.

I flinch. The expression in his eyes changes from anger to fear.

"You have to help me. He's coming," Rochester says, urgency in that fake American accent of his, the look in his eyes changing to acute desperation.

"I know, but we need to talk some things over before I can help you. I need to know what you know about—"

"No," he says. "You have to help me *now*. Before he hears, before he knows where I am. He'll find a way to … to put an end to me."

I throw a look at Detective Mosepi. There's unease in the detective's face, and it's infectious.

I nod slowly. "I understand," I say. "We have already implemented extra security measures to keep you safe, but you have to work with us in return. Do you understand?"

Rochester nods, squeezing my hand until it becomes uncomfortable, looking straight into my eyes. "Okay, all right. Ask what you came to ask." He releases my hand, and I'm able to pull Yena's journal and the distorted photographs I received from The Rabbi from my purse.

I place the photographs on the table, keeping the journal in my lap. "That's Yena," Rochester says, pointing to the distorted face on the nearest picture.

"I figured as much," I say. "We need a better description of Yena, though. Will you be able to work with a sketch artist for us?"

He shakes his head. "It won't matter if you got Picasso to do an identikit of Yena. He is utterly mediocre where his appearance is concerned. Figuratively speaking, Yena is able to slip into a crowd and become invisible."

I bite the inside of my bottom lip. The Rabbi had said something similar about Yena's appearance.

"What business did you and Yena have?" Detective Mosepi asks.

"He wanted organs and limbs for muti, obviously. Not the stuff I normally deal in, but I have connections in Nigeria, Kenya, and a few other African countries. South Africa is sometimes difficult when it comes to human muti, especially since most hospitals have those things incinerated faster than the doctor can call a time of death," he explains.

"Killing is not my game. I simply buy and sell for profit."

"How'd you two meet?" I ask.

"He came to me. I don't know where he got my name. There was something about Yena … I knew from the start I shouldn't cross him or deny his requests. The fucker cost me money at the end of the day." Rochester looks at the journal in my hands. "How'd you get your hands on that thing? He never went anywhere without it."

I clutch the notebook tighter, thinking it might be best not to make Rochester panic again. "This is my notebook, not his. Does he have one?"

"Looks identical, actually." He reclines in his seat as far as he could go, given his restraints. "I saw it in the glove box of his van."

"His van?" Detective Mosepi and I say in unison.

"Yeah. It's a regular black van. Registration num—" He sucks air through his teeth, creating a hissing sound. He sits upright and studies a cut on his thumb. A drop of blood swells the length of the superficial wound. He bends forward enough to stick his thumb into his mouth and suck at it.

"You were saying?"

He takes his thumb out of his mouth and starts again, "Registration num—"

Before he can say more, he jumps up from his seat as though a jolt of electricity has surged through him. The chair clatters to the floor, metal clangs against linoleum.

Detective Mosepi tries to talk him back into his seat, but without luck. Things are going south quickly.

More crimson blooms on the back of Rochester's hand, but something else seizes his attention—something neither Detective Mosepi nor I can see.

"Help me!" The desperation in his voice is enough to tell us things are terribly awry.

I stand and step away, searching for whatever is setting Rochester into a flat spin.

"*Help me!*" Rochester shouts. Another slice spontaneously appears on his skin, this time across his cheek. His hand flies to the new wound, but can't staunch the cut.

"Call for an ambulance," I urge Detective Mosepi.

The detective moves to the door and disappears into the corridor, leaving me to deal with this by myself.

Rochester flinches forward as though he's been struck by a whip across his back.

"Talk to me, Rochester. What's happening?" I search the interrogation room for anything remotely muti-related: a pouch of something, a sprinkle or dash of a suspicious substance, *anything* to explain the attack.

His shouts grow louder and his pleading more intense.

I crawl around on my hands and knees in search of the hex bag. When there's nothing to be found hidden under the surface of the table, or the chairs, I'm back on my feet.

By now, there are hundreds of lacerations cross Rochester's body. The locations vary, the wounds are jagged and deep. I watch in horror as blood blossoms through his orange jumpsuit, unable to help the terrified criminal.

"*Help. Me.*" Rochester hisses in pain.

Outside, the detective yells for medical assistance, but I have no hope for Rochester Ramphele to survive this ordeal.

In between the shouts, there's only the sound of metal jiggling against metal as Rochester tries to free himself. His wrists are mangled, his shoulders angling awkwardly. He flails and contorts to get away from the unseen entity. It's useless. Even if he got himself loose by some miracle, the attack would follow him. I'm positive of that.

I watch the slashes appear across his face, over his bare arms, on his ankles, maiming him. His flesh peels away wherever the cuts run too deep.

This is the possessed Ford Ranger all over again.

I want to close my eyes before the inevitable crash, but my eyelids aren't getting the message. I want to flee, but my legs won't work. There's nothing I can do except watch.

The screaming comes to an abrupt end. The quiet is far worse.

Rochester—now a bloody mess—falls to his knees.

I cringe at the sickly pops of his shoulders and deafening cracks of his arms breaking that accommodates the inhuman position he's fallen into.

Blood pools on the linoleum floor, seeping into the cracks, staining the yellowish color a blackish-red.

"Rochester?" I say, reluctantly taking a couple of steps closer.

There's no indication that he's alive anymore.

"Rochester?" I hesitate before touching his shoulder. My fingertips stretch out, slowly nearing his broken form.

"Next time." A rasping voice breaks the silence and I snatch back my hand.

Rochester's head lifts and turns, accompanied by more creaks and pops, until his glazed-over eyes are looking straight at me.

"Next time," he repeats.

The movement of his head reveals a slash running from ear to ear across his neck. Blood streams down his front.

"Next time, I'll hit you where it hurts. Find meeeee ..."

The last word is more an exhalation than speech, but I got the gist of the message.

Detective Mosepi returns with paramedics in tow.

"He's dead?" he asks.

I manage a nod before the paramedics squeeze inside to see if they could salvage some life inside Rochester Ramphele. I bend down to pick up my purse, rummage around for my cell phone.

"Are you okay?" Detective Mosepi sounds concerned.

"I'm done screwing around," I say, finding my phone and dialing the office number from memory. Heading toward the open door of the interrogation room, I say, "I've had enough."

CHAPTER 31

Ignorance breeds ignorance.

Citizens of First World nations often think South Africa is a primal, savage country. In many ways, it is. But while most of the world think us feral people, living amongst lions in our concrete jungles and fending off Ebola with sticks and stones, we're surprisingly more civilized than tourist brochures make us out to be.

If you stay in the areas allocated for tourism, industry, and suburban living, your chances of becoming a victim are slimmer than if you venture off the Yellow Brick Road.

Of course, South Africa is more than a crime statistic or an idiotic government. It's more than a statue of Nelson Mandela, Charlize Theron's Academy Award, or Mark Shuttleworth's space adventure. We are a nation of innovators driven to explore the known as well as the unknown. We strive to excel.

Competition is in our blood; survival embedded in our genes.

It should come as no surprise that I also possess a competitive streak.

As I step into the office building, I'm already dreading telling my grandfather how limited our options have become. He won't take my decision well—I know this for a fact. What other choice does SIRCIS have, though? It's either me playing the killer's game or someone else dying. If I have to become the bait, so be it.

"Ah, good," Precious says, poking her head out from the reception room. "I've received a call from the labs. The DNA results are being faxed as we speak."

"Fantastic!" I feel as though a weight has been lifted from my shoulders. "Thank God."

"I would advise against premature celebrations for the time being," she says, glancing to the stairs before she waves me closer to the desk.

I walk over. Exhaustion is a bitch, especially when you've seen someone murdered in front of you by an invisible hand.

Precious says, "Howlen looks like shit, and he's in a foul mood to boot. Any idea why?"

"Not in the least," I lie.

Precious clucks her tongue before looking me up and down. "You don't look much better. Something happen at the police station?"

"You can say that," I say. "Rochester Ramphele died under extraordinary circumstances."

"Oh? Tell me."

And so I do. I tell her all about the horrific day I've lived through and how all of it happened before lunchtime.

Precious doesn't inquire further than what I'm ready to divulge, but her eyes reveal how her mind is trying to find solutions to make my life easier. Precious would overlook my decision to play the killer's game as a viable option, like always, but eventually she'll come to realize we've crossed into that territory.

"Your grandfather is with Father Gabriel," Precious says when I finish my story. "You might want to go tell them what's happened."

"Will do, but first I need those DNA results." I stick out my hand and wiggle my fingers.

Precious looks at the fax machine before pulling the newly printed pages from the tray, and hands them over.

"Howlen," I shout over my shoulder, my voice drifting upstairs. "DNA results!"

"I'm coming!" he shouts back.

His footsteps move overhead, heavy and sluggish, as he makes his way to the staircase.

I walk to the banister, fanning myself with the papers. Howlen comes into view, a more disgruntled, disheveled, and annoyed version of the person I know.

"You look like you've had a *terrible* night," I say, smiling cruelly.

"Fuck off."

"Dearie me, one would think a girl named Cinnamon would have been able to put you in a better mood. She is, after all, a professional. Isn't she?" I pull the papers away before he can snatch them. "Considering you left me stranded in a really bad part of town, shouldn't I be the one in the bad mood?"

"I'm sorry, okay? Can we get over this, already?"

"No." I continue to smile, and flutter my eyelashes for extra effect. "Aren't you even going to ask how I got home?"

"You're here, aren't you?" he mutters. "You're alive. How bad could it have been?"

My smile falters. "If you weren't so good at your job, I'd have your ass fired so fast."

"Oh, get off your throne." He holds out his hand. "Do you want me to take a look at the results or should I wait until you're done throwing your tantrum?"

I throw the papers into the air instead of handing them over, and stroll away toward my grandfather's office. If I lingered, things could have quickly gotten out of hand. Then people would question why we were getting into a mud-slinging contest. That could lead to assumptions, and assumptions are always bad. Besides, Howlen isn't worth any of my emotions, anger included.

I knock on my grandfather's office door and wait until he permits me entrance.

"You're back earlier than I expected." My grandfather stands beside his desk, still dressed in his pajamas. Father Gabriel is hunched over something on the desk, studying it intently. "Do we have any good news?"

"Not in particular. Rochester Ramphele died before he could tell us the registration number of Yena's van," I say, walking inside. "The lab sent back the DNA results, though. So maybe we'll catch a break."

"If we don't?" he asks.

"I've decided if we don't find a lead to become the bait, I'll volunteer," I say.

At this, Father Gabriel snaps around to face me. Christiaan's jaw goes slack. Obviously they haven't even considered this line of thinking.

"Pops, what else is there to do?"

"I don't approve," he says.

"Neither do I," Father Gabriel chimes in.

"And I'm willing to take it to the next level if our current leads don't pan out. If they do, I'll withdraw my offer." I take a seat on the sofa. "I'm not—"

There's a knock on the open door before Howlen enters, still reading the results. "I've got some interesting news for you," he says. "Remember the sample we took from the customs officer you punched, Christiaan?"

"Yes," my grandfather says.

"Well, your little stunt pretty much solved a handful of our open cases," Howlen says.

"That's wonderful," he exclaims. "We should get the police out there immediately." He picks up the phone with shaky fingers.

"Is there anything about our current case in the stack of results?" I ask, studying my nails.

"Yena isn't in the system," Howlen answers. "But it seems our customs officer is a blood relation to the killer. In fact, according to these results, they're brothers."

That catches my attention. "You're sure?"

"As sure as the labs are." He shrugs and turns to Father Gabriel. "I couldn't figure out what's causing the Dead Zone phenomena. I've sent samples to some peers overseas to see if they can find a solution or an explanation, though."

"It's the work of pure evil, like I said." Father Gabriel uses an I-told-you-so tone.

"You withdraw your offer, yes?" my grandfather asks me, holding his hand over the receiver.

"For now, but we need to find Yena. Soon."

"Okay, okay, I'll make sure to get something out of Human-Tooth-Necklace-Guy." Christiaan returned to the phone call.

"You were considering offering yourself up to the killer?" Howlen says, walking closer. "Is this about last night?"

"What do you take me for?" I whisper. "Some pathetic damsel in distress? Sorry, Howl, but even if you didn't walk out on me last night at the club, we wouldn't have worked. You've got too many secrets, and I have no desire to complicate my life any further."

"How did you get home last night?"

"Does it matter?"

"If you knew why I stormed off in the first place, you might be more sympathetic."

"Doubtful. Very doubtful. But even if you did share your lot in life, what right does it give you to treat me with such callousness? Besides, I'm sure you were thinking up a buffet of excuses while you were banging Cinnamon."

"I can't talk to you when you're like this," he says.

"Oh please, if you wanted to talk about anything concerning your life, you had more than a few opportunities since Gramps employed you," I snap back.

"When you two are done whispering over there, let me know. We have to come up with a plan of action," my grandfather says. "I want these bastards in cuffs by Friday at the latest."

The plan of action is simple:

Detective Mosepi will be in control of a sting operation, along with cops from the Johannesburg Police Departments and airport authorities. Due to the unknown identity of the perpetrator, and not knowing his address, this will have to go down at OR Tambo International whether the hotshot airport guys want it or not.

Christiaan will be at the police station, ready to identify the guy out of a line-up, whereas Detective Louw and I will be stationed in the interrogation room, asking questions about crimes he's probably forgotten committing. There are eleven cases to which I can link the guy. That amounts to at least eleven lives he's ruined, or ended. Not counting the victims' family members or friends. And it doesn't include what his brother's been up to. We have to guess at the specific numbers until I can work through all of SIRCIS cases.

Howlen will stay at the office.

DARK COUNTRY

Nobody in SIRCIS wants to depend on him for anything. I have my own reasons why, but my grandfather's excuse is because Howlen's entered his *self-destruction season*. Whatever that means.

Father Gabriel has to be out of town for a week or two, due to some pandemic in Bloemfontein caused by a silly game called the Charlie-Charlie Challenge. This game supposedly makes kids think they're getting possessed by a Mexican demon or something along those lines. I'm not familiar with the semantics. Father Gabriel is the expert, and he said it's a load of bull. In other words, he'll quickly tell parents or teachers or the kids themselves that it's all in their heads, but I've seen how a bit of holy water and a prayer can make those types of people feel better.

Precious, on the other hand, is to hold the fort. We are still waiting for results to come through, for eyewitnesses to call back, for unexplained phenomena to be reported.

The plan of action will only be implemented in a couple of days.

In the meantime, I'm sitting on the floor in the musky, dimly lit storage room, sifting through case files for any further links to Human-Tooth-Necklace-Guy. So far I've only found two definite cases that the witness explicitly stated in the transcript where the attacker had worn a human tooth necklace. Everyone knows there are more links—we simply need the definitive proof of his involvement.

I drew the short straw on storage room duty.

Motes of dust swirl through the dank room where each box represents a case. There are, in total, one hundred and forty boxes relating to muti crimes. More boxes, dedicated to other paranormal and occult cases, exist, but those are thankfully in a separate storage room on the second floor.

The closet-sized space holding the muti-related cases is not my favorite place in the world. As I read through a file and evaluate evidence, I can't help feeling itchy. Those itches then turn to thoughts of spiders with judgmental eyes, large fangs, and a terrible disposition. When the spiders aren't enough to freak me out, my mind wanders to silverfish. In my personal opinion, silverfish are worse than any spider.

I shudder, scratch the back of my neck, and wade through boxes.

"Knock, knock."

Rynhardt's voice snaps me out of my concentration. I look up to find him standing in the door.

"I was sent to help, seeing as I need to familiarize myself with the cases before interrogation day," he explains.

"Oh, good," I say, shifting to the side to create space for him.

Rynhardt unclips his weapon from the holster and places it on the floor beside him when he sits.

I point to a stack of boxes near the door. "Those five boxes aren't related to Human-Tooth-Necklace-Guy. I still have a hundred and thirty two others to go through, though. Are you up for the challenge?"

"I am." He grabs one of the boxes I've already taken down for myself. "What am I looking for, exactly?"

"Check the transcripts for anything implying that the perpetrator wore a human tooth necklace. If you don't find anything there, you'll have to look through some of the lab results where trace evidence was collected. Push those to the side and I'll have Howlen see if they match to the results we got today."

"Okay." Rynhardt lifts the lid off the box. "It's quieter than normal here."

"Prep days are always like this," I say, flipping through a transcript. "Usually someone is sent here to dig up things we need, then I—or Gramps, depending if he's in town—go through the shortlist boxes again to make sure they do relate to whatever. If trace evidence stuff should be double-checked, they go to Howlen. Eventually the boxes come to me again when I need to go in and present the evidence to the police or sit in on an interrogation."

"Sounds like you could use a hand," he says.

I show him how our administration system works. Every box is compartmentalized for easy navigation. There's the overview file, which holds copies of the most important things. Then the summary of the case is stapled to the front of the file. Copies of the police report and lab results, and photographs of the scene, are also in those files. Another file in the box usually contains supplemental evidence, like transcripts and expert witness statements. The hard copies of audio or video recordings are in the boxes, as well, alongside any material evidence SIRCIS could find which the police overlooked. The last file contains our costs for the particular case. Some boxes have a lot of information, others are meager. When Rynhardt seems familiar enough with things, I let him be.

"A lot of work goes into your organization's running, huh?" he says.

"If we screw up the tiniest point, the case is thrown out and the criminal walks out of court scot free. Sometimes, even when we don't screw up, the guy gets off. It's crazy unfair how much fear these people create in the general populace."

"It's not an unfounded fear, though."

"No, it's not," I say. "Still."

"Still."

An easy silence settles in, where the only sounds are the rustling of paper, the shifting of our clothes, and our breaths on the artificial breeze coming through an overhead vent. Now and then, something hard in one of the boxes thumps against the cardboard, creating a hollow sound which only serves to enhance the endless quiet. For others, the tedious work paired with a soundless companion might've felt uncomfortable. Not to me. Not after the already difficult day I've been forced to live through.

We each work through several boxes, a time-consuming feat that would've taken longer had I been by myself, but Rynhardt eventually got fidgety.

"You're welcome to take a break. I've got things covered here," I say.

"I'm fine," he says, cracking the stiffness from his neck. "Mosepi told me what happened with Rochester Ramphele."

I mumble an affirmative.

"Anyone else would have been traumatized."

"I've been traumatized for the past two decades. Not a lot gets under my skin anymore."

"Not even someone getting killed in front of your eyes by something unseen?" The disbelief—or unwillingness to believe—is clear in his voice.

I turn to face him. "You've seen the video, then?"

"Mosepi had a difficult time explaining what was going on, so he sat us all down and played the video," he explains. "So, you're not experiencing any of the common signs of witnessing a traumatic event?"

"I was six years old when I saw my first murder victim." I close the file I've been working on. "My nanny had a bad case of food poisoning, and Mrs. Maura, my grandfather's housekeeper, wasn't available to look after me. Gramps was out of the country, too. This left me in the questioningly capable hands of my dearest dad, Detective Snyder.

"Detective Mosepi wasn't happy to have a kid on a call-out, I remember, but what else could they do? Leave a six-year-old with no supervision throughout the night? I think not.

"Anyway, so they park the car beside the other police cars and told me: 'Don't move,' but of course I didn't listen. Next thing I know, I'm staring at a dead guy with his guts spilling out of his body. Mosepi tried to cover my eyes, but I'd already seen the corpse, so …"

"What happened?" Rynhardt asks.

"I learned that I become more inquisitive when I'm traumatized, which is quite helpful when I'm on a schedule and need to be more productive," I say. "So, now you know."

"I'm not sure if I should be impressed or disturbed."

Answering him with a shrug is all I can do. I flip the file open in my lap again.

"What's the story of you planning something Detective Mosepi shouldn't worry about?" Rynhardt asks.

"I can't tell you about it. I'm sorry."

"All right."

"Thank you, by the way."

"For?"

"For not apologizing about what happened last night." I keep my tone light, even if it's a serious subject in my opinion. "For not making things too awkward," I continue. "It's refreshing."

"I don't think either of us have anything to apologize for. It's not how I usually act, but—"

"But it happened, and we can't take it back," I say. "I understand."

"I still want to take you out, if you'd like to?"

I smile. "I'm just an ordinary person with an unusual job, you know?"

Rynhardt straightens, pulls one of the boxes closer, and smiles back. "I know."

POLICE REPORT

Case Number: 081226558
Date: 27 May 2009
Reporting Officer: Deputy Patrick Nglobo
Prepared By: Thabo Oliphant

Incident Type:
Aggravated Assault / Attempted Murder

Address of Occurrence:
101 Loganberry Street, Bonteheuwel, Western Cape, 7764

Witness(es):
None.

Evidence:
Fingerprints (taken from window sill)
Footprint (size 10 Nike Air, tracks found leading away from puddle of blood)
DNA (collected from underneath the victim's fingernails)

Weapon/Objects Used:
Panga / Hunting Knife

Summary:
At approximately 23:00, on 27/05/2009, an unidentified male broke into the residence of one Celeste de Bruin at Bonteheuwel, Western Cape (through the living room window, by breaking off the burglar bars). The victim, who awoke to the noise, was roughly assaulted by the perpetrator after he'd gained entrance into the house. She was

subdued in her bedroom before being tortured and mutilated with a panga and a hunting knife. The victim, Celeste de Bruin, according to her statement, was bound to the bed and gagged by a masked assailant wearing a leather jacket.

The victim was repeatedly beaten by her assailant before she was threatened with the panga, and then physically assaulted with the hunting knife.

Medical reports indicate the knife was used to repeatedly stab and aggravate the victim's wounds through prodding and the twisting of the blade.

After sustaining multiple wounds, the assailant went on to remove the victim's tongue and breasts.

The victim's body parts were not found on the premises or in the surrounding neighborhood, making this a possible muti-related attack. Esmé Snyder, occult-crime specialist, was called in as a consultant on the case (Snyder International Religious Crime Investigative Services – Case File: #55-ES).

After the assault/attempted murder, the suspect escaped through the back door.

No witnesses have come forward in regards to the case.

Deputy Patrick Nglobo was the first officer at the scene, sent out to the residence after the victim dragged herself to the front door and screamed for neighbors' help. He arrived at the scene around midnight and immediately called emergency services to help the victim.

Celeste de Bruin was able to write a short statement while doctors stabilized her in the ER, but during her surgery, she passed away.

A partial footprint was identified in a puddle of blood near the bed, and fingerprints were pulled from the living room windows and burglar bars.

All trace evidence was sent to the forensics lab for analysis.

DARK COUNTRY

Closer inspection of the shoeprint revealed a size 10 Nike Air shoe. DNA evidence has also been collected from underneath the victim's fingernails and was sent for analysis at the forensic lab.

Victim Celeste de Bruin mentioned in her statement that the assailant wore a necklace of some kind, but she couldn't make out the pendant through his shirt.

Notes:
Refer to Addendum B for Celeste de Bruin's statement.
Refer to Addendum C for forensic results.

CHAPTER 33

Safety is relative.

The eight-foot high walls, state-of-the-art alarm systems, vicious guard dogs, overzealous burglar proofing, and whatever else people buy to make themselves feel safe are merely hurdles. The truth is: if someone wants in, they can get in.

There's very little anyone can do to stop the inevitable.

As Yena quietly makes his way through the bathroom of the Silver Lakes townhouse, he tries his best not to laugh at the absurdity of all these precautions. How much money did this woman spend to keep people like him from getting into her house? Yet here he is, making his way to her bedroom.

It'd taken him some effort to get this far, true. The security complex guards weren't too eager to take his bribe, at first, but they'd come around, as they always did. He also had to admit that he was getting too old to scale walls, but he'd made it over anyway. Everything after that came easy. The en-suite bathroom wasn't connected to the alarm system, so he'd pried open the window and climbed through. Voila. Simple.

He peers into the dark bedroom, and sees the king-sized bed with a single form lying on it. Soft breathing fills the quiet, and the air-con wheezes as it battles against the heat. The form shifts, then remains still.

There slept his grand finale.

Almost giddy with anticipation, Yena opens the bathroom door wide enough and slips through. Not even a creak sounds. Perfect. His footfalls are muffled by thick carpeting. Quietly, he treads up to—

"What the fuck?" a male voice comes out of the darkness.

Yena spins around and sees the silhouette of the man standing in the bedroom door, a shard of moonlight falling onto his white skin, making him appear corpselike. A sign from the ancestors, perhaps?

"Leila?" he says in an uncertain tone.

A lamp switches on, momentarily blinding Yena.

The high-pitched wail that follows rattles his brain and disarms him for the briefest moment, before he realizes it's the woman who's screaming. Well, shit. This is not how it's supposed to happen. His eyes adjust just in time to see the man barreling toward him, ready to tackle him through the closet. Where did this crazy motherfucker with the dog collar come from, anyway?

Yena doesn't expect the force of the tackle when the man's shoulder collides with his midsection. He flies back, the air in his lungs exiting in a loud *oomph*. An almighty crash resounds as his back strikes the closet, his head slamming against something hard. Adrenaline surges.

"Call the police," the white man commands.

No! No, this isn't how it's supposed to go.

Yena, while unable to think clearly, gives over to his instincts.

"Where's the phone, André? *Where's the phone?*"

He knees his opponent in the groin, earning an almost animalistic yelp from the man, while he somehow manages to find his hunting knife, clipped to his belt. The guy doesn't budge, though. Yena watches as the man pulls back and then straddles him, readying to punch.

It can't end like this. He would never be able to endure such a humiliation.

One, two punches, before stars begin dancing in front of his vision. Three, four punches, before he tastes blood. The guy grabs him by his ears, lifts his head slightly, and slams his skull on the concrete floor in the closet.

While the man's blood boiled, too engrossed with saving the woman, he doesn't notice as Yena angles the knife.

He jabs the blade up into the guy's ribcage, feeling soft flesh give way to hard muscle. The knife penetrates deeper. The man's eyes widen in shock, but he doesn't stop his assault. Yena twists his weapon and pulls it out and back before jabbing it into his body a second time. Again and again, he stabs.

"Lei ... la," he gasps, the fight finally beginning to leave him.

Blood and saliva mix on the man's lips, bubble onto his chin, and drip on Yena's face.

Yena grins through the pain, positioning his blade right against the man's ribs again and angling it upward. The tip of the knife breaks skin, slices through the man's body like it's made of butter, and hits home. He pull his knife back quickly, his grin turning into a smile. Resilience and determination—that's what the white man possessed more than anything else and Yena wanted it all.

The light in his opponent's eyes blinks out of existence so fast that Yena barely has time to register the moment. Dead weight falls forward, pinning Yena in place.

"André, where's the goddamn phone?" the woman shrieks from somewhere in the house.

Yena counts his blessings as he maneuvers the newly deceased man off, grunting with the effort. He shouldn't have doubted his ancestors' reasoning—he knows this better than anyone, but sometimes he's still bound by the way of man. He crawls out of the closet and scrambles to his feet, ignoring the pooling blood he walks through.

The back of his head throbs, his skull aches. Still, so much power courses through his veins now …

The woman suddenly appears in the bedroom door, out of breath, tears streaming down her cheeks. She freezes in place, her gaze moving beyond Yena to the closet. A heartbeat turns into an infinity as she slowly comes to the realization of what she's looking at.

"André?" His name is barely a whisper on her lips.

She looks back to Yena, gaping in abject terror.

A dead lover.

A fate sealed.

Yes, everything happens for a reason.

CHAPTER 34

In summer, the subtropical weather turns the Jacaranda City into an almost corporeal entity as nature changes from bland to an emerald green. On cloudless days, the skies are the brightest azure and the sun shines warm on the rich red earth.

When the clouds roll in, the skies first change into gossamer blue before swirls of silver breaches the pregnant white cover. The aggression builds at a slower pace, a fair notice for humans and animals alike to get inside, and then the clouds turn into a pewter-colored blanket. Hues of violets can, at times, be seen when lightning streaks through the heavens, and the thunderous claps will echo across the sheltered, fertile valley surrounded by the oblique hills of the Magaliesberg range.

Rainstorms, though sometimes violent, serve as a wondrous reprieve from the humidity.

The heavens, however, haven't dropped a single bead of water onto Pretoria this year.

Humidity would be a fine change of pace after this dry, intense heat, but the weather forecasts don't look promising.

What's more, it's still only spring.

If the temperature doesn't normalize soon, we are looking at an excruciating summer. We are looking at a drought—possible famine and further destabilizing of the economy. This will lead to more desperation, which will mirror a rise in the crime statistics. More ritualistic atrocities will be committed, which means more innocent lives will be ruined.

As I lie in bed in a flimsy nightdress, the covers kicked to the floor, I ponder the probable future of the country, the people, and myself. I'm worn out, but my worries keep me awake. The curtains hang in front of the open windows, unmoving, like they've been weighed down with lead. My hairline is damp with sweat again. It doesn't matter how many showers I take, I can't cool off. The unbearable warmth lies heavy on my chest, making breathing harder than it should be.

Hoping to relieve the pressure in my lungs, I turn onto my side and stare into the darkness.

The bed still smells like Rynhardt.

I push my face deeper into the pillow, inhaling the masculine scent he left behind. Traces of musk intertwine with the subtle deodorant he wore. It smells nice, almost homey. Perhaps if I can convince myself I'm not alone, sleep will be possible. It's worth a try, even if it's a long shot.

Ignoring the heat, I curl into the sheets, bundle the pillow beneath my face, and close my eyes to breathe the scent deeply.

In, out. In, out. In, out.

I imagine a body pressed against mine, molding to my form, a pulse beating in time with my heart, a hand draped across my waist. Slowly, I begin drifting away on a cloud. I enter that place between sleep and awareness, that dangerous place where the smallest creak in a distant bedroom could send you into full panic. My breathing grows deeper as I sink further into the comforts of my sheets, floating higher into my wildest dreams.

My fantasy is interrupted by the padded footsteps of *something* stalking through the house. Almost imperceptible clicks sound, as though long nails are tapping against the tile with each step taken.

I twist in bed, grapple for my cell phone, and dial my grandfather's number.

"Esmé." He answers the phone after several rings. "Do you know what time—?"

"There is something in my house." I cut him off with a hurried whisper.

As eccentric and excessively active as my grandfather could be at times, protective instinct overwrites his peculiarities. Whenever I truly need him, when my life is at risk, or if I'm scared enough to call him in the middle of the night, he's as clear-minded as any normal person.

"I'll be right over," he says. "Stay on the line."

On the phone, I hear him rushing around. I turn my attention to the approaching footsteps coming down the corridor.

"Hurry," I whisper.

As the clicking nails approach, I'm transported back to the nightmare I had weeks earlier. Green fog, demonic entities, gravestones in mall parking lots ... What if that thing from my subconscious had come to life?

"Are you there?" he asks.

"Y-yes." I reach out to the bedside table, switching on the lamp. I look back to the open bedroom door, waiting for the owner of the clicking nails to come into view. "Pops, if something happens to me—"

"Nothing's going to happen to you." The background noises turn to sounds of him driving. "I'll be there in five minutes."

A lot can happen in five minutes, and those footsteps have halted right outside my bedroom door.

I'm torn between the fight or flight response that every human experiences at least once in their lifetime. Considering I'm in a pretty secure house, flight is out of the question. That leaves me with fight. The problem with my supposed choice? I have no weapon except for my bare hands, which might not be enough, if my nightmare is anything to go on.

The padded footsteps and those unnerving clicking nails on the tiled floor start up again, entering my bedroom—

There's ... nothing.

"Esmé?" my grandfather says. "Are you there?"

"It's in h-here with me. I can't s-see it," I explain, searching the floor for whatever's intruded into my inner-sanctum. "P-pops ..."

A heavy body pounces onto the bed.

I shriek, still looking for something that doesn't seem to be there. Indentations appear across the sheets as weight shifts to one side, then to the other.

I throw my sheets over the invisible creature, and—judging from the silhouette under the covers—find it to be about the size of a large dog. Without hesitating, I leap out of bed, run toward the door with my cell phone still clutched tightly in my hand, and don't look back.

My left leg is suddenly caught, anchored to the floor. With my momentum broken, I fall, crashing into the hard tile before I can soften my landing with my hands. The cell phone clatters out of reach. All of this is accompanied by a banshee's warning, which I realize is my own scream of disbelief and pain.

I twist around on my stomach and kick out with my right foot. Flesh meets coarse hair, which covers solid muscle.

An inhuman growl answers my assault, warning me to back off.

I don't.

I kick out again, harder, and my foot connects with whatever the fuck's decided to intrude and do heaven knows what. This time, I shift its weight enough to scramble away slowly. If I can only get to the bedroom door ...

A sharp pain in my right leg makes me shout out in terror. I kick out again, this time with my left foot, before I move forward.

Sticky, thick blood leaks from the long scratches on my leg, the air taking on a metallic tang. I ball my hand into a fist, ready to throw my entire weight behind a punch.

Another growl warns me to not even think about it.

I don't think about it, I just do it.

With a twist of my hips, I bring my fist from far behind to meet the unseen creature where it keeps a firm grip on my leg. With an audible crack, my fist impacts with the *thing*.

An animalistic yelp cries out before the weight lifts from my leg, giving me an opportunity to escape.

I scramble backward.

Nails click across the bedroom, as if the creature is pacing like a trapped predator, sizing up its next meal.

Not wanting to become an invisible creature's takeout dinner, I lunge forward and grab the door's edge, pulling it shut faster than I thought humanly possible. I slide backward, to the other side of the corridor. Ignoring my bleeding leg, I pull my knees to my chest and wrap my arms around them. I watch the bedroom door through the darkness as the creature—muscle and sinew and coarse invisibleness—throws itself forward in an attempt to escape.

DARK COUNTRY

There's no telling how long I sit there watching the door, listening to the chaos, before the front door slams open and my grandfather rushes to my rescue. It couldn't have been too long, even though it feels like a lifetime.

Crash! Thump!

"Is that the—?"

"*Ja,*" I confirm, weary.

"What is it?" he asks.

I pull my shoulders up.

"You're bleeding," he says.

"I'm fine. It's just a few scratches."

"Come on, I'm taking you home." He helps me to my feet. "And you're going to tell me everything."

"Okay, Pops," I say. "I'll tell you everything." I'm too tired to argue, so I allow him to lead me out of the house and take me back to my childhood home.

And I do.

I tell my grandfather everything about my screwed up life while he's bandaging my leg. From Howlen and our stupid two-year on-and-off fling, to the uncreative paranormal activity following me around, what the message Yena left behind at Abraham Amin's dumping site actually meant, to Rynhardt's and my one-night stand. I end it by telling him about the words Rochester Ramphele spoke in Yena's voice.

If Christiaan Snyder is shocked at his only granddaughter's sordid life story, he doesn't show it.

By the end of my confession, I'm wiping away tears with the back of my hand.

"Are you disappointed in me?" I ask.

"You know what disappoints me?" he asks, frowning. "Trying to communicate with the place of everlasting darkness. It's disappointing and frustrating to talk some sense into their employees, let me tell you."

"Do you mean Eskom, Pops?"

"Of course I mean Eskom."

"Oh."

"Get some rest." He tucks me into my old bed the way he used to when I was a child.

I'm not sure if he fully understands the severity of the situation, because he certainly isn't acting the way I'd expected him to. Still, it's nice to share my burdens with him instead of hiding everything away.

"I mean it," he says.

"All right, Gramps. Love you."

"Love you, too, sweetheart. *Lekker slaap.*"

If only, I think, but fall asleep before I can say anything of the sort.

Dread taints the very atmosphere of the entire residential block the following morning.

I'm paranoid, yes, but even from afar, something seems wrong when I return.

On the surface, my house looks like my house. The charcoal-colored roof is intact, the sandstone walls are fine. My garden doesn't hold any discernible abnormalities in need of immediate attention. It's a regular middle-class house, situated on a panhandle property in a nice suburb in Pretoria-Moot. My neighbors keep to themselves, as all neighbors do these days, unless they can't, for some reason. Familiar faces pop up once in a while—the preteen boys who kick a rugby ball into the yard every so often, the nosy widow who peers over the wall whenever she feels the need, the teenage girl across the street who gawks at Howlen each time he comes around. As untimely as those faces seem, they show life beyond the walls everyone has built around their personal prisons.

Visually, nothing is amiss, but I sense danger. Regardless of the warning bells, I walk up to the front door with my grandfather without hesitation.

It's painfully obvious that my house is not a home.

A home, in my opinion, needs pets. Preferably a tail-wagging, tongue-lolling, happy-go-lucky beast of a dog, accompanied by a yapping pavement-special with a tendency to bite ankles. A home needs warmth, something décor alone can't provide when nights are filled with nothing but quiet. A home is a sanctuary, full of love and joy and patience. A home is imperfectly perfect with cracked tiles, sloping walls, sofa stains, and stubborn creaks. A home is where memories are made.

My house is a shell. A promising shell, but a shell nonetheless.

I have no pets. There is no method to my decorating. No sentimental value lingers in the rooms or things I've bought to make the house feel homier. If I wanted to, I could leave now with only the pajamas on my back and not care.

This is not my home.

The front door inches open.

I inhale a gust of sour air and my resolve to enter crumbles into nothing. The previous night returns in flashes, the fear I experienced of the *thing* makes me tremble.

What lies beyond that door? Is it still here, waiting?

My grandfather pulls me behind him and takes the first step inside.

I imagine the entity jumping out and devouring him whole, and my fear multiplies. I grip his wrist and he looks back, concern marring his forehead.

"Please don't die," I whisper.

He smiles. "Would it make you feel better if I said I don't intend on dying today?"

"I'm not joking. Be careful."

He winks and turns to face the living room.

I let go of his wrist. His bravado seems careless. Who knows what lurks behind the doors and furniture?

He scans the living room, fearless.

I follow him inside after he's gone out of view. Everything in the living room looks the same as when I'd left. I glance into the corridor as he peers into the kitchen.

"Looks clear," he says.

I close the distance between us, directing my gaze to the ceiling as I search for traces of the creature. Why it would be on the ceiling, I have no idea, but it's better to be safe. Luckily, there's nothing there. I hadn't imagined the attack. It was here. I have the scratches on my leg to prove it.

My grandfather stands in the passageway of my bedroom, his face unreadable.

I move to his side, expecting the worst.

"There's nothing here," he states. "Perhaps—" He stops himself, smiles, and shakes his head. "It appears we're both in dire need of a holiday."

"Seems so," I say, looking around my bedroom. Objects had moved from their original positions. Drawers were open, their contents spilling out of their respective places. The closet doors were ajar. Something had clawed at and thrown itself against the bedroom door until the wood buckled and cracked. My bedroom is undeniable proof I'm not going insane.

"Do you want me to wait for you?" he asks.

I don't answer. I walk inside and inspect my room with a quick glance. Something else is off. Something else is still here. But I don't want to concern my grandfather or Father Gabriel with this when I can handle it myself.

"I'm fine, thank you," I finally say. When I turn around to face him, a fake smile is already plastered into place. "I'll see you at work?"

"No, actually," he says, his expression changing, becoming stern and unyielding. "We're going to see Tweedledee and Tweedledum today. Get dressed."

"Who?"

"I can't pronounce their real names," he says. "Get on with it. We've got a long drive, and we still need to make sure we have a proper case against Human-Tooth-Necklace-Guy before we go after him tomorrow. Chop-chop, *pop*." He claps his hands together, twice, and walks out of my bedroom to give me privacy.

I grab a pair of cut-off jeans and a black tank from my wardrobe, underwear, some cowboy boots to cover the bandages on my leg, and head to the bathroom for a quick shower.

Once I'm under the waterfall, I close my eyes and try to focus on anything except my catastrophic love life. After coming clean to my grandfather the previous night, I can't help but recount all of my mistakes and the things he still doesn't know about.

My first real boyfriend was a scrawny, emo IT student at TUKS named Gareth. I was seventeen, a late bloomer. The reason for that is simple—I wasn't going to continue the family tradition of reproducing early in life. After all, my grandfather had been twenty when he had Dad, and Llewelyn Snyder was sixteen when I came along, so it's safe to say we're a rather fertile family, if not responsible. I had fun with Gareth for a while, until he realized I wasn't going to be fooled into his bed anytime soon. He broke it off, and honestly, I didn't care too much, apart from the fact that I didn't have anyone to take to my high school's matric dance. Luckily, I had Leila, who gave her date the boot and said we would go as the school's first bi-curious couple.

After high school, there was Martinus, Jason, Marc, and Rudolph, all university students who ran for the hills as soon as it became apparent that I didn't put out. Again, I didn't care too much.

When I graduated, however, things changed.

I met Pierre, a handsome clinical psychologist, seven years my senior, at the gym. His wavy brown hair and deep green eyes made me melt whenever he glanced my way. His smile lit up his whole face, drawing me in like a moth to an electric bug zapper.

That's a nice analogy, really, considering I was the moth and he the electric bug zapper who broke my heart.

As insensitive as it sounds, if I'd known Pierre was crazier than his patients, things might have worked out differently. He was and probably still is, a lunatic. His crazy didn't show immediately, of course. It never did, with men like Pierre. No, he'd bided his time and wooed me like a gentleman for months.

He was truly everything I could have ever wanted in a guy: kind, sweet, supportive, understanding, intelligent … The illusion was pretty fantastic, especially to a naïve girl in love for the first time.

Once we moved in together, his personality changed so quickly, I suffered from whiplash. He'd hit me once, only nine months into our relationship. Stunned, I didn't know what to say or do at that moment, but when the shock wore off, I left Pierre and pressed charges against the bastard.

I have too much self-respect to let a man threaten, let alone hit, me.

My grandfather doesn't know about Pierre. Neither does my father.

If they did, Pierre would probably be dead by now. Detective Mosepi, on the other hand, was all too aware of him.

After Pierre, I didn't actively seek out another boyfriend, but I found one anyway. It happened sooner than I'd expected, too. I was barely single for two months when John stepped into my life. He was nice in a brutish kind of way, and though he wasn't necessarily the smartest man in the world, he was hopelessly sweet. The rugby player had the most wonderful smile—among other things.

Unfortunately, John hadn't reserved his smile just for me.

I found him in bed with another woman after coming home early from a trip to Uganda.

Breaking up had never been easier.

After John, I threw my emotions, desires, and dreams to the wind. When loneliness threatened to consume me, I had a casual fling here or a one-night-stand there. I didn't get serious with any of my lovers. I was careful. It had worked for years.

I was happy, because I didn't have to tie myself down. I didn't *need* to tell anyone about what I did for a living.

It had worked until Howlen and I spent our first night together.

My personal life changed in a blink of an eye due to one drunken night. Gone was my handful of lovers, tossed to the sky without a drop of remorse. Hope leeched into my heart, the vault of "maybes and what-ifs" opening for the first time since John. Yes, I never felt for Howlen the same illogical love I'd felt for Pierre or John—the type of love that started in the pit of my stomach and bubbled into my heart and soul. But it would've been easier to date someone who knew the ins and outs of the job, opposed to going out with a civilian. Yes, we argued often, we still do—in a professional capacity about science versus pseudo-science, about what is real and what is not, about whether the pantheon exists, about *everything*.

Such a pity he had to ruin a good thing with a prostitute.

"Move it, Esmé," my grandfather shouts, snapping me back to reality. "Stop daydreaming in there and get dressed!"

"I'm coming," I shout back. I rinse off the soap and get out of the shower.

DARK COUNTRY

When I'm dressed, my grandfather rushes me out of the house and into his car. As soon as we're driving, though, his reason for having me in a confined space, with little to no chance of escape, becomes clearer.

"We might as well talk a bit. Here's a topic: Tell me about Detective Louw."

L ife isn't fair.

Some people are gracious in their acceptance of this inexorable fact, as difficult as it is at times. Others are prone to search for workarounds, regardless of who gets hurt. Lie, cheat, steal, kill—it doesn't matter what it takes to make their lives easier. In the end, they think it a small price to pay.

Yena, like most children who'd lost the only person who gave a crap about them, learned this lesson the hard way, and at a young age.

As he stands at his workbench, slicing through the soft organ he'd purchased for a hefty price, he thinks back to his humble beginnings. He thinks about what he'd sacrificed simply to survive another day, how he'd whored himself out for a piece of bread. Those hadn't been good times. Not at all.

Yena shakes his head, trying to rid himself of the bad memories threatening to consume his focus, but the seed has already taken root in the folds of his brain. There is no running away from the horrible experiences he's endured.

He looks over to the blonde-haired, blue-eyed woman huddling on the pallet, chained fast against the wall. Her buxom chest rises with each fearful breath she takes and falls every time she looses a shaky exhale. Whimpers escapes her gag while her body shudders with such vigor, the clothes she wears shiver in tandem. Her cosmetics streaks down her face as tears roll from her eyes. She is scared, with good reason.

And Yena bet she has never known what real hunger and fear and cold feel like. Even now, chained up like a dog, she can't begin to understand the hardships he's had to face for more than half his life.

Yena gets back to work, slicing and dicing, eager to shake the memories. He doesn't succeed. Flashbacks of his time on the streets pry his attention away from the work he wants to do. The hunger pangs, the crying, the filth, and the hatred. Every nightmarish moment, cast in black and white, reels across his mind in staccato. Yena stops slicing. His hands tremble from the fear of returning to such a state.

His ancestors aren't making matters better with their constant yapping.

"Want, want, want! Need, need, need!" Yena shouts, dropping the knife on the counter to clutch his head.

The woman screams a muffled scream, which makes matters so much worse. She screams again. And again.

A migraine is in its infant stages, situated behind his right eye but quickly growing into a potential problem. Memories and voices overlap in his mind, blurring his vision and making him nauseous. Yena slides down the wall until he's seated with his cradled head between his knees. He rocks back and forth in anguish.

If the magickal attacks don't let up soon, he'll be incapacitated when he can least afford to be. He's sent so many things after Esmé this past week—controlling the car she was in, killing Rochester before he could rat Yena out, threatening her through the dead man's vocal cords, and the tokoloshe—all in the hopes of grabbing her attention. And he needs to make sure she's finally gotten the wake-up call.

If she didn't get the message, he has to prepare himself for her next move—to dispose of her.

Simple.

But with the bad stuff flashing through his mind, every *kak* moment he's lived through and the buzz of voices telling him to do this and do that and to stop being such a pussy, he can barely breathe. Yena presses his fingertips hard against his skull, leaving imprints and possible bruises on his skin and trying to relieve himself from reliving horrors and nightmares.

It's not enough, though.

Not this time.

He rocks more violently, as though the action might soothe the pain blossoming in his head.

Yena screams, "Shut up! Shut up! Shut up!" His voice cracks halfway through the mantra, but it doesn't help. Screaming and rocking never help.

He's being tested by the ancestors again and there's nothing he can do about it until they decide he's had enough, that he's still worthy.

They won't hurt him permanently—he knows as much. Not while he's still useful to them. Who else would be so generous in their sacrifices? Who else aspires to be great, to be a god, in their names?

It'll let up soon.

Yena's sure.

CHAPTER 36

Tweedledee and Tweedledum, as my grandfather calls them, are actually named Thembekile and Thembelihle, respectively.

They are two ancient women, almost indistinguishable from one another due to their traditional clothing and deep wrinkles, and they don't seem to mind being called Tweedledee and Tweedledum. I think this is because of what they call Christiaan: *Mnumzane Hlanya*. One of them explained to me, in giggles, that it meant "Mister Crazy." I can't argue with the nickname.

Considering the third degree I received on the way over, about my sex life of all kinds of things, I'm inclined to adopt the nickname for him, too.

Then one of them explains it's for the best if I call them Tweedledee and Tweedledum because they get annoyed when people mix them up with one another. I'm not sure how logical their reasoning is on this particular point, but they are friends of my grandfather, so it's probably best not to question it, anyway.

"Sit, sit." One of the Tweedles practically forces me into a low seat.

We're outside of a dung and peach pit hut, on a privately owned agriculture holding near Hammanskraal. I decide she is Tweedledee, for the sake of keeping my head on straight.

She looks me over with her beady eyes and calls something to her sister before the other Tweedle—here forth known as Tweedledum—shuffles closer. She also studies me with narrowed eyes, and then the two of them have a conversation in isiZulu.

"You are in big trouble," Tweedledee says to me in English.

"We can fix it," Tweedledum says, sounding slightly unsure of her proclamation. "We're old, so it'll take time."

"Old? Ha!" My grandfather barked a laugh, sitting down on one of the empty low seats. "You two don't look a day over fifty."

"Tsk." Tweedledee smiles a toothless smile.

"Always trying to honey us up, huh?" Tweedledum scolds.

I feel like I should have a bowl of popcorn to fully appreciate these three together.

"You're being a shameless flirt while there's a bad man trying to hurt your little one," she continued.

"Very bad." Tweedledee goes into the hut.

"Powerful, too," Tweedledum says, puckering her lips up as though she's sucked on an especially sour lemon.

"Powerful, but foolish." Tweedledee returns from the hut with a rusty Ricoffy coffee can in her hands. "Possibly insane."

"It happens to the best of us." Tweedledum shrugs.

Tweedledee looks at her and nods. "Ancestral magic is dangerous if you don't know how to wield it properly. This man was never trained. His magic is raw, which makes him powerful, but ruthless. It's very dangerous."

"Very dangerous," Tweedledee agrees. "And he takes his ancestors to a bad place."

"It's slowly driving him cuckoo."

"And he seems to have directed all of his magic onto you." Tweedledee sits on her knees. She makes herself comfortable on the leather mat in the middle of the cleanly-swept courtyard and opens the coffee can.

"I don't think so," I say, and earn a reproachful look from my grandfather. "The places where the bodies are found are sucked dry of everything. We call them Dead Zones because everything dies in the area. Even the air seems to turn sour. I think he uses his magic to do it, to leave a trace of himself behind."

"No." Tweedledee shakes her head and throws the contents of the coffee can onto the mat in front of her. Old, discolored bones scatter across it. "That's the darkness his ancestors are forced to invoke, acting as sieves. They draw the power from the body, the land, the sky, and the creatures. Then they push the raw, purified magic into him. In turn, he uses it on you. It's a vicious cycle."

"Vicious," Tweedledum echoes as she sits beside her sister. "Good thing you have us."

"Twin sangomas are rare," my grandfather explains.

"We are two halves of one soul," Tweedledee says. "But our half souls are big enough to sustain one body."

"It means we're more powerful than this boy trying to hurt you," Tweedledum continues.

Tweedledee interrupts in her native tongue, speaking to her sister.

They go back and forth until Tweedledum rolls her eyes. "He's not trying to hurt you yet," she says, looking at the bandage around my leg. "That's because he lost control of his tokoloshe."

"Well, now it makes sense why you couldn't see what attacked you last night. Tokoloshes can become invisible when they drink water," Christiaan says, seeming more excited about this magical intervention than I am. "So, what are we going to do?"

"Why are you so excited about this?" I ask. "It's deeply disturbing."

"We'll purify your granddaughter, *Mnumzane Hlanya*." Tweedledee looks intently at the bones. "And then we're going to have to counter his upcoming attacks, which won't be easy."

"Not easy," Tweedledum says, shaking her head. "But doable."

"You're going to concoct something special for Little Red, here?" Tweedledee asks her sister.

"Mhmmm," Tweedledum hums, standing slowly. Her body creaks and cracks from age, but she doesn't seem to notice. "I'm thinking we'll have to delve into our Khoi shelf: *Waterblommetjies, sieketroos, hottentotsvy*—"

"Add in some bush-tick berry while you're at it," Tweedledee adds.

"One can never add too much bush-tick berry," Tweedledum agrees. "Two Happy-Chappy Cocktails coming right up."

"Two?" I ask.

Tweedledum disappears into a different hut.

"It won't kill *Mnumzane Hlanya* to take his medicine either," Tweedledee explains, staring daggers at Christiaan. I can only guess what she knows about my grandfather. "Now," she turned her attention back to me, "let's talk about the plan."

"What plan?"

"What plan, she asks." Tweedledum shuffles out of the hut carrying two brown glass mugs. She pushes one into my hand, and one into Christiaan's before slumping into one of the low seats. "What plan …?"

"Do you think it will be best to exclude them?" Tweedledee asks her sister. "Drink!" She points a finger between me and my grandfather but keeps her eyes on Tweedledum. They seem to communicate without words.

I lift the drink to my lips, hoping it doesn't taste as badly as it smells, and drink deeply.

The thick herbal mixture congeals in my throat. I push through, swallowing hard, and try not to think about what I'm putting into my body. The concoction knocks my breath away.

"Okay," Tweedledee says.

I'm still swallowing, not willing to stop for fear of my taste buds protesting.

"We've decided it will be for the best not to include you in the plan."

"What plan?" I repeat in a gasp as the tonic moves sluggishly to my stomach.

Tweedledum hands me a glass of water, seemingly produced out of thin air.

I take the glass, throw it back, and allow the tepid water to run down my throat.

"The plan of keeping you alive," Tweedledum answers.

"I like that plan," Christiaan says. "Let's do it."

"You don't know what the plan is!" I snap.

"You're high strung, Little Red," Tweedledee says. "We have a cocktail for that. Want one?"

There's this general belief that if you don't believe in something, it's unlikely you'll be affected by it.

This is nonsense.

Disbelief might be a natural barrier against esoteric attacks, but barriers of any kind are not indestructible. It's not a matter of religion, race, intellect, or any of the other things differentiating one person from another. It's about whether or not the unknown force is strong enough to break down the barrier to affect you, and if you're strong enough to resist. Life, love, faith, and the entire bloody universe aren't black and white or linear or logical. The force defies those known barriers. It's a squiggle, a fuzzy concept, an unknown variable.

The same can be said about muti and magic and the whole pseudoscientific world that swirls around it.

Did the concoction, prepared by arthritic hands, have any magical properties to it? Did the drink somehow purge whatever foulness was in me?

I honestly can't say.

Better question: Do I believe an herbal tonic is able to purify or heal a person?

Well, I won't say it's impossible. Improbable, maybe, but not entirely impossible.

"Did you know your mother is a doctor?" my grandfather says, pulling me out of my thoughts about the twins.

My words dry up. My mom is a taboo subject. Not because my father or grandfather don't want me to have a relationship with my mother, but because I don't want to know her. Anyone who walked out on her newborn baby's life and never even sent so much as a lame apology deserves to be forgotten. So, no, I didn't know my mother is a doctor. I don't want to know.

"She's a neurosurgeon. Best in her field, I'm told."

"What does that have to do with anything?" I almost yell.

"Talking about the weather seemed mundane under the circumstances," he says. "I'm just making small talk."

"No, you're baiting me. Why?"

"Concern makes me do silly things. Apologies." He sighs deeply.

"Pops?"

"You need a break from the occult consultation side of the business," he explains. "I know you don't like hearing it, but you need a break. If you don't want to take a holiday after we've closed this case, then I'm assigning you to something less important. I'm sorry, but you're burning yourself out and I'm—"

"I know, and I agree."

He glances at me, frowning.

"As soon as Yena's been caught, I'm taking six weeks off. I want to go visit Dad in PE., and then I'm going to New Orleans for a couple of weeks. I've always wanted to go."

"Alone?"

"Who am I going to take along?" I ask. "You need to keep an eye on the firm. Dad's got his … wife. Leila might be available, but I doubt it. There is nobody else, so I'm going alone. Yes."

"Okay. I'm sure Precious won't mind being boss for a while, though."

"Pops, I love you for wanting to come along, but the open cases will gather dust if one of us isn't there to keep them in line." I push my fingers through my lackluster hair. The heat's even screwing with my volume, now. Ugh.

"New Orleans, huh?" He changes lanes. "I thought you'd be more interested in Russia."

"Oh, Russia's definitely on my list of places to visit, but I've had this urge to see New Orleans for the longest time."

"It's not anywhere near Mardi Gras time, though. And I doubt you'll be in time for a Halloween visit," he explains.

I smile, and shrug. "I'm not interested in Mardi Gras or Halloween, Gramps. I'm going for the jazz and blues, and the history."

"They certainly have plenty of that."

I play with the hem of my denim cut-offs. "Pops, this is completely off-topic, but why do you keep making excuses for Howlen?"

"Well, Esmé, everyone's broken in some way or another. You are, I am, your dad is. But Howlen's just a tad more broken than most people. I know it doesn't seem like it at first, what with his swagger and skill, but he's got a past, love."

DARK COUNTRY

He inhales deeply and then continues. "When he was a kid, around twelve or thirteen, his biological sister was kidnapped. Howlen, his sister, and his grandfather were out and about town doing some early Christmas shopping when the eight-year-old girl got snatched away. They never found her, not a single trace. And Howlen blamed himself for her disappearance. He still does. His grandfather blamed himself, too—so much so that he eventually took his own life."

I look up to my grandfather, feeling like an asshole for being such a bitch toward Howlen, but this revelation doesn't change the fact that Howlen treated me like I was worth less than I am. "I didn't know."

"I'd appreciate it, as will Howlen, if you don't mention it," he says. "This time of year, heading towards Christmas, is always a bit tough on him."

"We're nowhere near Christmas, Pops, but sure. I won't tell."

Christiaan turns into Pretoria, where skyscrapers grow on the horizon, reaching to the heavens as though they're searching for salvation. Surrounded by green foliage and the purple Jacaranda blossoms which set Pretoria apart from the other capitals in the country, I can't help but feel a sense of devotion. No matter how bad this city's crime got, how corrupt the government became, how terrible the neglect was, my heart would always belong to Pretoria.

Christiaan must've sensed my emotions, because he softly said, "Every country has its secrets, every culture has its taboos, every house has its cross, but home is home."

P recious walks into my office, her arms folded and lips pursed in obvious disapproval.

I ignore her by double-checking some of the case files I'm preparing for Human-Tooth-Necklace-Guy's interrogation.

Precious crosses the office, her colorful maxi dress swishing as she walks, sits in the vacant chair opposite mine, and tuts.

"Tokoloshes?" she says, as if it's enough of an explanation for why she's pissed off.

Maybe it is.

Precious doesn't scare easily, but she's still a South African. Everyone's heard the stories and many fear the living shit out of the damn legend. Who wants to wake up to having a toe being bitten off? Nobody. Those little bastards create more havoc than just toe-biting, though. Leave tokoloshes to their own devices and before you know it, you're six feet under. Or, worse—someone you care for could be killed.

"Yes, Precious," I answer. "Tokoloshes."

"Do I need to be concerned for myself and my family?"

"No, Precious. Gramps and I've already sorted things out, I think."

"You *think*?" Precious' voice rises. "Esmé, I don't do tokoloshes. I can handle the other stuff, but I draw the line there. You understand me?"

"I do, but the killer doesn't even know you exist, so—"

"Don't assume," she cut me off. "You and Howlen both said we were dealing with something new as far as this killer is concerned. So, don't assume Yena doesn't know I exist."

The intercom system announces someone at the front gate.

Precious sneers, an automatic response these days, as she gets up from her seat. "We're not done here." She marches out of the office, heading toward the landing.

A second video system was installed upstairs during the renovations in case a receptionist wasn't downstairs to open the gate for clients, police, or whoever needed entrance. This made things easier for everyone except for Precious.

"We're upstairs," Precious says, before buzzing in whoever was out front. Precious makes her way back to me. "Louw," she explains with a thumb over her shoulder.

"Oh," I answer. "Okay, but you were telling me off about something before?"

"It can obviously wait." She throws her hands into the air and flips her weave over her shoulder in one fluid movement before she sits in the chair. Her devil-may-care attitude is cranked up to eleven. Sheesh.

Heavy footfalls bound up the stairs.

"What do you want now, Detective?" Precious says when Rynhardt is framed in the doorway.

"We got him," Rynhardt says.

"You've got Yena?" I ask.

"No, not Yena. We've got the other guy."

"What other guy?" Precious says. "Human-Tooth-Necklace-Guy?"

"Yeah, that one," Rynhardt answers.

"Wouldn't it be better if we call Human-Tooth-Necklace-Guy by his real name now?" Precious asks Rynhardt.

"In a perfect world, we'd know his real name. Unfortunately, he comes with seven forged IDs, a handful of aliases, and no priors we can get our hands on. So you may call him whatever you want," Rynhardt explains. "Even Mosepi's calling him Human-Tooth-Necklace-Guy, anyway."

"I thought we were planning a whole sting operation to catch him," I say, flipping through some files I might need during the interrogation. I'm not nearly as prepared for this showdown as I want to be.

"Our guys picked him up speeding down WF Nkomo," he says.

A file falls out of my hands, lands on the floor beside my desk, and papers scatter everywhere. I bend to put the file back together, but when I right myself in my chair again, my eye catches on the wall above the door. I stop dead cold, hoping my imagination is playing tricks.

"I wish they'd rather trailed him to wherever he wanted to be in Pretoria West. We might've picked up Yena along the way," Rynhardt continues, but his words grow distant and fainter.

My blood pumps hard while the hair on my neck stands at attention. Sour air blows through my office, tracing the contours of my shoulders. This sensation sends cold shivers across my flesh.

Brave of Yena to attack me in broad daylight, while there are witnesses. Or maybe Yena's just evolving, growing bolder.

How many different layers are there when it comes to megalomania?

"Precious," I say. Unmoving, I stare at the wall and wait for Precious to turn her attention to me. Rynhardt's voice fades into the background until I'm sure he's stopped speaking. "Please tell me I'm not seeing things." I keep my voice as level as possible.

"What? *Motherfucker*," she gasps.

Good, it's not my imagination, then.

A plume of red smoke leeches from a new crack in the wall, curling in various tints of crimson and scarlet and wine. The smoke doesn't rise to lick the ceiling or fall away to attack the door frame. It merely hangs there unnaturally, never growing in size and never fading, acting to disconcert those who witness it. Yena must be aware of the change in the game—why else would this display of power be needed?

The sour air smells noxious and reminds me of the nightmare I had a few weeks back.

"Leave," I command. Yena's here now, in some form or another. He's been watching me, calculating my every move to make the torment more sadistic. But I can't lose my head. And although I'm visibly shaking, I've already made my decision: I won't be bullied into fearing ghosts and monsters and unseen entities.

Acrid spittle sprays onto my face from nowhere and the smoke flares. I've had enough.

"*Leave*," I shouted my command. "You are not welcome here. You do not scare me!"

"I'm going to get Christiaan," Precious says, leaving the office.

Rynhardt peers into the corridor. "Doctor Walcott," he shouts.

"What's the commotion about?" Howlen enters.

Nobody needs to give him an explanation.

"I thought you've already dealt with this," he says to me.

"When would I have had the time?" I snap back. "Can you deal with this? I have to go to the precinct."

"Am I forgiven?"

"For ditching me at a strip club to hang out with a prostitute? Not in this lifetime."

"Jesus, Esmé. I have issues, okay?" He walks to my desk and slams down the paperwork he brought along. "I'm sorry for leaving you in a shoddy part of town, for going off with another woman, and for being a total douche."

The plume of smoke grows bigger, then smaller, then bigger again. It's as though it's breathing.

"I don't forgive you for that, but I'll be civil if you'll get your head out of your ass."

"Deal."

I look back at the wall. "I will revel in your defeat, Yena." I spit his nickname as I grab the files and stuff them underneath my arm. I move to Rynhardt's side, still staring at the smoke. "Let's go. I want to see if we can speed up this chase by a few months," I say.

He falls into step beside me, not commenting on the smoke.

Rynhardt seems to be taking everything in stride, but then again, the human psyche has strange ways of protecting people from incomprehensible and horrible things, until it stops. When that happens, their worlds shatter, and the resounding crash when everything catches up with them is something only a depressed poet can describe.

It would be a shame if the intergalactic wrecking ball hit Rynhardt's world too hard.

He drives us to the Pretoria West Police Station, a mix tape playing in the background while I try making sense of the files on my lap.

"Detective Mosepi has done the preliminary interrogation," Rynhardt says. "He'll debrief you as soon as we get there."

"Mhmm," I grunt. "Do you want to talk about it, Rynhardt?"

"About?"

"You know," I start. "About my proficiency in attracting trouble."

"Honestly?"

"If you want to talk about it—"

"I'm okay," he says. "It takes a lot to scare me, Esmé."

"Okay." I'm dubious of his so-called well-adjusted façade.

He sighs, pinching the bridge of his nose, before casting his gaze back to the traffic jam ahead. "Look, nobody knows this, not even my family, but I've encountered my fair share of *unusual* activity." Rynhardt glances at me from the corner of his eye, probably thinking I'd be surprised by his confession.

I'm not. Instead, I wait for him to continue.

"You don't seem impressed."

"Everyone's had their run-ins with the weird and wonderful, Rynhardt. People just don't readily admit it."

"Yes, but—" He shakes his head. "It doesn't matter."

"No, please go on, I'm listening."

Rynhardt grimaces. "I was born with—" He stops midsentence again. The suspense is killing me, but before I can say anything about him spitting it—whatever it is—out, he switches to Afrikaans. "*Ek is met die helm gebore.*"

"You were born with second sight?" I nod.

"You don't believe me. Forget I said anything."

"I do believe you. I'm thinking about all of the cases I've worked on relating to second sight. Some of them were quite interesting, while others were somewhat disturbing."

"You've worked on stuff like this before?" he asks.

"Oh yes, all the time" I explain. "Snyder International Religious Crime Investigative Services studies all of the fringe sciences. NDEs, HSPs, Shadow People, Ley Lines, Alternate Dimension theories—you name it."

He narrows his eyes. "NDEs and HSPs?"

"Near Death Experiences and Hyper Sensitive People," I offer.

"So you're actually a paranormal investigator?"

I frown. "No, I'm an occult crime expert. I have degrees in criminology and theology, and I'm starting work on my BA in anthropology next year."

Rynhardt is silent, then says, "I don't get it."

"What's not to get? SIRCIS is a business like any other. We were established to study the fringe sciences in particular, but like all businesses, we sometimes have to do things we don't like in order to break even every financial year. This is where ritual crimes come in. We consult on cases for the SAPS, act as expert witnesses in trials, and try our best to explain certain events as scientifically as possible for the general public. When we're not doing that, though, we're conducting studies and experiments to understand the world beyond our own. SIRCIS is trying to build a bridge between science and fringe sciences, so the unknown can be explored by more people."

"I get that, but your grandfather travels abroad to lecture and train police to investigate ritual murders. If he doesn't know what he's doing—"

"My grandfather is a complex man with many talents, but he knows what he's doing. The Vatican wouldn't have allowed Father Gabriel to be on our services if they thought Gramps was a lunatic," I say. "I need to get on with sorting these files before we get to the police station."

"Esmé—"

"Not now, Rynhardt. I have to focus."

MISSING TEEN ALERT
CHANTELLE MARIE PERKINS

Description:

Age: 17 Years	**SAPS Case Number:** OB06/06/06
Gender: Female	**Last Seen:** Monday, 06/06/2006
Build: Athletic	**Last Contact:** Monday, 06/06/2006
Eyes: Green	**Last Seen Wearing:**
Hair: Blonde	Pink sweatpants, with the word
Weight: 61 kg	'JUICY' bedazzled in gold, across
Height: 1.70 m	the buttocks. A white tank top and a
	black hoodie, as well as white
	Adidas trainers.

Chantelle Marie Perkins was last seen jogging down Columbia Road in Clubview, Centurion on the 6th of June 2006, around 0530 hours. She jogged a specific pre-approved route every morning before school and the neighbors always kept an eye out for her. A witness, Lesley Joyce, stated that on the day of her disappearance, a suspicious car (a black Volkswagen Golf) without a registration number had driven up and down the streets in Clubview. Police were notified of the suspicious activity, but had not arrived by the time Chantelle went out on her usual run.

Before Chantelle went missing, a brutish man was seen getting out of the car to walk down Columbia Road. Witnesses described him as a twenty-something-year-old black male wearing a leather jacket, big black boots, and a necklace with a tooth pendant.

DARK COUNTRY

At 0600 hours, when Chantelle had not returned to get ready for school, her parents became worried. By then, the suspicious car had also left the area.

If you know of any leads to Chantelle's whereabouts, or know of anyone who may be able to assist us in finding her, please contact your nearest police station.

Coming face to face with a criminal has always been a troublesome experience. Not because those men and women are sometimes accused of the most heinous crimes humanity has to offer, but because I'm always let down, for some reason. I expect monsters to do the things they're accused of doing, not regular human beings. It's like figuring out Adolf Hitler was just a man with a vicious appetite for violence and a knack for manipulation. But the horrifying truth is they're people, and that means everyone is capable of such extreme actions. Adolf Hitler was still just a man.

With Human-Tooth-Necklace-Guy, I'm confronted with the same disappointment.

Sure, he's a bit broader in the chest than most of the criminals I've seen, and he consists of corded muscles and sinew and he has a lot of height on me, but he's just a human. He possibly has a terrible undiagnosed chemical imbalance in his brain, or he lived a terrifying childhood. But he's a man, nonetheless. I'm not a psychologist or a brain surgeon, so I can't explain why he is the way he is, the same way I can't explain why I am the way I am. All I know is that he's flesh and bone. And like my grandfather had implied, everyone in the world has a black mark against their name.

I drop my files onto the metal table, earning a reproachful grimace from the perpetrator. I sit across from him and his lawyer, take in his features—a strong jaw, brown eyes, large forehead, but most distinctively a scar across his upper lip—before I divert my gaze to the files in front of me.

Detective Mosepi sits down to my left, silently allowing me the space I need to interrogate Human-Tooth-Necklace-Guy. Rynhardt leans against the wall behind us, for reasons unbeknownst to me.

It's time to get answers, fresh leads, Yena.

The lawyer will be a problem, but the rat-faced criminal defense attorney with his beady eyes and cheap charcoal-colored suit doesn't seem like the type to care. This case is the sort of case they give out as punishment to insubordinate lawyers. It's unwinnable, career suicide.

"My name is Esmé Snyder," I start, folding my hands on the desk. "How would you prefer me to address you?" I direct my question to Human-Tooth-Necklace-Guy, who looks away.

His pink tongue runs across his white teeth before he smacks his thick lips. That's all the response I get.

"You know that keeping your identity from us won't halt the investigation or prosecution. In fact, the more you piss them off"—I gesture in Detective Mosepi's direction—"the likelier it is they'll prosecute you under the name Pink Fluffernickel De Wet."

He doesn't break, which I expected.

"Let's get on with it. You know why you're here, right?" I say.

"Speeding." His voice is abrasive, like sandpaper against tree bark. If he hadn't been a real-life villain, he could've played one in a radio drama.

"That too," I say, glancing at the disinterested lawyer. Had he even given the guy counsel? "You're also a suspect in a lot of open cases."

Human-Tooth-Necklace-Guy sneers and shrugs.

"If you don't start cooperating, the police are going to charge you with theft, assault, kidnapping, rape, attempted murder, murder, and the illegal trade of human tissue. They have enough evidence to put you away for the rest of your life."

"Allegedly," the lawyer chimes in.

Human-Tooth-Necklace-Guy flashes me a wolfish smile that cuts through my confidence. "Three square meals a day, a free education, a lifelong gym membership, and I get paid for doing menial chores around the prison. And you think I need to be worried?" He snorts in amusement. "I'm not scared."

"You should be scared, though," I say. "You don't think you'll be in the general populace, do you?" I drop my hands to the white piece of paper outlining the charges. "With this rap sheet? No, no. You'll be in a dark hole where nobody will ever find you. The rest of the world might think the prison system in South Africa is a picnic, but people get lost and forgotten so easily, with the amount of prisoners in there. And the things that happen to those lost and forgotten inmates …" I shake my head and tut. "Let's just say they wish capital punishment was still an option."

"Miss Snyder, are you threatening my client?" the lawyer asks.

"I'm hardly the threatening type."

"I'm not scared," Human-Tooth-Necklace-Guy says again.

"Of course not, but people quickly change their minds when they see how it really is on the inside."

I slide the files into view, opening the top one to the photographs of the victim. Sumaya Sava, a twenty-nine-year-old Muslim woman who'd been brutally attacked in 2004, peers back through swollen and discolored eyes. All she'd done to deserve this was walk alone from the bus stop. I take out the photos and spread them over the table for the lawyer and his client to see. Displaying Sumaya's bruises, her gaping wounds, and the lacerations, as well as her defensive wounds, is probably shocking, but this is the least of the shame she's had to endure.

"Do you remember this woman? The one you raped and mauled like an animal?"

He looks away.

"No, you be a man and look at the things you've done."

Slowly, he turns back to face me, defiance glittering in his eyes like jewels.

"Before she was raped and disfigured, she had a life. She was a mother, a wife, a daughter, and a sister. You took all of that away from her. Her husband divorced her, taking their children with him. Her depression is so great, she's tried to commit suicide, which is a taboo to her faith. She's been ostracized from her family and her community."

Not missing a beat, I open a second file and take out the next set of photographs.

Henry Ndaba, a teenager at the time, who'd been targeted due to his albinism. He'd been partially castrated and he'd lost an arm. I remember interviewing him, remember how he'd said the man responsible had a possible cleft lip and definite demonic eyes.

I glance at the Human-Tooth-Necklace-Guy, searching for the demonic eyes Henry had mentioned, but don't find any trace of them.

"Do you remember this man?" I ask, suddenly unsure as to whether we had the right guy in custody. "Look closely."

"I know nothing." He spits out each word individually.

I'm not satisfied.

One after the other, I pull out photographs of the victims, bitching every time he looks away.

The lawyer is quick to say I'm badgering his client, but I have a sharp tongue, and apparently Rynhardt is well-versed when it comes to the law. Rynhardt keeps the proceedings in check with ease, much to my dismay. I would've enjoyed getting under his skin with a more brutal line of questioning. Finally, when every photograph is on display, something inside Human-Tooth-Necklace-Guy snaps.

Gone is the rage, the detachment, the defiance. All that remains is the broken man whose sins have caught up with him. Success is in my grasp.

"I'm not this man anymore," he says, barely above a whisper.

"I need to convene with my client," the lawyer chips in.

"No." Human-Tooth-Necklace-Guy taps at a random photo with his index finger. "I'm not this man anymore. I've done bad things, I know—"

"You need to shut up right now." The lawyer cuts him off, jumping from his seat.

"Sit down, Mr. Khumalo." Detective Mosepi's calm voice rings through the interrogation room for the first time.

The lawyer does as he's instructed, but doesn't seem happy about being ordered around.

"We all make mistakes," Human-Tooth-Necklace-Guy says. "These are my mistakes. I'm not like this anymore. I've grown up. I have a wife and a baby, and I have a job. I don't do this anymore."

"*You* have a life," I say. "But your actions have ruined the lives of not only these people, but also the lives of their families and friends. *You have a life, yes. They do not.*"

"Fuck you! We all make mistakes!"

"What is your name?" I ask, not allowing myself to be baited into another circular argument.

Human-Tooth-Necklace-Guy doesn't answer. A veil of insolence glazes his eyes, making his intentions clear. He won't answer any of the important questions. There's an unjustified loyalty between him and his brother, one I won't be able to break in one sitting.

After an intense staring contest between us, my cell phone vibrates in my pocket.

I fish it out, scroll to my messages, and find an MMS from an unknown number, with no explanation. The image of a man appears after downloading the message, but his face is warped as he's walking into a ruin. Colorful graffiti, gang tags, an image of a hawk, and *JOU MA SE POES* is visible against one wall of the desolate building. There's also a black van parked nearby, and overgrowth on the side of the building. Not a lot, but enough to hide certain illegal activities, if the occasion calls for it. The place looks familiar, for some reason, but I can't place it.

Detective Mosepi leans closer and looks at my phone before he whispers, "What is it?"

"We need to talk," I say, jutting my chin to the door.

"Emergency?"

"Possibly."

Without so much as a look in Human-Tooth-Necklace-Guy or his lawyer's direction, I exit the interrogation room with Detective Mosepi in tow. Rynhardt follows, too. When we're out of earshot, I hold out my cell phone for them to study the image.

"This just came in from an unknown number. The place looks familiar, but—"

"That's what used to be Lucky Luke's," Detective Mosepi says. "It's across the street, beyond the dip, and a few buildings over. Just opposite the Cash & Carry."

"I thought it closed down ages ago," I say.

"Oh, it did. Lucky Luke's closed down and fell into disrepair. Now it's a heroin house."

"Oh my god," I breathe. "The police station is right here. Why the hell don't you do something about it?"

Detective Mosepi's unreadable expression is his only response, because duh. I should know by now that logic isn't in everyone's nature, or in their vocabulary, for that matter. The SAPS is no different in that regard.

"Fine, can we go see if he's there?"

"You want to go snooping around in a heroin house filled with druggies who are stoned out of their minds, in search of a guy whose face we can't see?"

"A simple no would have sufficed, but yes," I say. "I would like to follow this lead."

"We can't. There are protocols—"

"Protocols haven't done jack in this case, so far."

"Don't get snippy with me, Esmé," Detective Mosepi warns. "Everyone's frustrated."

I wave my hand in the direction of the street for emphasis. "He's right here, Mosepi." My indignation amplifies my voice. "You know what?" I pocket my cell phone and straighten. "While you're following protocols, I'm going to catch a killer."

The two steps I take aren't enough to get me out of his reach.

Detective Mosepi clamps his hand around my wrist and says my name in a low, fatherly voice.

I turn to face him and feel my resolve wasting away.

"I need to clear things with the captain first, so give me a few minutes and we'll go together. Okay?" he says. "Okay?"

I exhale through my nose, nod, and his grip loosens.

"Rynhardt, keep an eye on her. I'll be back in a bit."

Rynhardt acknowledges the request with an unenthusiastic, "Yes, sir."

Detective Mosepi departs.

Rynhardt studies me in one quick look, the same technique he taught me just three days earlier, before leaning back against the wall again. "Are you still angry with me?"

I have a split second to make a decision—a decision I will likely regret in the morning.

Detective Mosepi rounds a corner, disappearing from sight. Now's possibly my only chance. The captain is unpredictable at the best of times, and I doubt he'd be in the mood to send some of his people on a wild goose chase.

I saunter up to Rynhardt, as close as I can without broadcasting my intentions to the whole world, before placing both hands against his chest. My fingertips draw circles against his crisp white shirt.

"Angry is too harsh a word," I say, keeping my voice low and seductive. "Mildly disappointed, maybe, but I'm over it."

Our gazes meet, and a somewhat familiar fluttering starts up in the pit of my stomach. The feeling catches me off guard, and I almost don't go through with my plan. Unfortunately for Rynhardt, people's lives are on the line.

"I didn't mean anything by it, you know?" he says, snaking one hand around my waist.

I take a step closer, press my cheek against his shoulder, and allow my hands to slowly move down his chest and to his sides.

"I know." My hands slide lower, until they come to a rest on the waistband of his pants. I tilt my chin up to look into his eyes again. "I *really* do like you."

"The feeling is mutual."

I blush. "Take me out to dinner sometime?"

"Just tell me when."

I move my left hand to his cheek before I draw him closer and kiss him deeply. Meanwhile, I move my right hand nimbly to his pocket, snatch his keys, and put them in my pocket. If I'd come with my own car, I wouldn't have resorted to this treachery, but life loves throwing curveballs. So, here I am, ready to commit grand theft auto for the sake of following a lead which may not even pan out.

I dash across the corridor and toward the back exit. Past the tarnished metal door leading to the parking lot, I run for the Ford Ranger—a beastly thing beside the rest of the vehicles.

"Shit. Shit. Shit. Shit." The mantra keeps my legs pumping, my boots smacking against the asphalt. I don't look back. I can't look back. "Shit. Shit. Shit."

I almost run past the Ford Ranger, needing to grab hold of the bullbar to stop myself from overshooting. As soon as the fob key's pressed and the locks spring open, I'm climbing into the driver's seat, singing my tune of obscenities. Then I start the engine and pull out of the parking space, finally allowing myself a glimpse at the door.

Nothing. Nada. Zilch.

Rynhardt hasn't figured out I've left the police station, yet.

I turn my attention to the road and drive out of the parking lot without so much as being stopped by the guard at the gate.

CHAPTER 40

I'm parked a few cars behind the black van, which stands in front of what used to be Lucky Luke's.

Leaning down across the seats to keep a watchful eye on the door without being spotted, I link my phone to the hands-free device in Rynhardt's Ford Ranger.

If I knew what Yena looked like, this would be easier. As it happens, I'm hoping my instincts will come into play when the murderer sets foot outside the door.

If all goes well, my mission will come to fruition before a cop pulls me over for stealing Rynhardt's car.

When the setup is complete, I call my grandfather to let him know what's up. His phone rings a few times before he answers with a disengaged, "Yello."

"Hello, Gramps," I say.

"How's the interrogation going?" he asks. "Is he talking?"

"No, I gave up on him when I got a tip off for Yena himself."

He mumbles an affirmative.

"Pops, could you stop whatever you're doing and pay attention for two minutes?"

An audible sigh follows, before he says, "Sure, darling. What's up?"

"Can you get together some bail money?" I bite my bottom lip, staring at the door of the heroin house.

A prolonged silence fills the conversation.

"Are you there?"

"Yes," he draws out the word. "Why would you need bail money, Esmé?"

"I might have borrowed Detective Louw's car without his permission, or knowledge, for that matter," I say. "But there's a perfectly good explanation for why I did it."

"I'm listening."

A man, wearing a remarkably similar outfit to the warped man in the MMS, walks out of the heroin house. He looks left, then right—a responsible, or suspicious, pedestrian?—before making his way toward the black van. Nothing about him screams "I'm a homicidal maniac," apart from him coming out of Lucky Luke's.

My heart pounds in my throat, my eyes widen, and my thoughts reel. Could it be Yena, or am I simply desperate enough, crazy enough, to follow anyone?

No, it's Yena. There's no way in hell it isn't Yena. My instincts are lighting up like Chinese New Year.

"Esmé?"

"Pops, I've got to go," I say, starting the engine, ready to follow the black van to the ends of the Earth if I have to. "Remember bail money, please."

I end the call, watching the van and preparing to follow.

The van slips into the lane first, behind a taxi, before heading west on WF Nkomo Street.

I keep two cars between us at all times.

We drive through the dip, past the Pretoria West Police Station and toward Quagga Centre, situated across the KFC and Debonairs Pizza. Taxis and vehicles turn off either to the restaurants—maybe looking for a lunchtime snack—or to the shopping center, for something entirely different.

We continue heading west, past the Pretoria West Golf Estates, although it's not *really* golf estates in anyone's opinion. Even the residents aren't deluded enough to be fooled by the massive signs proclaiming these two-bedroom, one bathroom properties as exclusive high-end homes. It's low-cost housing with "Golf Estate" in its address, for lower middle-class homeowners who want to feel important. Everyone knows this, but it would be in bad taste to mention it out loud.

At the WF Nkomo Street and Transoranje Road intersection, the robotor traffic light, as the Americans like to call it—catches the van before it can turn left. With two taxis and one *skedonk* between us, I'm still safe from being discovered.

I tap my fingers against the steering wheel.

When the traffic light changes and the cars move forward again, we turn left on Transoranje Road and head south. The road acts as a boundary between the Proclamation Hill and Pretoria West suburbs, but judging from the way the van navigates the roads, it seems we aren't heading to either.

"Where are you going?" I ask out loud, keeping a steady speed and distance from the van.

Soon we're turning west on Quagga Road, driving through a more industrial and rundown part of the area. The Consol Glass Factory used to be around here somewhere, as well as a soap dispensary and a fabric outlet. An array of other big companies, ranging from steel fabricators to second hand car dealers, makes their homes here, too.

My cell phone vibrates again. The car's stereo rings in unison, and Rynhardt's name pops up on the screen.

"Hello?" I answer as casually as I can, trying not to betray myself with something as silly as emotions. Indifference is, after all, an emotion I've mastered.

"You stole my car," Rynhardt exclaims.

"No, I'm borrowing it," I correct him. "Don't worry, Rynhardt, I'm an excellent driver. Also, I'll return it with a full tank of gas and there won't be a scratch anywhere."

"I don't know if I want to marry you or arrest you for *stealing my car!*"

"If you're trying to make me blush, it's working."

"Give me that," Detective Mosepi's voice chimes in.

The phone changes hands.

"Go switch on your tracker, you love-struck fool. The first girl who flutters her eyelashes at you, and you turn into a moron. What is wrong with you?"

"I regret that," I say loudly, hoping Detective Mosepi will hear.

"As for you," he says directly into the phone, "I'm going to wring your scrawny neck when I get my hands on you, Esmé."

"And suffer a police brutality lawsuit? I think not, Detective Mosepi."

"Don't start with your bullshit. I know your tricks almost better than your daddy does. Get your ass back to the police station or I'm putting out an APB."

He's not joking, but I'm not cracking yet.

"Esmé!"

"I heard you, Detective," I say in a singsong tone, keeping my eye on the van. We're still heading west on Quagga Road, coming up to Laudium.

"You are obstructing justice—"

"Only if it turns out this guy *is* the killer, but then all I'll get is a slap on my wrist, anyway. Why? Because I found the bloody killer. And if this guy doesn't turn out to be Yena, then I'll admit defeat and take whatever punishment you wish to bestow upon me."

"She's heading south on Quagga Road," Rynhardt says in the background. "Nearing Laudium."

"Detective Mosepi, if you put an APB out on me now, you lose your best chance at getting information which could possibly lead to an arrest," I say.

There's a moment of silence before he says, "You are not to approach the suspect at any cost. Is that understood?"

"Loudly," I answer.

"Don't get spotted. Keep three cars between you for as long as possible, and pull away if it seems he'll figure out you're following him," he continues.

"Yes. Understood."

"I'm on my way with backup to see if this guy of yours is Yena, and if he isn't, you're paying for the full cost of this exertion," Detective Mosepi barks at me.

"Now you're just being mean."

"And, Esmé, you're to stay on the phone with Rynhardt until I'm there with you." He ends by shouting, "Catch!"

"I'm angry with you," Rynhardt's voice replaces Detective Mosepi's.

"No, you're not. You're intrigued. Maybe even a little excited," I say. The background sounds change from office noises to echoes. They're already in the parking lot. "Hold up, we're coming to a robot."

I slow down and look around the interior of the Ford Ranger. "Do you have sunglasses or something?"

"Glovebox," he says.

I lean over, open the glovebox, and find a pair of sunglasses inside. In one smooth movement, I have my eyes covered and I'm tying up my hair up into a messy bun.

"You good?"

"Yup."

The traffic light changes color and the cars move forward again. By then, traffic has thinned out and I'm certain it's going to be harder to hide when the next few cars turn off.

Rynhardt and Detective Mosepi are in a moving vehicle—the police scanner and windy noises in the background proves as much.

"Talk to me," Rynhardt says when a few minutes have passed.

"We're heading into Erasmia, not Laudium." The Ford Ranger is becoming conspicuous as the rest of the vehicles disperse to other places, leaving only the black van ahead. "I need to focus on not getting spotted, call you later." I end the call without waiting for confirmation. As the vehicles both decelerate at a stop street, I calculate the van's probable location before switching on my indicator. The van heads forward, whereas I turn into a completely different street.

"The race is on."

I speed up.

The cell phone rings again.

My foot barely touches the brake pedal at the next four-way crossing before I turn right. Luckily, it's the middle of the day where little to no traffic is driving around in the suburbs. I speed up a fraction, hoping to get to the next stop sign just as the black van does. It takes me a few streets to catch up, but eventually we're driving on different streets at the same pace.

It takes everything in me not to toss my cell phone out of the window, it's ringing so much.

DARK COUNTRY

We're coming to the edge of the Erasmia suburbs, entering the more agricultural areas between Erasmia and Mooiplaats. The plots are mainly occupied by chicken farmers, but I'm sure some of these properties are self-sustainable agricultural holdings, farmed by hippies or hipsters or whoever the hell makes their homes there.

I don't mind the open air or being away from the buzz of the capital, though. These places are, however, riddled with dirty little secrets. Headlines of previous terrifying, unrelated cases in the media pop into my mind: SA DAD "HELD FAMILY HOSTAGE FOR YEARS," WIFE, SONS WATCH IN HORROR AS GANG KILLS FARMER, THE HORROR OF THANDI MODISE'S CANNIBAL PIG FARM, etcetera, et-fucking-cetera. There are too many places to hide criminal activities when it comes to farmlands.

I turn back onto the main road, the only one heading in or out of the region, hoping the driver's too oblivious to notice this massive Ford Ranger behind him. At least it blends into the whole scenery.

Five minutes later, the van turns down an unpaved road. Red earth shoots up from the wheels, dust billows around the black metallic exterior.

I drive straight on, not wanting to alert the driver.

I actively ignore my cell phone, which continues to ring.

When a few minutes have passed, I make an illegal U-turn and head back to the dirt road. I park the Ford Ranger at the open gate, looking straight into the steep incline of a little hill that provides both privacy and security. Long grass stalks wave in the slight breeze, mocking me as I sit helplessly in the car.

"Don't do it," I say to myself. I restlessly tap the steering wheel as I study the entrance of the plot. I still my hands, grip the wheel hard, and look around. "Don't do it."

I do it.

After switching my cell phone to airplane mode, I climb out of the car, and walk up the dirt road.

The sun beats down on the hilltop, biting the exposed skin of my bare shoulders and legs while I jog up the path. There are a few barren trees, spaced far apart. The grass and weeds have grown out of control—

so much so that I can easily hide in the bushes, if necessary. Dust clings to my sweaty skin, turning my pale complexion to a reddish brown.

My boots become filthy and my clothes heavy, making the exercise worse than it should be. It's not the type of day one wants to spend outside, but this is a matter of life and death. Or so I keep telling myself. I'm no cat burglar, or ninja, or spy, and I hate admitting it.

The dirt path opens into a lot after a five-minute jog, and I spot a few rundown outbuildings ahead. I kneel in the long grass, ignoring the itchiness of my thighs and searching for the black van. After a moment, I spot the vehicle behind one of the outbuildings, parked near a neglected house.

"I'm going to get myself killed," I whisper.

I resign myself to my fate if the decision to play cops-and-homicidal-killers backfires, and set off toward the large concrete block straight ahead.

CHAPTER 41

Dirty glass shards protrude from broken window frames like jagged shark teeth.

Against my better judgment, I step through the unlocked door and enter an abandoned office. A thick layer of dust covers the entirety of a reception desk, while a scene depicting a possibly violent game of musical chairs lies before it. Overturned chairs battle for space with listless pieces of paper and rubbish. Paint and wallpaper are stripped down in places, displaying bare patches of concrete.

The depressing state of the building is further tainted with the stench of rotting meat and rat piss, creating an ambiance of death and despair.

My boots crunch across debris laced with shattered glass as I make my way to the only other door in the room. I glance over my shoulder, hoping nobody has sneaked up on me. So far, luck's been on my side. If only my good fortune holds out until the police track the GPS of the Ford Ranger.

A painfully loud squeal comes from the rusting door handle and echoes through the whole building as I push down on it. It's followed by an even louder creak when the door swings open.

A gag-inducing odor greets me as I enter the darkness.

I cover my nose and mouth, but to no avail. With my free hand, I pull my cell phone from my pocket and find the flashlight app.

The light cuts through the inky blackness, illuminating the blood-splattered slaughterhouse with its shiny metal hooks and stained floors.

I wave my cell phone across the room, finding a workbench littered with instruments of horror and some unpleasant remains that I, thankfully, can't distinguish from my position.

"Shit," I whisper, coming to grips with the fact that I'm *not* prepared for whatever comes next. With shaky hands, I bring my cell phone closer, disengage the airplane mode, and dial Rynhardt's number.

He answers on the first ring. "What the actual—"

"It's Yena," I rush my whisper.

"Whatever you do—for God's sakes, don't get out of the car."

"I'm already in his workshop."

"Jesus Christ," Detective Mosepi cusses. Rynhardt must have placed me on speaker. The sirens are switched on while he continues to shout obscenities.

"Step on it, Elias!" Rynhardt barks. "Get out of there. Get out, *now*."

Only then do I hear a muffled scream coming from within the slaughterhouse. It takes every ounce of courage not to scream out in response.

"There's someone here," I say through clenched teeth. I move the phone away from my ear to use the backlight as a weaker torch.

"Get out of there, Esmé!" Rynhardt shouts loud enough to be heard even with the phone at arm's length.

The whimpers and screams and cries continue as I stepped deeper into the workshop.

The gory mess on the workbench, where pieces of flesh lie in coagulating blood, turns the rising bile in my throat to acid. A maleficent apothecary, where tiny jars of unidentifiable ingredients stand within reach, is a soulless rendition of a horror movie come to life. The low hum of a swarm of—hopefully—flies is noticeable only by ear. Scratching and squeaking—more proof of a rat infestation—surrounds me. I walk on, allowing the whimpers to guide me. The blackness is so deep, so physical, I feel like I'm walking through custard. My flashlight app doesn't shine bright enough to make the unknown seem any less frightening.

Finally, after what feels like searching forever, the cell phone's light falls on the blonde, terrified woman sitting in the back corner of the building.

My heart drops like a stone into my stomach.

"Leila?"

A shaky gasp escapes my mouth when I see her chained to the wall in the farthest corner of the slaughterhouse.

She's sitting on a pallet, where the straw has become crusty with feces and decomposing food. The bedding—if one could call it that—is filthy even in the bad lighting. But, of everything I've seen in this shithole, it's the terror in Leila's eyes that'll haunt me for the rest of my days.

Without considering what would happen if Yena decides to return and finish her off, I'm on my bare knees in the filth, pulling the saliva-soaked rag from Leila's mouth. Then I'm tracing the chain from the wall to her ankle. It's padlocked fast. Blood covers the metal, her ankle, and the pallet.

"Run," Leila croaks. "Go, find help."

"Help is coming." My throat is thick with grief and fear. "I'm not leaving you."

"He's insane, Esmé. He'll kill us both. Go."

"No, we're going to get you out of here."

Leila cries, stifling her sobs whenever they start to get out of control. When she's managed to pull herself together again, she says, "Even if you can free me, he cut my ankle. I can't walk properly."

"Then the fucker's going to have to go through me to get to you," I say. "I am *not* leaving you behind."

I'm on my feet again, using my cell phone to light the way back to the workbench. There must be a key here somewhere, or a hand saw—*something* to get Leila out of her chains.

With shaking hands, I rummage through the workbench, pushing aside jars and tools and trying to ignore the human tissue scattered across the surface. Cockroaches and maggots scuttle and squirm across the table. My muscles are hesitant, and every movement feels like I'm wading through more black custard.

"I can't find a key. Where's the key? Damn it!"

"Esmé, leave it."

"Pull yourself together, for fuck's sake."

Leila hiccups her tears away. "He killed him."

"Who?"

"André," Leila whispers.

I have no idea who André is, but clearly he meant something to Leila.

"Sorry, Lei." I give up on finding a key and settle on a hammer and screwdriver instead. A feeling of malaise falls over me as I return to Leila's side.

How am I going to get her out of here in one piece?

I don't want Leila to see how out of my depth I am, so I turn the padlock onto its rounded back, position the screwdriver, and start hammering. If we can just hold on until Detectives Mosepi and Louw come, all will be well. All will be fine.

Leila cries out, her broken nails digging into my shoulder when I accidentally pull the chain too far away and it cuts into her wound.

"I'm sorry, I'm sorry, I'm sorry. Hold on, okay?"

"Goddammit," she hisses.

"Relax, Lei." The hammer pounds against the back end of the flathead screwdriver. *Bam! Bam! Bam!* But the lock doesn't spring open as I hope.

"Es—"

I cut her off when the hammer comes down with a mighty, hollow blow.

"Esmé!"

CHAPTER 42

When Yena noticed the splash of crimson in the long grass, he knew he'd fucked up properly.

He blames his headache for not being as focused as he always is. How could he not have seen the tail? Blame shifting won't help Yena out of his predicament, though. No, he needs a plan, one he can use to turn the situation in his favor.

The headache hasn't improved, but there's no time to fix it.

He peers through the window of the decrepit house, seeing Esmé dash across the field and toward the slaughterhouse. She will find her friend there—the slutty one he'd had to keep gagged thanks to her incessant shrieking. Jesus, her voice could burst eardrums.

Yena stretches his neck one way, far enough to hear the crack, and feels the release in his tight muscle before he does the other side. He grabs his hunting knife from the table and slips it into the holster on his belt. The time has come to put an end to the game, even if Esmé is a few days early. Yena walks out of the decrepit house, clearing his throbbing mind of whatever negative clutter is running amok in there. He no longer has the luxury of losing his head.

He enters the office through the open door and quietly slinks across the room to the slaughterhouse. Their voices are somewhat muffled, but not enough.

Tsk-tsk. You're no good at sneaking, he thinks, allowing himself to be swallowed by the shadows. His eyes adjust to the darkness swiftly, giving Yena an advantage over Esmé and her need for a flashlight.

"Pull yourself together, for fuck's sake." Esmé's nervous voice fills his workshop while her friend exchanges sobs for hiccups.

He moves closer, quiet as the grave, barely breathing to keep himself from being noticed.

"He killed him," the blonde says.

"Who?"

"André."

Esmé whispers something to her friend which he can't quite make out. An apology? Maybe. It doesn't matter. Neither of them have figured out he's with them, yet, waiting to pounce.

Esmé hammers at the lock, but her efforts to free her friend are in vain. The woman cries out.

Esmé says, "I'm sorry. I'm sorry. I'm sorry. Hold on, okay?"

Yena moves a few feet closer, well hidden until he no longer needs to be. He knows this place like the back of his hand, every crack in the concrete floor, each meat hook in the ceiling—even the drains' positions. He knows exactly where to step and not to step, to remain a part of the fixtures.

"Goddammit," the woman hisses.

Nearing them, he slowly clips open the hunting knife's holster. Just in case Esmé isn't in the mood to listen ... or play. Whatever movements and sounds Yena might have made are drowned out by Esmé's desperate hammering.

"Relax, Lei," she says, pounding away.

Bam! Bam! Bam!

Yena moves within a couple of meters from Esmé's hunched-over form.

The other one looks up, straight at Yena. Even in the darkness, he sees how absolutely terrified she is. Her bottom lip quivers while her eyes stay glued to Yena.

"Es—" she starts to say, but the hammer comes down with a mighty, hollow thud again, cutting her off. "Esmé!" she shouts.

Yena smiles as Esmé turns slowly. She drops the screwdriver to snatch her cell phone from the blonde, but holds on to the hammer.

The flashlight suddenly shines directly into his eyes and he lets out a hiss of annoyance, covering his face with one hand. Yena didn't expect her to do that, but this momentary lapse will be the last.

Yena rights himself.

"Our final meeting was not scheduled for today, Esmé," he says. He makes sure his disappointment overshadows his accent. "I don't like surprises."

She doesn't respond with words. Her expression, however, is one of defiance and rage. Oh, yes. She wants to play. Good.

Yena sighs, the same way a father would sigh if his child were being irksome.

"Since you're here, I suppose we should get started. But please take note, I am not entirely prepared." He strides across the slaughterhouse, calculating his steps past Esmé and Leila and moving toward his workbench. Yena keeps an eye on her, the same way she keeps Yena in her sights at all times.

When he gets to his workbench, he senses how she itches to attack him with the hammer, but common sense keeps her feet frozen in place.

"Have you ever known anyone to achieve a godlike status?" he asks, reaching for a glass jar without needing to look.

"I cannot say that I have," Esmé answers.

Yena nods, glancing at his hand where a fat cockroach scurries. He shakes the insect off and opens the glass jar.

"That will change today." He throws the contents of the jar into a filthy mortar. "I will free myself of this mortal shell, these chains made of flesh. And you, my dearest Esmé, will witness it."

He tosses pieces of chopped organs into the concoction, opens a drawer, and finds a special herbal elixir. "It's the grand prize for finding me. You should feel honored for getting this far."

"I feel disgusted," she hisses.

"That makes two of us," her friend concurs.

Yena sneers at the blonde's remark. She's never been worth his time, but she will be useful for this last hurrah.

"It's a pity you feel that way, Esmé. Perhaps I can change your opinion on the matter." He dusts his grimy hands off over the mortar and slips the hunting knife out of his holster.

Then he steps away from the workbench and toward Esmé. "I just need one more thing from your friend. Do you mind?"

"Don't come near us." Esmé makes a show of wiggling the hammer in her hand, but the action only amuses Yena. "I'm warning you."

"Now you're being childish. Step away," Yena says, walking closer.

"*I'm warning you!*" she roars, clutching the hammer.

Yena doesn't so much as flinch. He keeps going, fearless. She won't hit him. No, if anyone was interested in the evolution from man to god, she would be the one. Esmé Snyder has always been the one.

She aims to hit him square in the face, but when she pulls the hammer back, he flicks his hand in her direction and the weapon flies out of her hands. It falls an impossible distance away, clattering loudly against the concrete.

Better safe than sorry.

He sees Esmé stare into the darkness where her hammer landed, dumbstruck.

Yena bypasses her, chuffed with his ability to entertain, heading straight for her friend—who's been placed in this situation because of Esmé's failure to humor his simple request to find him. It is her fault, after all.

"No!" She charges Yena just as he angles his knife in his hand, bending over to take the blonde woman's heart.

But the blonde isn't as helpless as he'd thought.

As Yena is tackled from one side, the blonde is up on her good leg, wielding the screwdriver Esmé had dropped earlier. She would have killed Yena, too—the flathead was aimed at his heart—but Esmé's attack shifts him. As it happens, the tool finds his shoulder instead, burying itself hilt deep between muscle and tissue and arteries and veins.

Yena roars in pain. Momentum drives him to the side and backward onto Esmé.

The blonde woman cusses in victory, falling to her knees as Esmé and Yena wrestle nearby. They're a flailing ball of limbs scrambling to get the upper hand.

With the knife still angled, still gripped tightly in his hand, he realizes a decision needs to be made. Esmé has gone rogue, off-script. He has two options: kill her and search for a new opponent, or let her win this bastardized version of *his* game.

With his head still pounding and the ancestors still screaming, he isn't thinking as clearly. Then, before he can make up his mind, his knife plunges into her torso, fast and easy. It is as if fate has chosen for him.

It's as if she hadn't felt any type of pain. Esmé continues to attack him or defend herself, though, and the battle continues.

He needs to kill Esmé now, absorb her powerful essence into himself and accept his godlike powers. To do this, he needs her heart. Yes, the blonde would have sufficed, but why waste a more potent ingredient when it's within reach?

The blonde bitch screams in her dying-cat voice, tugging at his clothes, trying to pull Yena off Esmé.

He smacks back with one hand, hoping to catch her off guard, but the world has gone off-kilter.

No. No! NO!

Footsteps rush from the other side of the slaughterhouse. *Fuck!*

A male voice shouts commands. Beams of light project into his eyes, blinding him. Nails rake down his face before an almighty wall crashes into him.

Yena, lying under a great weight, feels his lungs being crushed, and can't figure out what was happening until Detective Mosepi's voice barks out his rights.

Before Yena has a chance to fight, the overweight detective has already turned him onto his stomach and is forcefully twisting his hands behind his back.

Yena never admits defeat, but he won't allow himself to be shot, either. Instead, knowing he is beat, he quietly consents to being handcuffed and watches Esmé bleed out on the cold concrete.

"What a waste," he sighs.

The younger detective, the one he'd seen accompanying Esmé at the Crocodile River, tends to her. His hands are pressed against her side, but she doesn't respond. Even the blonde is more concerned with Esmé's well-being than getting loose.

"Stay with me," the young detective says repeatedly, nervously.

Before Yena can find out if Esmé is alive or dead, Mosepi—now finished reciting his rights to him—punches him repeatedly in the face with his immense fist, until he blacks out.

ALLEGED PRETORIA SLASHER IN POLICE CUSTODY
Sapa | 30 September, 2015 18:47

Police have arrested the alleged Pretoria Slasher who is accused of the kidnapping and murder of Valentine Sikelo, Carol-Anne Brewis, and ANC MP Abraham Amin, Pretoria police said on Wednesday.

The Pretoria Slasher's identity is being withheld from the public. However, other information was released by the SAPS.

"The elusive Pretoria Slasher who evaded police capture has finally been arrested," said Detective Elias Mosepi.

"[The Pretoria Slasher] was arrested this afternoon on a small, abandoned plot in Erasmia at about 15:03. He has been at large since the beginning of September. The suspect will appear before the Pretoria Magistrate's Court soon."

The Pretoria Slasher, 35, had been on the run since the assault and murder of Valentine Sikelo on the 4th of September 2015, in Pretoria West.

A relative who has allegedly participated in previous cases related to the Pretoria Slasher was arrested in Pretoria West, earlier on Wednesday.

More details to follow as information is released.

– LiveTimes
Comments have been disabled for this article.

SLIPPERY PRETORIA SLASHER BEHIND BARS
2015-09-30 18:53

Police have arrested the Pretoria Slasher who is accused of the kidnappings and murders of Valentine Sikelo, Carol-Anne Brewis, and Abraham Amin.

"He [the Pretoria Slasher] was arrested in Erasmia, more details will follow later," said Detective Rynhardt Louw.

The suspect (35) had been on the run since the assault and the murder of Valentine Sikelo on the 4th of September, 2015.

Meanwhile, a man believed to be a relative of the suspect was also arrested in Pretoria West earlier this morning.

"The suspect is expected to appear before the Magistrates Court on Friday pending further police investigations," said Louw.

He added that the police recovered further evidence of more victims at the homestead.

"A team of independent investigators, with the assistance of the police, is combing the area for further clues of who these victims are and where they may be located," said Louw. "Police investigations are at an advanced and sensitive stage, and more arrests are imminent."

– News24/7

Join the conversation!
24.com encourages commentary **submitted via MyNews24/7.** Contributions of 200 words or more will be considered for publication.

We reserve editorial discretion to decide what will be published. **Read our comments policy** for guidelines on contributions.

FAMILIES RELIEVED BY PRETORIA SLASHER ARREST
Article By: Almarie Badenhorst   0 Comments
Wed, 30 Sept 2015 20:00 PM

"The capture of the so-called 'Pretoria Slasher' is a big relief for the victims' families," Pretoria police commissioner Ludwa Mamba said on

Wednesday.

Earlier, authorities captured the suspect after the killer evaded police for almost a month.

The Pretoria Slasher is accused of kidnapping, torturing, and murdering Valentine Sikelo, Carol-Anne Brewis, and ANC MP Abraham Amin.

Further investigations of the agricultural holding where he was found living yielded more possible victims. Police said they will question the suspect and formulate charges against him.

He and another man, a family relation according to insider sources, will appear in court on Friday. The Pretoria Slasher could also face charges of murder, rape and evading arrest.

Two hostages: a civilian and an occult expert who had been consulting on the case for the SAPS, were found at what is now called "The Carnage Farm." Both hostages sustained minor injuries and were taken to a hospital for treatment.

The Pretoria Slasher did not resist arrest when police found him.

Officials are now looking to piece together a puzzle of muti and murder.

– EWN

PRETORIANS CHEER AS SLASHER IS ARRESTED
31 September, 2015 | 10:32 a.m. 21 Comments
By Andrea Miller

Yesterday was a good day for Pretoria residents.

First, news came in that the Pretoria Slasher has been taken into custody and that police saved one hostage from a fate worse than death, and an investigator from bleeding out. Then, scattered thundershowers across the city finally broke the insufferable heat. It's as if God Himself was celebrating the police's victory.

DARK COUNTRY

Sources within the Pretoria West Police Department claim the Pretoria Slasher is cooperating with authorities, for the most part, but so far he's still being elusive about his true identity. But, there's a twist! The Pretoria Slasher's half-brother is *also* in custody. Police allegedly picked him up for speeding yesterday morning and linked him to a buffet of crimes.

This leaves the question: Is this a matter of nature vs. nurture, or something entirely different?

For those readers who don't know, the Pretoria Slasher has been a busy guy as far as kidnapping and murders are concerned:

His first known victim—Valentine Sikelo (28)—was found brutally mutilated and murdered in a field in Pretoria West on 4 September, 2015. The young mother, wife, daughter, and sister had been walking to the taxi rank on the same day she'd died, before the Pretoria Slasher whisked her away and tortured her for muti.

The second victim—Carol-Anne Brewis (12)—was found on Gert van Rooyen's property, her body broken and her brain missing. She was taken out of her bedroom in the middle of the night, and killed in his van. Why? According to our inside source, the Pretoria Slasher just said: "She was the perfect sacrifice."

Abraham Amin (39)—a politician for the ANC party—was the third victim. His body was found gutted, hanging from the Daspoort Tunnel's ventilation shaft. This rising star in the political party was a beloved figure in his community, as well as in the party. Whatever his future held, it came to an abrupt end when he was kidnapped from an ambassadorial mansion in Moreleta Park, held captive, and killed while trying to escape.

These are *just* the victims we know about. Numbers have been thrown around by investigators as to how many people the Pretoria Slasher has killed in his lifetime, ranging from between 8 to 39.

"It's difficult to be sure, because [he] also seemed to buy a lot of body parts and organs on the black market," our source divulged. "So far, we have enough evidence to link him to at least 15 murders, but the investigation is far from over and the number is likely to change."

International readers might be thinking I'm making this stuff up, but the truth is, ritual murder is alive and well in South Africa. Muti—made and distributed by traditional healers—are basically homeopathic remedies. Usually, "muti" are tinctures and tonics made from indigenous plants, but there *are* people who take things too far … This is where witch doctors, witches, and the like come into play.

Now, so far, there is no word as to whether the Pretoria Slasher is, in fact, a registered traditional healer, but the Traditional Healers Association of Africa has already distanced themselves from the killer.

As for the Pretoria Slasher's half-brother, well, that's a whole other story. Apparently, he's been raping, mutilating, torturing, killing, and heaven knows what else, for almost as long as brother dearest.

"They'll both be prosecuted to the fullest extent of the law," the source said. "And their stays at casa C-Max will be extended."

C-Max, the maximum security prison in Pretoria, however, may not be equipped to handle either prisoner. According to other gossip around town, they both seem to have some sort of mental disorder. This is purely speculation, but is it truly so farfetched to say they suffer from schizophrenia? I don't particularly think so.

Then again, no insanity plea has ever been won in South African law history … Maybe they won't try the trick for their respective defenses? Who knows?

I'll keep you updated on what's what as more information is released, so subscribe to my blog and stay in the know!

Yours truly,
Andrea Miller

EDIT I'll be doing a vlog series on muti crimes in the near future. If you want to know more, follow me on my Youtube channel. Handle: TrueCrimeSA.

– TrueCrimeSA.co.za

Log in to leave comments.

New Orleans, Louisiana
December 1st, 2015

The piano plays in harmony, fading out slowly for the trumpet to take over as the tune reaches its crescendo. The cellist plucks at the strings of his instrument while the singer sings a haunting song to an upbeat melody.

I sip a cocktail—Sazerac, the waitress called it—tentatively, relaxing in the front row of the jazz club, watching the show. Here, in this city of carnivals and culture, I can forget about the jagged red scar on my abdomen. I could forget about Kenneth Mtetwa—otherwise known as Yena—and Simphiwe Mtetwa—also known as Human-Tooth-Necklace-Guy—and the terrible deeds they've done.

I can forget about everything bothering me, if only for a little while.

It's why I came here in the first place: to enjoy a different culture, to see the sights, to heal safely in another country, and to forget of how foolish I can be, at times. My actions almost cost Leila her life, as well as my own.

Still, we got the guy. They put him behind bars and he's going to stay there for a long time—the rest of his life, if there's any justice in the world.

Rynhardt touches my hand gently, leans over, and whispers, "I've got to run to the men's. Don't go anywhere."

I smile. "Okay. Enjoy yourself."

He rolls his eyes, smiling back, before giving me a quick peck on the cheek. Rynhardt leaves the table.

The set ends and I applaud loudly, beaming as the musicians take a bow.

This is what pure joy feels like, even if I'm recovering from a possible life-threatening wound. Rynhardt took time off work to join me on the three-week holiday in New Orleans, and it's been great so far. We may have only arrived the previous day, but so far I am happy that I didn't end up coming by myself. After the whole ordeal with Yena, of me almost dying, Rynhardt forgave me for stealing his car, but only if I promised never to do it again.

I never explicitly promised a thing, though.

There's a possibility we're also in an actual relationship now, although neither of us have talked about it. We just, kind of, fell into a routine. Whether it'll grow into something more, I'm not sure. Right now and here, I don't even want to think of the future.

A waitress saunters over, places a dish filled with oysters in front of me, and smiles.

"I didn't order this," I say.

"It's been paid for," she answers in her heavy accent before sauntering off to tend to another table.

I study the dish, but before I can take some, a man with short bleached dreadlocks, dressed in white from head to toe, sits down opposite me.

His skin contrasts profoundly against his ensemble, but that's the point. He commands a whole room with his daring appearance.

I pull my hand back into my lap and square my jaw.

"Oysters Rockefeller," he says in a Ugandan accent, pointing to the food in front of me. "Best in the city."

"Shouldn't you be preparing for your criminal case?" I ask.

The Rabbi grins. "I was acquitted of all charges, thanks to lack of evidence."

"Congratulations," I say, my throat tightening.

"You still owe me a favor and I've come to collect."

"I'm on holiday, recuperating after my run-in with Kenneth Mtetwa."

"I heard. Had it not been for the twins' protection, I'm sure you would have been dead," The Rabbi says. "You have some good friends in them."

"Or maybe I was just lucky enough to survive a lunatic's attack?"

"Be that as it may, I am cashing in my favor. I have a friend who's in trouble, you see? A friend who has been accused of a horrific ritual murder which I know she didn't commit. There are good, there are evil, and then there are the neutrals. I am one of those neutrals who do not pick a side. She is a neutral, too. Seeing as you're one of the best, I was thinking you can extend your services to help get her off the hook and find the real killer, while you're at it."

"If I say no?"

"You won't say no. You live for this stuff ... You aren't called the Crimson Huntress because of your hair, Esmé."

I slump back into my chair. "Can this at least wait until I'm back in South Africa? I really need this break."

The Rabbi fixes his jacket. "Your request would be difficult to implement, considering she's right here in New Orleans." He flashes a wolfish smile, the kind that makes me wonder if he's about to eat me alive. "Perhaps you should brush up on your voodoo trivia tonight, in between humping your detective. I'm not sure how well you know the culture."

"I know enough," I say.

"Good, then I'll pick you up at your hotel first thing in the morning. Bring your boy-toy along for the ride, if you want. What's it they always say? The more, the merrier?" The Rabbi stands. "Fate is a funny lady, don't you agree?"

I answer him with a glare that could've lanced boils.

The Rabbi winks, pointing at the oysters with his index finger. "You won't have experienced New Orleans until you've had those. They're absolutely delicious."

I'm about to respond with a snarky comeback about sharks, but The Rabbi disappears into the incoming crowd.

"So much for having a relaxing holiday," I say to myself, picking up one of the oysters.

"Oh, you ordered without me?" Rynhardt sits down.

I hand the oysters over to him, which he accepts with a smile.

"I have some good news and some bad news," I say. "Which would you like to hear first?"

"Good news," he answers.

"Well, we might have to extend our holiday, which is proudly sponsored by ... You guessed it! Snyder International Religious Crime Investigative Services."

"I like the good news. What's the bad news?"

I bite the inside of my cheek, inhale deeply, and decide to ease him gently into my life as an occult crime expert. "What is your standpoint on voodoo as a theology?"

EPILOUGE

27 May, 2021

It's been five years to the day since the commencement of my incarceration for the so-called "murders" of five people. The courts and the media called me a monster, even attempting to have the constitution revised to recall the death penalty.

I do not see how they can judge me.

Is it wrong for a person to step on an ant? Do we call them murderers, as well?

I'm kept in solitary confinement, where my only company is this diary and a soft tip pencil, which I sharpen against the nail-scratched walls—courtesy of the previous desperate and weak inmates who once occupied this poorly lit cell.

I am considered a danger to the other inmates. Even my one-hour daily exercise is in an empty yard, watched over by several armed guards.

Good thing, too.

If anything, solitary confinement has strengthened me—physically, mentally, and spiritually. My connection with the ancestors has never been stronger. They keep me company, day and night, whispering their wants and needs and ideologies. Plans: so many plans.

All I need is one more opportunity to kill, one moment to fill me with power again!

I am patient, though.

My time will come.

Soon.

South African Terms

Bakkie: Pickup Truck

Boerseun: An Afrikaner boy or man; a farm-boy, a 'son of the soil'

Braai: Barbecue

Cooldrink: Soda / Pop

Electricity Socket: Electrical Outlet

Eendracht Maakt Macht: Afrikaans representation of the Latin phrase *Ex Unitate Vires* 'From unity (comes) strength', the motto on the South African coat of arms.

isiZulu: The Zulu language

Ja: Afrikaans word for "yes"

Kak: Afrikaans word for "shit"

Lapa: A traditional South African garden structure crafted from African hardwood poles and finished with a genuine thatched roof.

Lekker slaap: Afrikaans for good night or sleep tight.

Magic vs. Magick: **Magic** is much more liberal in what it accepts to be magic: anything which uses willpower to manifest change can be classed as magic. **Magick** on the other hand refers only to things which use will power to better the person and move them towards their 'True Will.'

Matric Dance: Prom

Muti: Traditional Medicine

Shebeen: Pub or bar

Skedonk: A banger; an old, battered motor car.

Skinnerspruit: A stream in Gauteng, South Africa.

South African City Nicknames:

The Mother City: Cape Town

The City of Gold: Johannesburg

The Jacaranda City: Pretoria

Taxi Rank: Where taxis wait for clients

WF Nkomo: William Frederick Nkomo was a freedom fighter during the Apartheid years.

Acknowledgements

First of all, I would like to thank the wonderful staff at Vesuvian Books for going above and beyond in getting *Dark Country* into tip top shape. L.K. Griffie, you are simply magnificent for *still* putting up with me after all this time. Thank you so much for your patience and loveliness! Holly, thank you for making this book come alive. I know I'm not always the easiest writer to deal with, but you always make the editing process painless. To all the proofreaders who worked on the project to find those hidden gremlins, thank you *so* much. You rock! And then there are all the other Vesuvian authors who support and cheer and are there to make me feel part of the family … I am so very grateful for you all becoming part of my life. Thank you, thank you, thank you. *blows kisses your way*

To Italia Gandolfo, my agent and friend, I love you to bits. Your gentle nudges in this or that direction has made me not only a better writer and editor, but also a better person. Thank you so much for always being there for me, darling. I appreciate everything you do immensely— *everything* including answering a midnight Whatsapp message about the super-massive promo stuff. You are, simply put, my guardian angel.

Scott Roberts, cover artist and illustrator extraordinaire: You brought this cover to life when I didn't even know what I wanted to have on the cover. I absolutely *love* everything about it (and how you always seem to know exactly what I need). Thank you!

To my husband, the light in my life, you always play such an intricate role in my writing. Making me hundreds of mugs of coffee so I can meet a deadline, cheering me on when all I want to do is give up, being my beta-reader and helping me find those pesky plot issues before sending my books out. I love you so much and can't imagine a world without you. Thank you for it all, my lovey.

Thank you to my mother for working so hard to give me and my sister the best opportunities in life. None of this would have been possible without the sacrifices you made and your tireless efforts. I love you!

To Aunt Marietjie: Not only do you champion my books, but you're always just a phone call away when I need a chat about this or that. Thank you so much for your constant support and love. ☺

Last, but certainly not least, I want to thank everyone I haven't mentioned by name thus far. You know who you are and how much you mean to me. Yes, yes, I'm fully aware I can be a handful and that you totally deserve your name in print, but space is limited and there's a whole series worth of acknowledgements I need to curate, at some point … That said, I want to thank you for always being there for me no matter how annoying I am when I start babbling about books, writers, and the industry. Thank you for loving me, cheering me on, and helping me with this or that. I love you all so much (and I promise I'll give you a personalized shoutout in the next book's acknowledgements). *super hugs*

About the Author

Monique Snyman is an editor and the author of Bram Stoker Award® nominated novels, *The Night Weaver* and *The Bone Carver*, as well as the South African occult crime/horror series, *Dark Country*. Monique was born in Pretoria, South Africa and grew up on the western edge of the city during the post-Apartheid Era when the ideological dreams of a Rainbow Nation was at its height. As a result, she was fortunate enough to be exposed to various cultures, languages, religions, and class differences from a very early age. While Monique's first language is Afrikaans, she dedicated her career to specializing in English creative writing. Monique resides outside of Johannesburg with her husband and daughter.

MoniqueSnyman.com